THE CONFRONTATION

There was a moment of silence before Kayler found some of his earlier courage and snarled, "You haven't even got a gun. Or you think you kin take me with your fists?"

Checker looked back at Kayler, who had placed his hands on the pistols in his waistband to reinforce his point. His lariat lay on the floor in front of him. Without hesitation, Checker walked toward him again, his eyes locked onto Kayler's own menacing gaze.

"That's true, I don't have a gun, but you do."

"I'll shoot you, Checker, or I'll beat you to death. Which way you want it?" Kayler grasped the handles tightly but didn't pull either weapon.

Checker closed the short distance between them in four steps. The room forgot to blink. . . .

Other *Leisure* books by Cotton Smith:
BEHOLD A RED HORSE
PRAY FOR TEXAS
DARK TRAIL TO DODGE

Cotton Smith

BROTHERS OF THE GUN

LEISURE BOOKS NEW YORK CITY

A LEISURE BOOK®

February 2002

Published by

Dorchester Publishing Co., Inc.
276 Fifth Avenue
New York, NY 10001

ISBN 0-8439-4968-6

The name "Leisure Books" and the stylized "L" with design are
trademarks of Dorchester Publishing Co., Inc.

Printed in the United States of America.

Visit us on the web at www.dorchesterpub.com.

To those great people who helped me along the trail.
You know who you are and I will never forget you.

BROTHERS
OF THE GUN

Chapter One

"Here comes trouble, an' it be carryin' a lynchin' rope."

Along the bar of the Lady Gay, the closest men nodded agreement with the first drinker's observation. They watched George Washington Kayler strut through the batwing doors of the crowded saloon and dance hall. His swagger was that of a man expecting attention. An oily yellow glow from wall gas lights made his fearsome scowl even more intimidating.

"Now do jes' what I said," he growled without looking to the seven grim-faced men behind him. "We're gonna git us an army of real Texans."

They glanced at him nervously. Each carried a rope and firearms, in open defiance of the town ordinance. Since the Dodge City trial, the big-shouldered trial boss had been preaching the values of a lynching. In his left fist was a coiled lariat. A new one. Butts of two pistols were visible above his waistband. Kayler's new blue-striped, store-bought suit was too small for his huge frame, but no one told him. A loosely tied bandanna, resting low on Kayler's chest, was in sharp contrast to the city attire. He reeked of lilac water from a fresh haircut and whiskey from a long afternoon. Stories of his ending arguments with a single roundhouse punch were plentiful.

Along with his six Circle J drovers was a Triple-C rider with a toothy, self-conscious grin nailed to his tanned face. Wearing a red shirt with white embroidered stars on both pockets, he cradled a double-barreled shotgun in his arms. A coiled lariat hung from his right forearm. His too-handsome face reflected the quart of whiskey he had consumed to give him courage to join the others. He didn't notice two other Triple C riders, Sonny Jones and Harry Clanahan, sitting at a back table. They saw him and were surprised to see him with Kayler, but they quickly returned to their own conversation.

Whispered declarations of support passed along the ornately carved, mahogany bar lined with cowboys drinking or waiting to pay seventy-five cents for ten minutes of dancing. "It's about time we showed 'em some Texas justice." "Yeah, let's string up the bastards an' git outta hyar." "Figured Kayler would get 'round to it sooner or later." "Hear tell he's a mean 'un." "Yeah, nobody ridin' Circle J says much 'bout him." "Their beeves looked a mite peeked comin' in. I'd say he pushed 'em too hard." "Well, who cares, he's right 'bout this. Let's git 'er done." "That's a Triple C hand with him." "Which one?" "That un, with them stars on his shirt." "Well,

I'll be. You think John Checker is for this?" "Not hardly."

A skinny cowboy in the middle of the bar nervously gulped his whiskey and hurried toward the back of the room to get as far away from the situation as possible. Most Texans, however, were unaware of Kayler's entrance. Instead, they were concentrating on dancing, games of chance, free food at the bar, drinking, playing billiards, ogling the women serving whiskey and dancing, or just talking to each other to push the night into another dawn.

The loud band, seated in the upper balcony, gave Texas cowboys all the justification they needed to hold the dance-hall women tight and move them around the floor more or less in rhythm to the music. Dressed in bright, skimpy dresses that showed off bosoms and legs, the powdered and painted girls laughed in a practiced manner as the men screamed out Rebel yells. Outside, an autumn Kansas sun had surrendered to the tension of nightfall. Gas lamps were weakly imitating the vanquished sunlight throughout the south-side glut of saloons, casinos, and pleasure houses.

Like the Lady Gay, most were frothing with cowboys who hadn't yet left for Texas. But this wasn't another boisterous evening of celebrating a successful trail drive. This was a night of swelling fury as Dodge City tingled with whispered talk of a lynching. Trail drives were finished for the year and these Texans were now staying around for only one reason: a hanging—now four days away and an eternity for the hard men who waited. They wanted to see the Star McCallister gang get what they deserved for murdering Triple C drovers and rustling their precious cattle.

Waiting for the niceties of civilized justice was growing less and less acceptable, usually in direct relationship to how much money a cowboy had left from his trail-drive pay. Being broke in a fancy town tends to make a man downright angry. Increasingly, the cowboys' carousing had an edge to it. From the moment the trial ended a week before, lynch talk blossomed with the primary justification for the action; it would do the job just as well and they could be on their way home to Texas all that much sooner. Besides, it was a way to show the arrogant Dodge City residents who lived on the north side of town what the Texans thought of their superior-acting ways. All it would take was somebody to lead the way, somebody like Kayler.

Waiting theatrically for the right moment to take charge, Kayler patted the side of his leg with his lariat, as if counting down to a prearranged beginning. Too-short coat sleeves accented his size, as did knee-length, mule-eared boots. Buttons on his vest struggled to keep it in place around his thick chest and belly. He was a man who knew his size made most men fear him; he had always liked that feeling.

"Here we go, boys. Here we go," he growled, and his most grimacing expression appeared. Only the Triple C drover dared to voice his support.

Kayler's heavy eyebrows arched their defiance and his reddened eyes narrowed in purpose as he mentally prepared himself for the first step in leading fellow Texans in a worthy cause. His chest rose and fell in a long inhalation. With a predetermined manner, he drew a pistol from his waistband, cocked it, and fired it over the heads of the band members.

They scrambled for cover, stopping in midnote of a raucous rendition of "Camptown Ladies." A cornet flew into the air, bounced off the railing, clanked on the bar below, and skidded to the floor. A lanky Texan grabbed the cornet from the floor and blew into the mouthpiece. The man at his side told him to shut up and listen. He nodded agreement and held the instrument in front of him with the open cone facing up. Soon he was using it as a handy spitoon.

Whiskey-laden heads turned toward the pistol-brandishing Kayler with his two rope-carrying side-kicks. Half of the Texans kept dancing and yelling, unaware of the absence of song or determined to ignore it; the others stutter-stepped to a halt and yelled their anger at the interruption. One screamed loudly, "Texas necktie party, a-alright!" At the bar, every Texan turned toward the rope-carrying three-some, except an older man who appeared to be asleep, leaning against his elbows on the bar.

Gradually the room became quiet, and all the Texans finally stopped dancing but continued holding their partners close to them. A whispered "Not now, cowboy" from a black-haired woman to her amorous partner brought muffled laughter followed by immediate demands for silence. Appraising the attention he sought, Kayler swallowed and coughed.

Swelling his thick chest, he raised his big left fist, showing a coiled lariat, and, in a whiskey-enhanced voice, he bellowed, "I'm G. W. Kayler, and I say we show this damn town what Texas justice is all about. We've waited long enough, Texas is waitin' for us to come on home. Let's go get Star McCallister and

13

his bunch—and string 'em up—right now! Me 'n' my boys, we just bought brand-spankin'-new ropes for the doin'. Who's with us?"

Twenty hard voices signaled their agreement and fists rose in the air to support the declarations. They were mostly from the dance floor and along the bar. Except for a few, men at the billiards and gaming tables returned to their entertainment, leaving their involvement to gruff observations about the recommended task. Through the bars of the upper bannister, frightened band members peered and whispered about what they should do next. Indecision ruled and no one moved. A bald-headed cornet player gazed longingly at his instrument in the hands of the Texan who was now waving it in the air.

The trial of the Star McCallister cattle-rustling gang had been remarkably swift—although the hundreds of Texas men who crowded into and around the courthouse would likely attest to its not being swift enough. Townspeople couldn't remember seeing so many Texas cowboys happy and excited—while sober—after the convictions of murder and cattle rustling were announced. Of course, the sober part hadn't lasted long after that.

Warming to the enthusiastic response, the Triple C rider, who liked to be called Tex, stepped forward and yelled, "I ride for the Triple C, and I say the time has come to make 'em pay! We lost good men on the trail because of that bunch over there. I'm joinin' Kayler 'n' the Circle J to get justice!"

A new ten-dollar white hat was pushed back on Tex Whitney's head, revealing a whitish band of skin below his hairline. The sun hadn't been allowed to touch there for a long time, but damp curls of

brownish hair were released to rest upon his forehead. Tex glanced at the big French mirror behind
the bar as he moved, admiring his appearance. He
adjusted his hat, glanced again at the mirror, and
smiled at what he saw in the reflection.

On both sides of the mirror were large oil paint-
ings of naked women. Tex glanced at them, then at
the women standing with partners on the dance
floor. They were watching! They were watching him!
He smiled again. Being the center of attention felt
very good.

At a table in the far corner, Sonny Jones and Harry
Clanahan were paying little attention to the heated
exchange. They'd heard such empty, whiskey-
aroused challenges before; a nightly ritual it seemed,
regardless of the saloon. But none of their fellow Triple C drovers had been involved before. John
Checker had warned them against it; the former
Texas Ranger had ridden with them on the long,
dark trail to Dodge. No one figured he was bluffing.
Tex had been too consumed with his performance
to see either of his trail friends so far.

It didn't matter. Sonny Jones, the ever-happy rider
with the outlaw past, was listening to his Irish friend
tell him about a waitress in this saloon whom he had
met the day before. Clanahan was obviously smitten.
At the moment, she was serving drinks to a table on
the far side of the crowded, smoke-laden room.
Clanahan's eyes caressed the thin, redheaded
woman as he described her, secretly happy she was
serving drinks at the moment and not dancing with
some cowboy.

"Sonny, me lad, ye should see this fine lass! Oh
what a beauty she be—and from the green isle she

comes, too! Minnie. Minnie Oliver be the name of this angel of light. Look at her now! Is she not a beauty! Sure, and she be agreein' to meet meself after she gets off tonight," Clanahan exclaimed. His voice was barely audible above the thundering clamor for a lynching.

"That's great, Harry. She sounds like a nice girl," Sonny said, grinning widely. Yellow light drew flickering lines down his broad face, over his flat nose and wiry mustache.

To look at the easy-laughing, always-singing drover with the hard-traveled derby hat, it was difficult to believe he was deadly when pushed—until one saw him pushed. Only John Checker knew his real name was Cole Dillon, a name feared by many along the border. A name that grew out of the frustration of losing the War of Northern Aggression and found justification in becoming an outlaw and a hellion with a gun. Sonny Jones had left those days far behind, and his given name as well. Checker had accepted that change as fact, even though he had once tracked him across the windswept Staked Plains of Texas as part of his Ranger duties.

"Aye, she be—and a sweet one to gaze upon, I tell ye," Clanahan continued, his eyes locking on her movements.

She glanced up at him and smiled softly. Tinted-red hair was piled high with bouncing ringlets. Her mouth was bright red, her eyelids were laden with kohl, and her flat cheeks carried circles of cinnamon. Minnie Oliver was thinner than many of her sister workers, but her rumpled green dress did the job of accenting small breasts and dark-stockinged legs. Sonny groaned inwardly and tried not to show what he felt. The woman was a whore; he had paid for her last week. Surely his friend knew what she was—or did he?

"Whoa, pardner! That woman's got her hooks into you," Sonny exclaimed, and slapped his friend on the shoulder. "That could get mighty costly." It was as close as he dared come to the subject until he saw how Clanahan reacted.

Unlike his Irish friend's new city business-suit attire, Sonny was wearing trail-worn, narrow-legged shotgun chaps and large-roweled Mexican spurs. But his ever-present derby looked reasonably good after cleaning had removed layers of dirt and dried sweat. The sleeves of his shirt were gathered by dark leather garters around his upper arms. Matching leather gauntlets protected his wrists. His shirttail was already out, flapping under his unbuttoned vest, like it usually did when he was riding. And, as always, the happy cowboy's vest pockets were jammed with cartridges, chunks of hard candy, coins, leather strips, and an old watch. A Colt .45 was shoved into his waistband at the back, out of sight of ordinance enforcers, but handy.

"Don't ye be givin' such joy to yourself from the teasin'. Minnie be a drink-serving lass, Sonny, an' ye be knowin' it. No dirty leg she. Aye, a good lass," Clanahan said, his face turning a deep red. "Oh, oh! Don't look! Don't look, Sonny! She be coming this way, me friend," He chugged the remainder of his whiskey as an exclamation, then added, "Begorra! Ye be on your manners now, ye black-faced rascal."

Minnie Oliver slid through the crowd of cowboys, smiling at the occasional pinch or touch or whiskeyed proposition, and stopped in front of their table.

17

Her smile was wide and loving, and her eyes sought those of the suddenly bashful Clanahan. Sonny watched silently and hoped Minnie wouldn't act as if she remembered him, if she did.

"What can I do for you, cowboys?" she said, glancing seductively first at Clanahan, then at Sonny, who bit his lower lip.

Her eyelashes fluttered, and, for a moment, Sonny thought she was going to say something to him. Her performance in bed popped into his mind, and he shook his head to send it away. Whether or not she took that for a signal not to recognize him, Minnie looked back at the Irishman.

Clanahan swallowed and said, "Minnie, darlin', wee sweet lass that ye be, bring me an' my friend a bottle of fine Irish whiskey now—and make plans for going back to Texas with me later."

"That sounds like a marriage proposal, Mr. Clanahan," she said impishly. Her eyes embraced his gaze, and the Irishman's face deepened its crimson hue.

"Aye, I am supposing that it does."

"Ask me that in another week," she said, then she leaned over and kissed him lightly on the cheek and disappeared into the crowd.

Sonny started to say something but decided against it. Whatever he said to his friend would be misinterpreted. It wouldn't be the first time a cowboy fell in love with a whore. That was often the price of loneliness. Suddenly, the ugly thunder of the lynching rally caught his full attention. Perhaps he was looking for a distraction, but his usual happy manner disappeared into a taut face. Instead of their customary joy, hooded eyes were bright with worry.

18

This was more than the usual bar bragging; this was trouble.

"Sonny, darlin', a fine politican our Tex be makin'. Hisself be gittin' all puffed up like a red rooster in the barnyard, he be; askin' the chickens to follow him to paradise," the slump-shouldered Clanahan drawled, sensing his friend wasn't in a mood to discuss Minnie Oliver any further at the moment.

"He does like prancing in front of a crowd," Sonny growled. "Damn fool. It's a good thing Checker isn't here. He'd boot him all the way to the Red."

Clanahan laughed heartily and glanced around to see if Minnie was in sight. He couldn't see her for the standing men. He squinted and slowly stood on his one good leg. His broken right limb was fully splinted, an injury from the night their herd was stolen by the McCallister gang. His head jerked back and forth in an attempt to see if she had reached the bar yet.

Sonny studied the knot of men growing around the seven would-be lynch mob leaders; his right fist opened and closed like a heartbeat, a nervous habit that usually preceded trouble. He knew of Kayler from hearing about him beating up an unfortunate cowboy last week. Something to do with a card game. Kayler's Circle J crew wasn't thought of highly as cowmen—mostly the dregs nobody else wanted. His herd came in scrawny from being pushed too hard. Word had it that he had bragged about making John Checker back down around San Antonio.

The band hadn't resumed its playing, in spite of the encouragement by a bartender and a sweaty cowboy with an arm around a blond lady in a bright blue dress. She was more concerned about pulling on the bodice to keep it in place and thus calling more attention to her heavy bosom.

From beyond the milling crowd of cowboys, a voice at a poker table bellowed, "What about John Checker?" It rattled across the saloon like a thrown saber.

Tex's face turned as red as his shorter companion, and his nostrils flared. With his hands on his hips, he repeated the question loudly, turning it into a challenge. "What about Checker?"

Embarrassed at being singled out, the seated cowboy glanced at his friends at the table and said timidly, "I hear tell the Ranger isn't going to stand for no lynchin'."

Tex snapped, "Are you afraid of John Checker?"

"Damn straight I am."

The crowd laughed, supported by other exclamations of agreement. Frowning, Tex looked at Kayler for help. With a disgusted snort, the big man said, "John Checker's not here. We are. He can do what he wants and we can do what we want. I say we show this town some Texas justice. If'n he don't like it, I'll make him wish he did. I've done it a'fore."

A short, stout Circle J cowboy chimed in. "Yessiree, we kin do that!" He waved both arms in the air and the ropes in his fists swung wildly, knocking off his hat. He immediately stopped to retrieve it.

"Grab your ropes an' let's go, boys!"

The declaration came from the middle of the group and was immediately supported. Reinforcement rippled through the aroused saloon. Tex's face was flushed with the moment; he turned his attention toward Minnie Oliver, waiting at the bar for Clanahan's bottle.

"Sweet lady, us Texans are gonna take care of some business that needs tendin' to—and then I'll be back to tend to you. What'd ya say?"

Long eyelashes fluttered her answer. Tex smiled broadly and glanced at himself again in the mirror. The bartender closest to him caught the observation and grinned, but Tex didn't care. He was the center of attention and loving it. He spun toward the main part of the saloon and roared, "For Texas, men! For Texas!" Then he smiled back at Minnie. His eyes dropped from her face to her bosom and back to her face. She smiled knowingly, and he thrust out his chin and said, "Follow me, men." A grizzled cowboy closest to him heard the words and chuckled.

"Harry, this is getting bad. I'm going to find Checker. I told him where we'd be, but he's probably at the hotel. You stay here," Sonny declared.

Clanahan wasn't listening. He was leaning one way and then the other, trying to see Minnie Oliver, but the swirling mob shielded her from him at the moment.

"Harry, I'm going to find John. Wait here," Sonny repeated, jumping from his seat.

"What? Faith 'n' I be goin' with ye," Clanahan said, turning his head back toward Sonny.

"You've got a busted leg, you dumb Irishman, so stay here. Invite that girl to sit with you while I'm gone—or something. But don't try to stop this bunch. We'll cut 'em off at the jail if I can find John soon enough."

At first glance, Sonny's thick frame appeared doughy, but that was deceiving; he was as strong as

21

he was fearless, the one most likely to charge an enemy and laugh at the challenge. Yellow light drew flickering lines down Sonny's broad face, over his flat nose and wiry mustache. Sonny was the one who made up songs on the trail about anything and everything, and laughed even quicker. He was likely to wake up smiling in the middle of a drenching rainstorm.

He was a head shorter than Clanahan and darker skinned. His late father had been a top vaquero for one of the great Mexican ranches; his mother was a proper Englishwoman, now remarried and living in Amarillo. The physical contrast between his parents was most evident in Sonny's blue eyes and light brown hair that covered his ears. Clanahan was well aware of his trail-driving friend's tendencies to challenge anything and everything with a bold laugh followed by a fierce attack. He knew Sonny was intending to face the lynch mob alone, if need be—and only because Sonny's friend, John Checker, wanted the court's declaration done by the law, not by some cowboys seeking revenge.

Still standing himself, Clanahan looked toward the doorway, grinned, and grabbed Sonny's arm as he passed. "Methinks ye won't be going far to find our Ranger friend."

Sonny frowned at Clanahan's hand on his arm, then realized the significance and stared back at the saloon entrance through a tapestry of smoke.

"Be that the man hisself coming—or is Harry Clanahan a wee leprechaun?"

"Good eyes, my friend. Let's make sure he knows we're back here," Sonny said, "and wait for his play."

Few saw John Checker step into the saloon, except the two Triple C riders watching him from the rear of the saloon. He stopped and stood for a moment, his arms crossed. His dark eyes sought immediate answers. With them came a sudden sense of cold. Without anyone really thinking about it, the tall ex-Ranger had become the leader of the Triple C trail hands since their trail boss was badly wounded during the McCallister raid.

Dressed now in a dark blue suit with a matching vest and white Stetson, Checker had joined the drive because it was going where he wanted to go, to Dodge. His reason for coming was personal. There were no signs of his carrying a weapon of any kind. Shoulder-length black hair brushed against his shoulders as he positioned himself just inside the doorway. A bartender glanced up at him and his eyes widened, the color of his face instantly matching the white apron he wore.

Checker nodded and continued to look around, letting the fervor of the cowboys build without interruption. His lean, tanned face was accented by an arrowhead-shaped scar on his right cheek. His intense study caught Sonny and Clanahan signaling to him from the back. Nothing in Checker's face was readable, even by them. He made no further attempt to communicate with his two trail friends, concentrating instead on the throbbing crowd to uncover its master.

Sonny whispered to Clanahan, "Do you have a gun?"

"Nay, my friend, 'tis with my saddlebags."

"When I yell out, you shove your hand inside

23

your coat like you're ready to pull one—and keep it there. Got it?"

"O sweet mither of God!"

"It'll be all right, Harry, we'll just wait for John's move," Sonny said, and chuckled, in spite of the seriousness of the situation.

"What be the man, Checker hisself, about to do? Take on all of Texas?"

"Just watch and do like I say."

The former outlaw and former Ranger had become good friends, drawn together by each other's courage, on the Triple C trail drive from deep within the belly of Texas. Checker knew Sonny's past, and Sonny knew John Checker was half brother to Star McCallister, the convicted head of the rustlers who had stolen the Triple C herd. He knew Checker's only reason for coming to Dodge City with the Triple C herd was to be reunited with his long-separated sister, Amelia, and her family. She, her husband, Orville Hedrickson, and their two small children lived on a small horse ranch south of town. Amelia and Checker were the bastard children of J. D. McCallister. He cast off their mother when he was tired of her, never marrying the woman or recognizing the children as his, and letting them live in horrible poverty.

The simple facts had come from Checker; the rest, from Amelia Hedrickson at a party for the Triple C drovers after the herd was recovered and Star and his men arrested. She told Sonny about the fourteen-year-old Johnny Checker attempting to kill the elder McCallister after their mother died pitifully. He wounded one of his men and was saved from their vengeance by a saloon prostitute, who took pity on the boy.

Sister and brother were forced to part shortly after that. Neighbors took in the younger Amelia but wouldn't risk keeping the boy. He had acquired a terrible enemy in J. D. McCallister, and they were afraid his vengeance would be directed at them as well as the boy. Checker was forced to leave his sister behind and ride quickly out of town. Three McCallister men came after him, but only two came back, reporting the boy was dead. Amelia assumed the worst for years until one day she overheard a Texas cowboy talking about a fierce Texas Ranger named John Checker. Her letter to Ranger headquarters had finally triggered his return.

He had ridden with the Triple C drive, giving him a less lonely ride in exchange for his gun. Discovering that his half brother was behind the rustling of their herd had been as hard as discovering that his sister and her family had been wonderful.

"It's Checker!" a startled cowboy yelled, and frantically pushed his way toward the back of the saloon. Statements about lynching and justice were swallowed, helped along by "shhh" and "shut up." The room looked for its courage and became quiet.

Kayler glanced over his shoulder and smiled.

Chapter Two

"Nobody's hanging anybody tonight."

Checker's hard challenge came like a rifle shot snapping at the heads of the standing cowboys. Someone whispered, "He doesn't have a gun." The men closest to Checker tried to ease away from him without appearing to do so, pushing against the furious knot that had formed in the center of the saloon.

Tex saw his opportunity, strolled confidently in front of the surprised Kayler, and said, "Checker, those bastards killed our friends. We're going over to the jail and see that justice is done. Right here 'n' now. You don't have to go if you don't want to. Kayler's going to lead us."

A few of the braver heads nodded agreement. In the middle of the crowd, a growling voice supported Tex with "Let's go, Texas! We've had enough of this!" Checker ignored the second challenge and stepped toward the curly-headed Triple C cowboy. Tex froze in place, forgetting he held a shotgun. His gaze faltered from Checker's glare as he closed the gap between them. The room became aware of the encounter and fell into a soft rattle of isolated chatter.

With words so low only Tex could hear, Checker said, "I want you to leave, Tex. I want you out of Dodge—by tomorrow morning. Tell Randy I said you could have two horses from your string."

Tex's eyes ballooned into heightened fear; his hands forgot they held a shotgun and a lariat. Both slid to the floor. The heavy weapon hit first, and the rope flopped on top of the stock. Ten men jumped, and he looked at the gun as if he was discovering it for the first time. His chest burned, and he knew he was going to be sick. Within the crowd, someone said, "What's Checker doing? What's he sayin'?" That was followed by an urgent "Shut up, you fool."

Shaking his head, Tex stuttered, "J-J-John, I—I—I..."

"You knew the rules, Tex. All of us talked about it after the trial. Don't let me see you again—here or in Texas. I don't like people who don't keep their word."

"B-b-but, J-J-John, I . . . this was d-d-different. I—I—I thought y-y-you wouldn't care, I—I—I really did. John? John . . ."

If Checker heard Tex's explanation, it wasn't apparent. As his last words lashed at Tex's courage, Checker turned away to find G. W. Kayler now absorbed by the crowd. Tex's stomach recoiled and he spun toward the bar, retching on the boots of a Circle J cowboy. The smaller man stumbled backward

27

Cotton Smith

to avoid the vomit and crashed into a blond waitress with a tray of filled drinks and a bottle.

Whiskey and glasses flew over the bar and slapped wetness across the closest men. The bottle exploded against the side of the bar; shards and chunks of glass, mixed with brownish liquid, spewed everywhere. Angry and wet, the waitress cursed him loudly. Laughter was sparse and forced, providing only brief relief from the tension. Red-faced, the cowboy demanded a towel from a bartender to wipe off his boots. Leaning over, his hands on his stomach, Tex left the saloon without a glance to either side. The shotgun remained on the floor where it fell.

Trying to regain control of the room, and still feeling secure with thirty cowboys around him, Kayler snarled, "There's only one of him." The threat was enough to trigger Sonny's loud response from the back of the room. His hard words shoved their way through the crowd.

"I wouldn't count on that, Kayler."

Heads jerked around to see Sonny Jones, with a cocked revolver, standing on top of their table, and Harry Clanahan beside it. Clanahan's right hand was perched inside his coat pocket. The Irishman sought Minnie's attention with his eyes and nodded for her to move away from the bar. Checker walked into the center of the stunned crowd of men and they stepped aside to let him enter. He walked straight toward Kayler, stopping inches from him. Checker's eyes tore into the bigger man's soul.

"Who wants a lynching?" Checker's voice was low and biting.

No one answered. Agitated drovers, surrounding

28

the would-be leader, lowered their heads and eased away from him. A few appeared defiant but said nothing.

"I said, 'Who wants a lynching?'"

Kayler stutter-stepped backward to resecure space between himself and the Ranger and muttered, "I—I did. W-we've waited long enough. D-damn it, Checker, we've waited long enough."

Without responding, Checker turned and addressed the half-circle of men. His words came like they were used to being obeyed. "Any man who joins these fools will be judged a murderer in the eyes of the law. Kansas law. Texas can't help you here. No one can. You will be hunted down and hanged yourself. Are those cowardly bastards in that jail worth giving up the rest of your life? Think about it, boys. This is no time to let whiskey do it for you. If you're tired of waiting, head for Texas. No one is keeping you here."

He paused to let his words sink in. The room was unable to breathe. He looked around at the gathered men, tilted his head to one side, and continued, "Nobody wants to see that bunch hang more than I do. Nobody. But I want the law to do it. That's the law's job, not ours." He paused again, then added, "If that's not clear enough, I will stop any man who tries to start a lynching again—any way I have to."

A thin cowboy with a pockmarked face snarled, "I hear tell Star McCallister is your ree-lation. That why you're trying to stop us?"

Checker's face was a storm for an instant, then the anger passed. He strolled over to the drover and said, "What did you say, friend?"

"I, ah, nothin'. Ah, nothin'. I didn't mean nothin',

honest," the cowboy answered, his Adam's apple jerking up and down with his retreat.

Through gritted teeth, Checker spoke in words that moved slowly into the room, like they were being examined carefully first. "I'd go find the man who told you that—and tell him you looked at death tonight. Don't ever say something like that to me again."

"N-n-no sir. No s-sir, I sure won't," the cowboy said, staring at his boots.

There was a moment of silence, and Kayler found some of his earlier courage and snarled, "How you going to do that? You haven't even got a gun. Or you think you kin take me with your fists?"

Checker looked back at Kayler, who had placed his hands on the pistols in his waistband to reinforce his point. His lariat lay on the floor in front of him. Without hesitation, Checker walked toward him again, his eyes locked onto Kayler's own menacing gaze.

"That's true. I don't have a gun, but you do."

"I'll shoot you, Checker, or I'll beat you to death. Which way you want it?" Kayler grasped the handles tightly but didn't pull either weapon.

Checker closed the short distance between them in four steps. The room forgot to blink. It was happening so fast, no one even dared to flee. In the back, Sonny jumped down from the table and ran toward them, pushing and shoving his way wildly through the thick mass of men.

Stopping two feet from the leader, Checker said, "Give me your guns, Kayler."

"The hell you say. No, you git on outta here—and let a real man take care of things."

Afterward, the closest men argued whether Checker first grabbed one of the guns from the man's waistband or threw a short, thunderous right jab under Kayler's chin that snapped his head back like it was on a hinge. Either way, the two blurring moves were followed by a vicious blow with Kayler's own gun in Checker's right fist. The barrel struck Kayler's temple and sent him flying into a web of startled men. No one attempted to break his fall, and the big man's head slammed against the polished floor. But he was unconscious before he hit. He didn't move. No one attempted to help him either.

"Now I have a gun. Anyone else want to play this stupid game?" Checker said casually. There was no answer.

The metallic click of the pistol's hammer cocking in place was a singular sound of warning. He looked around the room, seeking challenge in the crowd of men. His face had the cold stare few had seen in Dodge but most had heard about. Over his shoulder, he saw Sonny burst through the last line of men. The former outlaw took in the scene instantly and stepped beside Checker with a half-smile on his face.

"What's it going to be, men? It's your call. Not many of you are going to be left to start a lynching," Checker advised.

"You can't get us all," a stocky Circle J cowboy with long, thick sideburns said. It was almost a question. Several turned to stare at him in disbelief at his statement.

"Maybe, maybe not," Checker said. "But you won't know whether we do or not—nor will your fat friend there on the floor. My first bullet takes you. My second takes him. Who gets the third? You? You? Is it worth it to guess?"

A lanky drover with a new shirt, now sporting a long, brown tobacco juice stain, held his hands away from his sides and said, "Checker, you make good sense to me. If'n it's all right by you, I'll be a-leavin' this hyar saloon. Got myself a hankerin' to do some dancin'—elsewhere."

On the heels of his words, a bespectacled cowboy added urgently, "I don't want no part of you, Checker. I ain't carryin'—and I ain't a-gonna. You got my word—as a Texan."

A chorus of voices brought various kinds of supporting statements. In minutes, the billiard tables were busy, as were the faro tables and the bar. Finally, the band members decided it was safe for them too. Feeling confident with Checker in the saloon, the cornet player came down and asked for his instrument back. The cowboy turned it upside down to let the brown juice run out and handed it back. Soon the rhythms of "Camptown Ladies" were again punching out renewed gusto, and the dance floor came alive with swirling motion and forced laughter. Furtive glances at Checker by the frustrated Texans, and the grumbling that went with it, gradually diminished into a night of resumed lust.

After a few minutes of indecision, the same stocky cowboy hesitantly walked over to the crumpled Kayler and tried to wake him. He whispered encouragement, but there was no response. Across the side of Kayler's forehead, a split-skin, red mark was growing fat and oozing blood, indicating the force and angle of Checker's blow with the gun barrel.

Checker walked over to the Circle J cowboy, struggling to get his leader awake or at least on his feet, and said quietly, "Tex knew better, and I told him to get out of town. I'm going to chalk this up to Kayler and not the rest of you Circle J boys. But I won't come in talking if there's a next time."

"I—I think ya done kilt him, Checker."

"No. He's just going to have a bad headache— most of the way back to Texas," Checker said. "You get some help and carry him out of here. I want the Circle J gone by tomorrow night."

"Tomorrow night? B-but . . ."

"If you boys aren't gone, I'm going to figure you want to fight. Understood?"

"B-but he won't be able to r-ride . . ."

"Use some of those new ropes you bought to tie him on a horse."

For a moment, the cowboy's eyes flashed a thought of further challenge, then they flattened into dullness.

"Yessir. Yessir," the stout Circle J rider answered, and waved for the rest of the Circle J men to come over and help him. In minutes, four of them carried the big man out of the saloon with the stout cowboy and another, taller cowboy walking behind them. None spoke or looked at each other.

Checker glanced around for Sonny, and the happy-go-lucky Triple C rider laughed and said, "Well, you do know how to make an entrance, Checker."

"Just happened to pass by. I was headed for the hotel. Kayler's a fool."

"Well, got to hand it to him, he was making thunder and lightning with this bunch. Went from bar talk to trouble real fast. I was headed out to find you when Harry saw you at the doorway."

"Should've figured it would happen. Too much time with nothing to do for most of them. And there's always a Kayler around."

"Yeah, and too much whiskey."

"Wish they'd head back to Texas, instead of waiting around."

Sonny continued to explain the situation as they walked back to Clanahan, who had sat back down at their table. Several cowboys stopped them to assure Checker they hadn't been involved. The Irishman was talking with Minnie, who had brought his order to the table. Sonny quickly advised Checker of the situation, including her being a whore.

As they approached, Clanahan glanced their way, grabbed Minnie's arm before she could walk away, and said, "Wait, honey, I want ye to be meetin' hisself John Checker."

"John Checker, I'd like ye to be meetin' the prettiest girl in Dodge herself, Miss Minnie Oliver," Clanahan said, beaming.

Checker touched the brim of his hat and bowed his head slightly. "Nice to meet you, Miss Oliver."

"The pleasure's all mine," she purred. Her eyes caressed his tanned face and invited him to get to know her better.

Sonny grinned and glanced at Clanahan. The Irishman hadn't caught the exchange; he was pouring Irish whiskey for the three of them. Checker frowned at Sonny and said politely, "Miss Oliver, don't let us keep you from your many responsibilities. We know you're busy. It was nice to meet you.

I'm sure I'll be seeing you sometime—when you're with my friend, Harry."

Uncertain that she had been dismissed, Minnie curtsied and walked away, swishing her rear as she went. After five steps, she paused and half turned to the side to look back. Disappointed none of them were watching her, she stomped toward the bar. Seated at the table, the former Ranger withdrew three cigars from his inside vest pocket, gave one each to Sonny and Clanahan, then bit off the end of the remaining smoke and placed it in his mouth. A flame from Sonny's match lit all three cigars.

"Here's to Texas," Sonny said, lifting the glass and puffing on the new smoke at the same time.

"To Texas," Checker supported.

"And to the beautiful green isle herself," Clanahan added.

All three laughed and downed the fiery whiskey. Talk wandered back to the McCallister gang trial. Triple C drovers sat on the front row, as a place of honor for capturing the rustlers. A wary resolve grew among this small band to see the men who killed their friends go the way of dust and get the terrible tragedy behind them enough to move on.

They had recovered their herd, but that didn't bring back the riders who went down under the McCallister gang's vicious ambush. Nothing would— not even watching the killers hang—but, at least, it was better than knowing they were somewhere alive and laughing. They had also determined, through Checker's guidance, there wouldn't be any interference in any way with the proceedings. They made that vow together at a toast for their friends left behind on the trail.

Within the heart of the town, the leading businessmen had been caught off guard about Star McCallister's criminal involvement. Some were not yet convinced and thought the Texans were nothing more than savages, intent on destroying anyone or anything that got in their way. Of course, this wasn't said where any Texan could overhear the statement. Sonny brought up that townspeople who remembered Star McCallister's late, wild, terrorizing father were quick with "like father, like son" observations, all pronounced with great sanctity, of course.

Reluctantly, he added that the same Dodge City old-timers whispered about a young lad named John Checker who had long ago tried to kill J.D. McCallister and been chased out of town by his gang. They were surprised he was alive. Hearing stories of his reputation in Texas brought wizened nods of expectancy. The only question they couldn't answer was why he had really returned. Only his trail-riding friends knew it was exactly what Checker said it was, to reunite with his long-separated sister and her family. Only they knew that Star McCallister and John Checker were half brothers.

Finally, Clanahan asked about Sarah Ann Tremons as a way to get the conversation back to Minnie Oliver. "Ye be squirin' the doc's fine daughter any these days?"

Sonny choked and coughed into his fist holding the cigar. He knew his lawman friend better than most but would have never brought up the subject of Sarah Ann Tremons. That would have been for Checker to do, if he wanted to. Out of the corner of his eye, he watched the former Ranger to see how he would react.

"Well, yes, I have, Harry. Had supper over there tonight. Checked on Dan. He's coming along fine. Thinks he can start back to Texas in a couple of weeks or so. He's a tough ol' rascal, as good as I've seen. I hope to convince him to ride in the wagon with Tug—at least part of the time."

"What's Doc Tremons say about that?" Sonny asked.

"Oh, in a roundabout way, I'd say he agrees."

"What do you mean, 'in a roundabout way'?"

"Well, first he yells at Dan about not listening to him; then, a few minutes later, he tells me quietly that it would all right if Dan took it easy."

Sonny laughed and sang out, "Oh, come along, Dan, an' listen to the Doc, he'll tell you about your troubles with a whole lotta talk. Coma ti yi yippy yippy yea . . ."

Clanahan smiled, then turned the discussion back to the subject fully occupying his mind. "Would ye be ever thinkin' of marryin' the sweet lass herself, the fine Miss Tremons, an' not goin' back?"

Suddenly the soft scent of Sarah Ann Tremons filled Checker. She had lived within his mind since they met. Always there, waiting for him to return. He had known that feeling only once before, and that was prior to joining the Texas Rangers.

Sonny expected Checker to say something about the subject being personal or scoff at the idea. The former Ranger drew evenly on his cigar, and the silence seemed like days to Sonny, longer to Clanahan.

Finally, the Irishman could hold his joyous thought in no longer and burst out, "By all that's holy, I be thinkin' on it! I be seein' the fine Miss Oliver as me bride. I be seein' meself on a small farm

37

with youn'un's all around us." He looked at Sonny, then at Checker, a little embarrassed by his revelation of something so intimate, yet exhilarated by the release of the statement.

It was Checker who responded first, and it was obvious his mind had not left Sarah Ann. "Those are mighty good thoughts, Harry. I feel sorry for the man who doesn't have them. Maybe it'll work out for you, but I'm afraid Miss Tremons needs someone with a little more to offer her than a horse, two pistols, a rifle, and shirts with pin holes. She deserves far more."

"Don't you think that's something for her to decide, John?" Sonny said, surprising even himself. "Why, I'd be right happy to sing at your weddin'. How's a few verses of 'Dixie' sound? Like . . . ah, I wish I was in the land of Checker . . ." His voice boomed, then broke into a broad laugh.

Checker shook his head and grinned, but Clanahan appeared miffed and said, "Aye, how 'bout the weddin' for meself 'n' Millie? I swear by me mither's grave, I be jes' likely to up 'n' ask the sweet, young thing tonight."

"Harry, you don't know a thing about her, dammit. You just met her. She's a—"

"A very pretty gal," Checker interrupted, and gave Sonny a look that made it clear he shouldn't tell what he knew about her. "Sonny's right, though. You've been riding a long, lonely trail. We all have. It's easy to get caught up in all that loneliness and see something that isn't there. All of us do it from time to time. Sonny's a good friend. He's just looking out for both of us."

"Oh, for the love of St. Peter an' his angels! Me

comrades, now Harry Clanahan is not one of the wee ones born yesterday. I know a thing or two about lasses, I'll tell ye," Clanahan snapped. His eyes sought Minnie Oliver, but she was not in sight at the moment; his face registered disappointment.

Pouring another round for the three of them, Checker changed the subject, his hardened face reflected the different topic. "You know, this lynch talk could be triggered again—at any saloon. Any time. I'm thinking we'd better start guarding the jail ourselves. We can rotate every few hours so nobody has to give up a night's sleep—or a day's play. I'll take the rest of this night an'—"

Involuntarily, Sonny glanced back at the doorway and interrupted, "Well, the way you handled Kayler tonight will likely keep the rest in line—but it's better to be sure. I reckon the boys will help. Well, maybe not Tug. You never know what he'll be thinkin'."

Anxiously studying the crowded room for signs of his waitress sweetheart, Clanahan asked, "Marshal Rand hisself be havin' two deputies inside all the time, is that not the truth?"

"Yeah, they're there. How long do you think they would have lasted against this group tonight?" Checker said.

Neither Sonny nor Clanahan spoke. Sonny examined his cigar to see why it wasn't drawing properly, and Clanahan was half standing, trying to see Minnie Oliver. Checker waited for their response, sipping his new drink.

"What be the good in having one or two more men ag'in the devil's mob hisself?" Clanahan asked without looking at either friend. His brow was deeply furrowed as his eyes continued to seek Minnie. His eyebrows popped up in delight as he discovered her on the far side of the saloon, talking with a tableful of cowboys.

"Maybe we all should stay there until this thing's over," Sonny suggested. "I don't think they'd rush the whole bunch of us."

He withdrew a pocketknife from his crowded vest pocket and hacked off a portion of the cigar where he held it in his mouth. After removal of an inch of the wrapped tobacco, he ran his fingers along the cigar, placed it in his mouth, and relit the smoke. Two long puffs proved his examination was accurate, and his toothy grin was evidence.

"Two men can do it—if they're alert and fresh," Checker said. "If anything looks suspicious, one will fire a double-barreled shotgun into the air. That'll bring all of us running."

"You think the boys at Ham's will hear that?" Sonny asked, irritated that his cigar was again drawing poorly. Checker chuckled, reached inside his coat, and produced a new smoke. He handed it to Sonny, and the former outlaw nodded his appreciation.

"Maybe, maybe not. But I think our being there is all that's needed to make 'em stop and think. I'll tell all the trail bosses we expect them to keep their men in line. This isn't our town. We're only guests here."

"High-payin' guests," Sonny said. "You plan on tellin' Kayler too?"

"Already told his men to get out of town—tomorrow."

"You think they will?"

Checker nodded his head.

Clanahan tossed down his whiskey and said, "Would ye be tellin' the marshal of our wee plan? What if hisself be against it?"

"He won't be. I want to see Star McCallister—and his bunch—hanging from a rope. Legal-like," Checker said. Each word was a stabbing.

Shoving the new cigar into his mouth, Sonny studied his friend in the oily glow of the saloon. He realized he'd never seen John Checker look so determined. Ever. He shivered. Clanahan, oblivious to Checker's manner, shoved his chair back and stood. His eyes were locked onto Minnie Oliver. She was sitting in a cowboy's lap, laughing.

"Me darlin's, ye won't be needin' meself this night, I take it. Me lady, she be callin'."

"Now, don't start some damn fight," Sonny growled, and laughed. "At least until we get over there—to help."

Chapter Three

Ominous hammering of a gallows being built welcomed the gray morning, making everyone in Dodge even more aware of the coming event. News of last night's saloon confrontation had spread throughout the town and changed somewhat in detail over the telling, at least in some places. A few townspeople thought the Texans had taken control of the town; a few even believed the mayor and the marshal had been hanged; a few were convinced John Checker had shot a dozen men by himself to stop the rioting. Many were not surprised at the real news about a lynch mob; they figured Texans were little more than savages anyway, intent on destroying anyone or anything that got in their way, though they would never let a Texan hear them say that.

As usual, no one was walking near the jail, situated south of the railroad tracks and north of the town's designated area for revelry. It stood like a sentinel separating the good from the bad—the respectable citizenry and their merchants from the wild fare for the incoming drovers—within the Front Street thoroughfare, almost a hundred yards wide. Inside the small structure were jammed eight gang members and Star McCallister, awaiting their sentences to hang. Far to the east were the vast cattle pens and the loading area for the railcars headed out.

Crossing the muddy street, a tired John Checker had just left Sonny Jones as the morning guard in front of the jail. The tall man spotted Harry Clanahan and Minnie Oliver walking down the planked sidewalk outside of the Great Western Hotel. Clanahan was using a crutch to assist his broken leg, but the smile on his face indicated he was feeling no pain.

"Top o' the mornin' to ye, me darlin' John!" Clanahan shouted gaily.

"Well, good mornin' to you, Harry—and to you, Miss Oliver."

Clanahan frowned slightly and said, "Pardon my sayin' so, John, me lad, but ye be lookin' a bit weary this fine morn. 'Twere it quiet at the constable's during the eve?"

Checker ran his hand across his unshaven chin before answering, "It was too quiet. Let's a man think too much."

Minnie Oliver was hungover; her dress was rumpled and her piled-up curls had fallen down on one side of her head. Her red-lined eyes looked directly into Checker's face and offered herself. He blinked and looked away.

"Headin' for a wee bit o' sleep ye be?"

43

"Well, later. Right now I'm going to get some breakfast and then see if the rest of our crew will help with the guarding. I think we owe the town that much."

"Aye, Harry Clanahan, ye be countin' among your sojurs."

Checker's shoulders rose and fell. "Thanks, Harry. I know you want to help, but I think we've got it covered. What with your bad leg and all—"

"Nawww, bleeming nawwww! John, me mither's son be better'n any lad ye be havin'—even with one leg!" Clanahan interrupted. His face was flushed with immediate temper.

Checker smiled. "All right, all right, you've got the watch tonight between ten and one. You'll relieve whoever's there and Sonny will take over from you at one. I'll take it from four on."

"Say, how did hisself, Constable Rand, be takin' the news about the fine Triple C lads playin' sojur an' guardin' hisself 'n' his boys?"

"Hard man to figure. I suppose he didn't like the thought that he and his men couldn't handle it alone. He didn't seem worried, that's for sure," Checker said. "He's all right, though. When he realized we were serious, he said we should watch from that alley by the hotel."

"What fer should we be doin' that?"

Checker glanced at Minnie, who burped, giggled, and burped again. He answered, "It makes sense. We can see everything going on around the jail—without standing on the porch and making a mighty tempting target. Sonny, you an' me are staying at the hotel, so we'll hear a shotgun warning easier too."

Clanahan glanced at the jail and waved at the coffee-drinking Sonny. In the former outlaw's right hand, at his side, was a double-barreled shotgun. Sonny waved his coffee cup and sang out, "Come an' get it, all you long-eared, hairy-assed, rope-lovin' clowns!"

Chuckling, the Irishman looked back at Checker and asked, "Movin' to the alley will Sonny hisself be?"

"Don't know. I told him what Rand suggested. Sonny kinda likes standing there, daring somebody to come at him, I reckon."

Clanahan agreed and noted that the rest of the Triple C crew wouldn't likely hear anything, regardless of where the guard stood. Tyrel Bannon and Pete Jackson were bedding down in the loft over Ham Bell's Livery, along with a lot of other money-short cowboys. In the case of both young Bannon and Jackson, it was a decision to save their money, not a decision of last resort. Randy Reilman, the drive's foulmouthed wrangler, and Tug, the hard-of-hearing cook, were sleeping with the trail drive remuda and chuck wagon on open flatland just across the Arkansas River. Both had been slightly injured during the rustling of their herd but were getting around fine.

However, the badly wounded trail boss, Dan Mitchell, was still being tended to at the home of Dr. Tremons, at the doctor's insistence. The rest of the crew had been murdered by the McCallister gang. Clanahan noted he had seen Tex leave early this morning as well as the Circle J hands. They had Kayler tied to a horse to keep him on. Checker acknowledged he had seen the disgraced Triple C drover leave as well. That brought more giggles from Minnie, who told Clanahan to tell how he happened to see Tex leave. The Irishman blushed.

"John, me be thinkin' ye were a mite hard on 'im," Clanahan said. "Tex never means nothin'. Hisse'f be needin' the stage, that be all. The man be too purty for his own good, I be thinkin'. Ye know, only a few of us Triple C men be left, an' he be one o' us, bless his soul."

"Yeah, maybe so, Harry, maybe so. If you want to ride after him, you can give him the word he can stay."

"A wee buggy ride this fine morn Minnie 'n' me be takin', John, me darlin'."

"He'll go to our camp first. I told him he could have two horses from his string. Randy'll pump him for the 'why' an' curse him for being so stupid. He'll have to repeat it for Tug because he won't hear half of it, and then Tug'll insist on cookin' up something for him before leaving. That'll take some time, I reckon. You shouldn't have any trouble catching up with him—if you leave soon."

"Methinks John Checker be thinkin' hisself about Tex."

"Are you sure you want to go out there? I can do it."

"Sure as me sainted mither's grave, I be."

"Thanks, good friend," Checker said and smiled thinly.

Clanahan smiled, took Minnie by the arm, and walked on. After a few strides, she turned her head to make a coquettish connection with Checker, but he was walking into the closest restaurant and wasn't watching them at all. She frowned, burped, and giggled. Clanahan looked over at her and patted her arm entwined in his. They strolled on, enjoying the sights of Dodge City struggling to come awake. Minnie gladly agreed to go with him to the Triple C camp, he would rent a carriage at Ham's Livery Stable.

Behind them came an intriguing song of jiggling bells, snorting horses, and creaking wagon wheels. They turned to see a brightly colored patent-medicine wagon rolling into town. Two prancing bay horses brought the enclosed wooden wagon down Front Street with flair and style. Painted crimson with accents of gold and purple, large scrolled lettering announced "Dr. Gambree's Patented Medicines."

Smaller letters added "Proven cures for thin blood, coughing, rheumatism, baldness, sores, feminine illness, and more! Thrill to Salome and her dance of seven veils! Enjoy the word of God preached by Dr. Gambree, ordained minister of faith." Matching rows of tiny bells lined the main harness of both horses.

At the reins was a striking-looking man with a black top hat, shoulder-length, light brown hair, and eyeglasses. Beneath his black duster, he was stylishly dressed with a tailored, three-piece broadcloth suit, a fresh white shirt and collar, accented with a crimson sash, and a matching silk cravat. Out of sight, a short-barreled Colt .45 with yellowish pearl handles and a matching knife rested in his belt, covered by his vest and sash.

"Greetings, you fine citizens of Dodge, I have come to heal you!" he shouted as the wagon jingled along Front Street. "Come and see the wonders of medicine and the charms of Salome! Learn how God wants you to live in good health."

Beside him sat a well-endowed woman in an elaborate, glittery gown that appeared to be more like a second layer of skin and hid little of her bosom. On her head was a small crown that caught the morning sun and sent it dancing away. Thick ebony hair lay over her shoulders. She waved and smiled at the gathering of people, mostly cowboys, as the wagon passed. Among the men, the talk was immediately about her.

"Hey, Doc! Ya got anything that'll put hair back?" a cowboy yelled, and pointed to his bald-headed friend.

"Ah, yes, my son, indeed, we do," Dr. Gambree answered authoritatively. "I have nostrums to cure everything from poor blood, to lifelong coughing, to most of life's aches and pains, to lumbago and kidney troubles—to saddle sores and a lackluster love life. And, yes, baldness and feminine ills as well. Come and see for yourself."

Bored cowboys and curious townspeople stopped their morning travels to watch the touring entertainment center enter their lives and take up a position at the corner of Front Street and Bridge Street, the town's major intersection, sometimes called "The Plaza." False-fronted stores with wooden awnings and eight-foot-wide wooden sidewalks adorned the area. On the north side of Front Street—the "deadline" for Texans—stretched out the respectable community of Dodge for at least eight blocks. Behind them sat the toll bridge over the Arkansas River. The streets were blossoming with people, horses, wagons, and carriages. It was a most suitable place to make a grand entrance. Even some of the hard-faced freighters reined their mules to watch.

Standing on the wagon seat bench, the black-haired woman began to move her hands and body slowly to unheard music. Her midriff was bare except for a glittering red jewel in her navel. Cowboys cheered and were immediately told to be quiet by their captivated comrades. She waved a long, see-through, rainbow-colored wrap, each color becoming its own separate tail. Slowly around her body the wrap was woven. Her gyrations were suddenly accented by a tambourine that appeared in her hand.

The long-haired Dr. Gambree jumped down and quickly brought out a large black leather suitcase from its place in the rear of the wagon. On a small portable table he rested the valise and opened it to reveal a colorful display of packaged, patented medicines: Hamlin's Wizard Oil, Blood Pills and Cough Balsam, Lydia Pinkham's Compound for Female Weakness, Dalley's Magical Pain Extractor, Doan's Pills, Carter's Little Liver Pills, Castoria, Bromo-Seltzer, and even Dr. Pepper's Tonic. With a polished style, he lined up a full row of his own branded products in dark bottles with bright yellow labels: Liniment & Worm Syrup, Blood Pills, Instant Back Pain Reliever, and Hair Restoring Oil.

"Gentlemen with heart troubles should look away—for I bring you a dance that has been handed down from the ancient days of the Bible. Ancient days, when the seductress Salome danced her way into the heart of the king of Egypt and away with the head of John the Baptist. Yes, I bring you now the great-great-great-granddaughter of the world's most beautiful woman—carrying the same seductive name as her illustrious ancestor—before your very eyes . . . is Salome!"

At the back of the fascinated crowd stood two more Triple C riders. One was Tyrel Bannon, the young Texas farm boy who had found his first trail drive to be far more than he had expected. At his side was the three-legged, black cur dog, Captain, who had taken to spending time with Bannon since his master, Dan Mitchell, was injured. The other rider was his good friend and mentor, Peter Jackson. The tall, thick-framed, black cowboy was holding a newly purchased prize, a sack filled with three new books.

Bannon was proudly wearing new chaps and spurs, a new hat, and a brand-new shirt. Unlike many drovers, he didn't want anyone to mistake him for a townie, so business suits were of no interest. But, so far, he had saved most of his money to give to his mother when they returned to Texas, including a special bonus for helping save the herd. Mr. Carlson, the herd's owner, had lent him worn chaps and an old set of spurs to make the drive, and Bannon was eager to return them.

His selection for the drive had been a veiled way of giving money to Tyrel's widowed mother, wife of a late friend. Carlson "advanced" the boy's pay to his mother before the drive began, telling her it was a standard practice. Later, he wired Checker to pay the boy in full again, plus a bonus. Trail boss Dan Mitchell never expected the farmboy, a green hand he didn't want along, to end up saving his life, but Bannon did just that.

To show his gratitude, Mitchell offered him a full riding job for the Triple C and gave Bannon a brand-new Colt .45 and gunbelt, and a new Winchester, from Zimmerman's Gun Store in Dodge. Jackson had actually done the purchasing, because the wounded trail boss was in no shape to do so on his own. The new guns were on Bannon's mind all the time. He knew the rules against being armed in the city limits and had reluctantly left the revolver and rifle with his other gear at the chuck wagon, along with the old Army .44 cap-and-ball revolver and homemade holster he had worn on the drive. Every day he rode out to the chuck wagon camp just to practice with the new weapons, especially the handgun.

His blond hair was freshly barbered, setting off his angular, sunburned face. Under a wide-brimmed, white Stetson, pulled low on his forehead, a tiny band of freckles had refused to leave his hawkish nose during the drive. Average-sized and slimwaisted, he looked younger than his eighteen years. But the veterans who rode with him on the long, dark trail to Dodge considered him one of them and respected his ability to fight, to stay with whatever task he was given—and to handle a gun.

Tyrel Bannon had seen a medicine wagon once before, back home, but it was nothing like this magnificent presentation. His face was bright with fascination. There was something strangely familiar about this Dr. Gambree, but he couldn't decide what it was. Obviously he'd never met the man before. But his interest in the medicine man was far surpassed by his interest in the woman on the wagon seat. Once she caught his stare and welcomed him with a brief connection.

He blinked, turned red around his neck, and im-

51

mediately looked around to see if anyone had noticed. If Jackon had, he didn't show it, and Bannon's view gradually returned to her and she smiled. He grinned so wide it hurt his face, and he was disappointed when she turned her attention to getting down from the wagon. He thought about rushing over to help her but was too shy to try.

Jackson watched the proceedings with an eye on the medicine itself. His back was bothering him most of the time these days, and he wondered if he should try taking something for it. None of the doctors in town would see a black man, and he couldn't bring himself to bother Dr. Tremons with his aches, not when he was helping heal his boss. That wouldn't be right, even though he was one of Dan Mitchell's most dependable men and had been on every trail drive Mitchell had led.

He glanced over at his young friend and said in his liquid southern accent, "Well, yo-all don't see this back home, do you, Ty-rel? Mighty fancy folks."

A gentle smile was there, like it usually was. So was an old scratched pipe sticking out the corner of his mouth. Strings of white smoke curled across his dark round face, danced along his wire-rimmed spectacles and past gray-speckled hair under a blackish hat with a half-inch band around the wide, flat rim.

Contrary to most celebrating cowboys, he continued to wear his trail clothes. No one seemed to know what he was saving his money for, but he clearly was. Over his beat-up batwing chaps and a patched red shirt, he wore a long gray coat with big pockets that Tyrel once thought carried anything a man could ever want. A big, faded blue kerchief was tied loosely at his neck. In one coat pocket was a book he was currently reading; in the other, a pistol.

Usually quiet around the others, he and the young farmboy hit it off on the first day of the drive—the older man seeing a young man eager to learn, and the boy realizing he'd found a good tutor. Bannon had never met a colored man before, but what he'd heard sure didn't fit in this man's boots. Not at all. They were good friends and more; Tyrel trusted Jackson to keep him out of trouble on the trail—and now in town.

Bannon liked to listen to the older man's smooth talking and watch his savvy way of handling a horse. Jackson's love of books had even sparked an interest for learning to read within the young rider. Among his gifts to take home, in addition to dress cloth for his mother and sister, were two almost-new books. Jackson had helped him read most of one already.

The thrills of Dodge City had been a new challenge for both of them: Jackson trying to keep his young friend from overdoing and Bannon trying to taste all of this wondrous new world. Bannon had his first real saloon drink and didn't like it; his first game of monte and won twice before Sonny encouraged him to walk away. He had experienced his first time with a woman and loved it. Jackson hadn't been with him for any of these passages. Tex, Clanahan, and Sonny were the guides. It had taken some scolding from Jackson to keep the young rider from spending more of his money on whores or gambling.

Bannon hadn't liked the advice but decided, by himself, that a real man had to learn to resist these temptations if he wanted to be somebody someday.

But he also told himself it was important to have done them all so a man could know just what temptations he was to avoid. He was still trying to reconcile with himself that being with a woman should be one of them. After all, how could anything so nice be bad? Maybe just once more would help him decide. He had never seen anything like her before. Not even the popular cancan dance at the Varieties Theatre was as exciting as this. Jackson touched him on the shoulder, and Bannon jumped.

"Come on, Tyrel, let's go see Checker."

"Aw, can't we wait until she finishes? It wouldn't be polite to leave in the middle."

"Tyrel."

"Oh, all right."

Bannon reluctantly agreed, and they walked away. The farmboy glanced back at Salome, who was now reversing the multicolored wrap from around her slithering body. His mind placed himself close to her. Out of the corner of his eye, he spotted Dr. Gambree busily selling medicines from his small table. Walking in rhythm to the drumming, he decided to ask Jackson about what he thought of Salome later. He glanced back once more but was disappointed that she was facing the other direction.

Jackson saw Clanahan limping toward them with a woman on his arm. He notified Bannon of his discovery, and they left to greet them with Captain bounding beside the young farm boy.

"Top o' the mornin', me darlin' Tyrel—and the saver of me life, Jackson! Methinks John Checker'll be needin' to see ye soon," Clanahan sang out cheerily. Jackson had helped Clanahan get away safely, with only a broken leg, after his horse was shot and fell on him during the McCallister gang raid. Clanahan had given him a leather-bound volume of poems, from one of the general stores, as a thank-you.

Bannon and Jackson greeted the Irishman with equal enthusiasm and tipped their hats toward Minnie. Clanahan introduced her to them, then explained what had happened the night before and Checker's decision to watch the jail to keep a lynch mob from taking over. Jackson had heard this morning that Checker had killed a dozen Texas cowboys but didn't figure it was right; Clanahan assured him it wasn't. Young Bannon was instantly eager to find Checker and volunteer.

"Is Sonny carryin' iron?" he asked.

"Aye, an ugly shotgun be with the happy lad— and a pistol fine as Mister Colt hisself be makin'," Clanahan answered, pursing his lips as he spoke. "Hisself got it from John when the lad took over the watch this morn. Don't know where John got it. Didn't look like Tug's. He'll be askin' ye to help."

His eyes wide, Bannon blurted, "Jackson, best we ride out to camp. Git our pistols an' such. Gonna need 'em."

Jackson relit his pipe, nodded agreement, and asked Clanahan for details about the evening. Tyrel interrupted, "Harry, did Checker stop those Texans by himself?"

"Aye, with a wee bit o' help from Sonny and meself. But make them see the error of their ways, did he."

"Man, I'll bet he had that Colt of his flashing."

"No, lad, John not be carrying last night. The city's fine ordinance, ye know."

"But . . . but how did he stop them?"

"A wee o' hard words, a bare-knuckle fist, an' a borrowin' of another fella's gun, 'twere. 'Twas a sight for all the Texas lads' eyes."

"Wish I'd been there!"

Minnie studied the young rider intently, finally catching his attention, giggled, and said softly, "You're the one, aren't you. You're the one that Thunder Agnes was tellin' all about, first time 'n'—"

Suddenly she realized what the significance of her knowing about Bannon being with a prostitute meant and stopped in midsentence. Crimson-faced, Bannon swallowed and stared at her, not sure what he should do or say. His mouth dropped open, but nothing came out. He pulled on the brim of his hat again, crossed his arms, and stared at the ground for an instant, then looked back at Minnie, hoping against hope that she would be gone. She smiled meekly and said, "Oh, I must be mistaken. I thought you were a relative of a friend of mine who just came into town." She glanced furtively at Clanahan, but he was too busy talking with Jackson to notice her mistake.

"No, ma'am. No kin that I know about."

"Oh, I'm sorry."

"No apologies necessary, ma'am." Bannon smiled a lopsided grin. She courtsied and sought Clanahan's arm for reassurance.

He looked at her, smiled, and declared, "Got to hurry along, me lad. Headin' out to camp, we be. John be wantin' me to talk with Tex. A wee argument they be havin' last night, an' forgiveness I be deliverin'. Don't want to miss the lad an' be havin' to ride all the way to the Red to catch up with his-self." He chuckled at his joke. Both Jackson and Bannon wanted to ask more about the incident between Tex and Checker, but the Irishman was already walking away. Minnie jump-stepped to keep up.

Behind them, Dr. Gambree was making another announcement. "And now, I am proud to bring you medicines and curing potions from all over this wondrous land. Step closer and see for yourselves, my friends. Never before—anywhere—have the world's great healing secrets been so displayed, and all for your convenience this fine day. As the Lord sayeth in the Good Book, 'Go and do thou likewise.' Luke ten, verse thirty-seven. Come closer, my friends, just today and today only . . ."

Chapter Four

A brooding darkness came to Dodge soon enough, bringing cool breezes, streaking shadows, and renewed energy for the south side's dens of wickedness. By early evening, talk of a lynching was nowhere to be found anywhere in town, whether it involved creating a mob to attack the jail or wondering if there would be an outbreak of so-called Texas justice. Even among the most hardened Texans, the talk was about more important matters: horses, cattle, women, land, and playing cards. Dodge citizenry were busy with matters of commerce or family and quite eager to put the jail's occupants—and the reason for being there—out of their minds.

Unspoken, for the most part, was the town's desire to get the hanging over so the cowboys would have no reason to stick around. Trail-drive riches had shrunk to parsimonious transactions for the most part, and heavy indulgence in the free lunches offered at most of the south-side saloons, billiard parlors, and gambling houses.

Quietly, during the day, three separate sets of trail-herd drovers pulled out and headed home, at the orders of their respective trail bosses. Leaving early seemed like a better percentage play than staying and losing a drunken hand to gunplay. Several other trail bosses promised their drovers an extra bonus if they didn't get involved.

Triple C riders accepted their guard roles without grumbling. No one said anything to the returning Tex about his performance the night before. Checker paid him the ultimate compliment by trusting him with guard duty in the late afternoon. Bannon, Jackson, and Tex had taken the daylight hours. During the night, the guard would be doubled: Clanahan and Tex would have the first watch to midnight; Sonny and Jackson, the second until four A.M.; and Checker and Bannon would take the hardest part of the night, from four on to morning. Clanahan would relieve them, by himself, at eight. Checker decided not to involve either Tug or Randy Reilman but to let them stay on duty at the chuck wagon camp.

Bannon was excited, and anxious, about standing watch with the former Ranger; Jackson told him it was quite a compliment because Checker obviously expected trouble—if it came—to be then. After supper, Bannon and Jackson went to find the medicine wagon; Jackson wanted to buy something for his backaches before he went on guard duty; Bannon wanted to see that woman again, so he eagerly agreed. Unfortunately, the wagon was closed and no one was in sight. A small printed sign said: "Begging your pardon, we are gone for a while. We will return to care for your needs soon. Thank you for your patience—Dr. Gambree." Bannon wanted to wait, but Jackson shook his head and headed for the livery and sleep. Reluctantly, the farm boy followed.

While Jackson and Bannon were at the medicine wagon, Harry Clanahan and Tex stood watch in a darkened alley next to the Great Western Hotel and across the street from the isolated jail. Both agreed with Checker—and Marshal Rand—that it made good sense to stay in the alley beside the hotel and not in front of the jail. If lynch mob trouble started, one was to fire the shotgun twice into the air. That would bring Sonny and Checker charging from their rooms.

Checker considered moving Jackson and Bannon into the hotel as well, for the two nights remaining until the hanging, and paying for it himself, so they would be closer if needed. However, hotel management wouldn't accept a black man under any circumstances, not even Checker's not-so-subtle threats. The manager expressed understanding but said he had to answer to the townspeople the rest of the year and just couldn't do it. The townspeople would more likely understand a lynching than a black man in his hotel.

Tex hadn't changed from his trail clothes, including chaps with large white stars at the lower flaps. Only a pistol belt, from his gear in the chuck wagon, had been added. Over the last hour, he had pressed Clanahan for a complete recital of his conversation with Checker about himself.

"Come on, Harry, what did Checker really say about me?"

"Well, me darlin' Tex, all of the words that be said I've told you now. Two times it be," Clanahan said feistily. "The big man didn't be sayin' all that much. Saints 'n' begorra, ye be a lucky lad who found the wee shamrock—a fair boss. John Checker be fair. Tough as Satan hisself, but fair."

"Checker isn't my boss. Dan is."

"Well, then, me lad, ye kin jes' be tellin' Mr. Checker that hisself."

"Oh, you know what I mean," Tex deferred. "I don't mean nothin'. You wouldn't tell what I said, would ya?"

"Nay, me silly friend, I would not. On me sainted mither's grave, I be promisin'."

"G. W. Kayler, now that's a real trail boss," Tex mumbled, glancing to see how the Irishman would react to the words.

"Kayler be headed for Texas a wee humbled, me lad," Clanahan snorted. " 'Tis a lucky man he be. Checker let him live."

"Kayler said he buffaloed Checker once down near the border."

"If'n ye be believin' in such a yarn, me friend, ye should be seein' the wee green ones soon."

The handsome cowboy was disappointed Clanahan wasn't impressed with Kayler and that Checker didn't have more to say about him. He tried a different angle: "Kayler's right. We should string up those bastards to show this town who's boss. Who cares if they live a few more days or not?"

"Checker—an' Sonny. Maybe Jackson. Meself, I be carin' that Sonny and Jackson be a-comin' when they be supposed to," Clanahan replied. "Aye, the sweet hour of midnight cannot be a-comin' too soon fer this mick."

The slump-shouldered Irishman was hungover from a serious case of lovesickness. Minnie. Minnie Oliver. His loins responded to the memory of their day together. Anger followed at the thought of her being around other cowboys at the saloon. But he tried to convince himself this was just her job and she had to do it. He could hear the tinny music from the dance hall down the street, or thought he did. It sounded so great and made him even more anxious to be with her.

"Tex, what time would it be nearin'?" he fumed out loud, took the brand-new silver watch from his new vest pocket, clicked open the lid, and checked the time. 10:37.

"About five minutes since you asked me before," Tex snapped, and strolled away toward the middle part of the alley to relieve himself. As he left, Clanahan began singing to himself: "When all around a vigil keep/The West's asleep, the West's asleep/Alas, and well may Erin weep . . . When Connacht lie in slumber . . ."

Urgently, Tex's peripheral vision sought movement among the shadows at the far end of the alley. He stared intently until he was satisfied, then nodded approval and motioned that he was returning. He glanced back at Clanahan and saw that his friend was staring down the street. It had been a long day—and an amazing one for him. First, he left town in disgrace, headed alone for Texas, all because of Checker's bullheadedness. The next thing he knew, he was helping his Triple C friends again— and guarding against the very thing he had tried to arouse the night before. Now he was going to help Kayler break into the jail and show Checker who was the real boss in Dodge. The gruff cattleman had teamed up with an unlikely supporter, the medicine show doctor.

Truly a strange day, Tex thought. *Who would've thought a medicine show doc would help with a lynching!* He turned his head away from the shadowy figures crouched ten feet away and smiled. Clanahan wouldn't like this, but he would have no choice but to go along.

Clanahan stared at the pocket watch and ran his fingers along the attached silver chain. It was a purchase from Wright, Beverly, & Co.'s general store, the first thing he did after getting paid, even before getting a bottle of whiskey. It was the first watch he had ever owned. His broadcloth suit had come from there, too. Under the store-bought vest, a revolver was stuck in his belt, rather than a strapped-on gunbelt, his bow to civilized society. Unlike Tex, who was wearing cross-belted pistols.

Tomorrow Clanahan planned to return to the jewelry store and buy that pretty brooch he'd seen and give it to Minnie. He would have done it today, but Sonny suggested that he wait, give it another day. Sonny counseled not rushing into anything. Tex agreed when Clanahan asked for his advice. But all Clanahan could think of was Minnie and her becoming a part of his life.

"Ah, me sweet mither, would ye be a bit proud of your lad if'n you could see him now, all dressed he is in the finery of a gentleman and sporting a fine new silver watch hisself," he muttered to himself.

"Tex, even ye be a wee jealous of this Irishman's beautiful silver watch."

"Yeah, it's a good-lookin' piece. Would really be nice if it had a star on the lid," Tex said as he strutted back to Clanahan.

Returning the watch to his vest, Clanahan withdrew two cigars from inside his coat pocket, handed one to Tex, and lit them with solemn concentration. White smoke encircled their heads, rattled around Clanahan's new derby and Tex's wide-brimmed Stetson, and ran for the dark sky. Clanahan leaned against the windowless side of the building to give relief to his splinted broken leg. His crutch and the double-barreled shotgun also leaned there.

"This be a night when a knowing man might be seein' a leprechaun, fer sure," Clanahan said, and squinted into the darkness. Silently, he told himself that if he saw one, he'd ask for his help in winning over the lovely Minnie.

"Don't be silly, mick." Tex chuckled. "Hey, is there somethin' across the street?" He motioned subtly with his right hand for the men in the shadows to advance.

"Where, Tex? I don't be see—"

Clanahan felt the strong hand across his mouth and the bursting of his neck at the same time as his mind caught the significance of the flash of a knife from the black-coated stranger behind him. Clanahan's hand rose halfway to his throat, and he wimpered. His body trembled as life rushed from the gaping hole. His frightened eyes caught Tex's terrified expression for an instant.

"No! No! You said—"

The assailant spun and pressed his hand over the

handsome cowboy's mouth to keep any shout from escaping. Tex's shirt erupted into crimson as the killer drove the knife into his stomach and shoved it sideways. Down-the-street sounds of men laughing and tinny music playing wrapped their irony around death in the alley. Tex collapsed to the ground, his blood spreading into the soft Kansas earth, taking the rest of his breath with the flowing red. Tex reached out to touch Clanahan, but his shaking hand only wobbled in the air and fell to the earth and was still.

Dr. Gambree stood over his fallen prey in silent admiration of the smoothness of the completed task. The second man, G. W. Kayler, was stunned and finally uttered, "Did ya have to kill them? Tex was with us—an' I—I thought you were just gonna knock out the Irishman."

Dr. Gambree straightened his red cravat and glanced at the bloody blade in his hand. Under his black top hat, shoulder-length, light brown hair glowed from the strokes of moonlight. He spoke with a guttural snarl.

"Would you rather be facing Checker right now?"

"Well, ah, no, but . . ."

"Then shut up."

Kayler shrugged, his eyes wide with fascination at the two dead men before him. His own swollen face was blotched with purple welts from his fight with Checker. Seeping blood headed for his boots, and he stepped back to avoid its assault. His big chest pounded against the undersized suit. A loosely tied bandanna, lying against his vest, rose and fell in rhythm. His crude, boisterous manner was swallowed beneath the fierce intensity of this strange

medicine wagon doctor who had approached him—
through Salome—about lynching the McCallister
gang.

The idea was simple: Instead of making the lynching into a loud circus, they would be invited into the
jail, with the doctor offering his spiritual services to
condemned men. Kayler enjoyed hearing that even
the marshal was in on it. Dr. Gambree's assistant
would bring extra Kayler horses to the back of the
jail. The gang would be tied and taken to a grove of
cottonwoods where Kayler's riders waited to hang
them. It was a perfect plan, except Kayler missed the
thought of aroused men following him, doing what
he ordered. It wasn't the same if no one knew what
they were doing.

"Now, for the next step. Kayler, are you sure your
men are waiting east of town by those cottonwoods?" Dr. Gambree said, and wiped his bloody
blade on Clanahan's coat, then returned his pearl-
handled knife to a sheath beneath his vest.

"Sure, sure," Kayler responded eagerly. "Ropes is
all knotted real purty, jes' a-waitin'. You done figgered this real good, Doc. Had no idea how you felt
about it. It's a shame folks can't see it, though."

"Checker has no right to be telling people what to
do. He's not the law," Dr. Gambree said. "The
sooner that McCallister bunch is strung up, the better. Marshal Rand agrees with us. Of course, he
couldn't say so."

Kayler smiled. "Can't wait to see that damn
Ranger's face! He'll know who runs this town then.
Everyone will, by God."

"Help me drag this Irishman up against the alley.
He'll look like he's sleeping to anyone passing,"

Dr. Gambree ordered, and stepped toward Clanahan's lifeless body. He paused and glanced upward at the darkened hotel with its windows pointed at the street. Inside, somewhere, John Checker and Sonny Jones were staying. Although Sonny had been spotted earlier in the night at the Lady Gay, Checker had been seen going into the hotel two hours ago.

Methodically, they dragged the lifeless body to the wall of the hotel and propped it in place so any passerby would think a drunken cowboy was merely asleep there. Furtively, Dr. Gambree glanced upward at the dark hotel as if he would see through the walls.

"Right under Checker's nose," he said, then chuckled to himself. "Lynch mob, my ass, John Checker. You should've been expecting family." He bit his lip to hold in the laughter that wanted out.

He replaced the derby on Clanahan's head, adjusting it downward over his eyes to make it appear as if the dead Triple C rider was sleeping. "How's that, you silly fool. You need to look your best for Checker."

After one more adjustment of the hat, Dr. Gambree examined his hands. Both had touched oozing blood, leaving red streaks. He cursed under his breath and tried to wipe the stain on the cowboy's clothes. Kayler shivered and looked away. He wondered if they were going to do the same thing with Tex's body but couldn't bring himself to ask. Veins pounding angrily in his forehead at the blood's reluctance to leave, Dr. Gambree yanked off Clanahan's coat, rubbing it over his hands, but the stains remained.

Dr. Gambree's steely gaze darted toward the jail

and saw a shadowed figure opposite the building waving at him. "Good. At least the fool can take orders." The medicine wagon doctor snorted his disrespect at the anxious command, grabbed the shotgun leaning against the wall alongside Clanahan's crutch, and jammed it barrel-first into the mud. He watched the weapon shiver in its new placement, laughed to himself again.

"What about . . . Tex? Yah gonna leave him here?"

"No, you're gonna carry him to the jail."

Kayler's face exploded into a mixture of anger and fear. He stammered, "W-what fer? T-that don't make no sense. I—"

"I thought you wanted to embarrass Checker," Dr. Gambree said. His eyes had a friendly look.

"Well, of course I do, but . . ."

"Imagine him seeing his own man dead in the jail and the gang gone. Get it now?"

Kayler chuckled harshly, shook his head, and said, "You think o' everything, Doc. That'll be real fine."

"All right, you get Tex there and stay in the shadows. We've got a hanging to tend to," Dr. Gambree said. "As soon as we're in control inside the jail, my assistant will bring around the wagon to put those bastards in."

"Yessiree, Doc, let's go," Kayler replied, and leaned down, grunted twice, and lifted the motionless weight into his heavy arms. He avoided looking at Tex's empty eyes and opened neck. He felt warm blood ooze down his shirt and shivered.

Inside the jail, two wall lamps stubbornly offered yellow light that slid gently over the occupants wherever ever-advancing shadows allowed. A strange melody of snoring made it clear Deputy Will

Atkins and his older associate, Deputy Orville Hazewell, had both nodded off, as well as most of the prisoners they were guarding. It was easy to do as the boring weight of the evening lay upon their minds.

Young Deputy Will Atkins was asleep with his legs propped up on Marshal Jubal Rand's desk. Once neatly-stacked dispatches, receipts, and warrants had oozed sideways from the weight of his clay-encrusted boots. Atkins's hands were folded across his rail-thin stomach, which rose and fell in gentle syncopation to his soft snoring. A scrawny mustache did little to belie Atkins's twenty years; even the artificial blackening hadn't helped much. Red acne entrenched on both cheeks was further proof of his age, in spite of the swagger he had developed in walking the town's streets while on patrol. Nestled between his fingers was a cigar, casually taken from the box on the marshal's desk. It, too, had succumbed to the evening, with its cold ashes splattered on his vest.

Deputy Orville Hazewell, a portly man who spent much of his off-duty time in pleasure houses, sat in a chair ten feet from the cells. A double-barreled shotgun lay across his lap. Hazewell should have known better than to let himself sleep while on duty; he'd been a lawman in three other Kansas railroad towns before coming to Dodge. He was nearly bald, and his wide-brimmed hat was pulled low over his fat-cheeked face. A faint smile indicated a dream about a red-haired dance-hall girl seeking to please him.

In the farthest cell, the convicted gang's shrewd leader, Star McCallister, was asleep on a bare cot.

His stylish gray suitcoat had been removed and folded into a pillow. His bowler hat with the coordinating silk band lay on the floor beside his bed. With his knees slightly bent, he looked frail and sickly, but then he always did. It had been hard for many of the town's businessmen to believe Star McCallister was an evil man capable of heinous crimes. Some still didn't.

The other eight outlaws were jammed into the remaining two cells. Four were asleep on cots or the floor, their snores joining the soft whines of the deputies' naps. One was Andrew Tiller, the rustler Checker had wounded in the shoulder the day he led the arrest and retaking of the herd. Leaning against the far wall, O. F. Verner, the quiet Negro cowman, stared through the small barred window at the full moon, coolly aloof from the timid stars surrounding it. No one knew what the initials stood for or how old he was. Considered a solid cowhand before getting injured by a bull, the former slave spoke only when asked a direct question and took orders only from Star McCallister. Ferguson, a nervous man with a tendency to pick his vein-swollen nose while talking, and the big-shouldered Iron-Head Ed Wells were talking and laughing about women.

The remaining outlaw, a short mullato cowboy with a long scar sliding across his right cheek through his eyelid and all the way to his forehead, was spitting tobacco juice through the bars at the sleeping Deputy Atkins. Joe Coffey's trajectory was only half the required distance no matter how hard he tried. Anger at his failure was swelling within the copper-skinned killer like an overworked boil. On the floor, a brown puddle grew as testimony to his persistence. Occasionally, Coffey would add an off-color comment to the conversation between Wells and Ferguson, always about something he had done to a woman—and usually involving the woman bleeding.

Even though Ed Wells towered over the diminutive Joe Coffey, both were feared by the other gang members. Wells was a loud bully who used his physical strength to get what he wanted. His ham-like fists were layered with white scarring from fighting. His nickname, "Iron-Head Ed," had come from ramming a door with his head to get to a man he was after. Joe Coffey was a pure pistol-fighter, whose insecurity about being small and his skill with a gun or a knife had manifested in a love of killing.

Joe Coffey gathered all his strength and spat again. This time he hit Deputy Atkins's arm and the lawman stirred. Coffey threw up his fists in a sign of victory, and the others laughed. Even Venner turned away from the cell window and smiled.

During the trial, Deputy Atkins had become totally captivated by the intimidating presence of John Checker and had told Deputy Hazewell so much about it that the fat lawman had finally asked him to stop. Checker had presented the case against the gang and left McCallister and his attorney with little room to wiggle around and much to whine about. The crowning blow had been the testimony by gang member Henry Seals, who agreed to tell all in exchange for a fast horse out of town.

Deputy Atkins decided right then and there that he wanted to be a lawman like Checker, not like his boss, Marshal Jubal Rand, who always had his hand out to the south-side purveyors of whiskey and wickedness. The deputy was observant but had always been wisely silent about such monetary matters. Deputy Hazewell was more pragmatic and suggested, prior to asking him to find another subject to talk about, that the young deputy would be better served imitating Marshal Rand. It was much more profitable and much safer.

A rapid knock on the office door jarred the two deputies from their sweet slumber. Hazewell jumped from his chair, swinging his shotgun into position but swallowing the chaw that had sat in his mouth. He choked and tried to keep his eyes from burning as the chunk of tobacco slugged its way down his throat. Unfortunately, it also cleared his head of the bewitching images of the redheaded girl. Atkins awoke with a similar jerk, grabbing instinctively for the Colt holstered on his hip without really knowing where he was or what was happening. His hand touched his gun before he realized what the sound meant. The cold cigar bounced on a planked floor, forgotten for the moment.

"Atkins! Hazewell! This is Rand—open up."

The brittle, precious voice was Marshal Jubal Rand's. It was a voice that always tried hard to sound important and forceful but usually reminded a person of dry wood crackling over a fire as the words popped methodically from his mouth. Atkins shook his head to clear away the wisps of unconsciousness. What did Marshal Rand want now?

Deputy Vincent and the marshal weren't supposed to relieve them from guard duty until midnight. That was hours away. Marshal Rand himself was usually home and in bed by this time every night since he married Widow Holman a month ago, returning to late-night guard duty only to impress the town council with his diligence. His new wife's wealth—from her late husband's holdings—made up for her lack of appearance, or so Marshal Rand had told Deputy Atkins on his wedding day.

Atkins looked at Hazewell for guidance, and he nodded approval to go to the door. Hazewell coughed and swallowed hard to rid his mouth of the remaining jolt of tobacco. Behind him, most of the gang were awake and stretching themselves. He ignored their bantering.

"Hold on, Marshal, I be a-comin'," Atkins said, rose, and picked up the door key on the desk.

For an instant he thought about straightening the scattered papers, but he decided the chewing-out would be worse if he was slow than if he was sloppy. At the door, he slid aside the security latch and peered out through the small opening. Rand's wide-brimmed hat was pulled down and barely allowed his slate-colored dullish eyes room to peer back. But it was definitely Marshal Jubal Rand, his florid face redder than usual.

The narrow-faced man with a handlebar mustache, closely cropped hair, and a sour manner was wearing a black duster that completely covered his frame, down to the top of his scruffy boots; Atkins had never seen him in such a coat before. It was buttoned up, hiding a normally prominent and constantly shined badge. Standing alongside the marshal was a slender, bespectacled man in a long black coat and top hat. Atkins recognized him as the medicine wagon doctor. Expressionless, the man held his hands behind him in a patient stance of pious concern.

"Come on, come on! Open up, Atkins, I do not have all night!" Rand spat anxiously, each word with its own crackle.

"A-ah, yessuh, but I was jest doin' what ya always tolt me to do, makin' sure afore I done opened up," Atkins stuttered.

"This is Dr. Gambree, the preacher and medicine man. He came to pray with the prisoners and give them some spiritual . . . help," Rand advised. "He's got to get back real soon to help his regular customers, so he needs to see them now. Let's go."

"Yessuh," Atkins said, and leaned his head back and yelled, "Rand's got a preacher with 'im. From that medicine wagon that rolled in today. Ain't that sumthin'! The preacher done wants to pray over Star and his bunch. Whadda ya think o' that, Star? You, too, Big Tom, ya kin done use some serious prayin'!"

Slamming his open palm against the cell bars, Iron-Head Ed Wells yelled back, "Keep that Bible-thumper away from me. I don't need no whimperin' and wailin'."

The always angry Coffey echoed the response: "Tell that fool we's already in hell." He spat in the direction of the empty deputy's chair and hit the desk.

Disturbed by the noise, Deputy Hazewell frowned, sputtered an obscenity, cradled the shotgun in his arms, and walked toward the stove in the corner, which had been allowed to go to sleep along with the jail's inhabitants. Tonight's air—even the stale version in the jail—needed a little warming, he decided, and headed for the adjacent stack of fire-

wood. A hot cup of coffee sounded good, too. But
the blackened coffeepot, resting on the stove, contained only the stale remains from earlier. Once he
got the fire going again, he'd make a fresh pot.

Atkins unlocked the door and swung it aside.
Movement toward his holstered gun was only a reflex as the marshal's fist-held pistol delivered a fierce
blow to the deputy's head. Deputy Atkins crumpled
to the floor, and a circle of dark red blood immediately sought direction from the wood-planked wood
floor. The gash in the young Atkins's temple was
evident even in the oily light.

At the instant of the blow to Atkins, the black-
coated Dr. Gambree slid into the office, swung a hidden pistol into firing position, and blasted away at
the far deputy's midsection. Thickly wrapped with
Clanahan's coat, the gun's harsh lead-belching was
muffled by the beehive-thick protection. Three times
it gave off a stunted thud and drove Hazewell
against the wall. His shotgun danced by itself in the
air for an instant before clanging to the floor. Hazewell gurgled a wistful cry and slid to the floor, cross-
legged, with his head resting on a bloody chest.

Sweat washing his face, Kayler entered a few steps
behind, carrying Tex's body. Rand holstered his gun,
pushed the door shut, and locked it again. He
avoided Kayler's stare. The big trail boss's eyes
couldn't believe what was happening. It wasn't how
he imagined it would be. He had always seen himself as a Texas hero. This was murder, not justice.
He wanted to drop the body and leave, but he knew
it was too late for that.

"Looks like you're going to need some more deputies," Dr. Gambree said laconically. "Where is my no-good brother?"

Rand pointed toward the far cell.

"Where are the keys?"

"Over here. I will get them." Marshal Rand hurried to the desk and opened the drawer where the keys were kept.

"Of course you will," the black-coated Dr. Gambree said.

"Did you say 'your brother'?" a stunned Kayler asked.

Dr. Gambree turned around, smiling, and walked toward the puzzled cowman. "That was a figure of speech, Kayler."

"Oh, yeah."

"Put that body there."

"Over her—"

Dr. Gambree's pistol thudded again and the lynch-driven cowman's face exploded into crimson. Again the pistol bucked in his hand and the muffled sound belied its lethal intent. Kayler buckled and fell to the floor, on top of the body he was laying down. Dr. Gambree stood over him and said, "Sorry about the lynchin' party, Kayler. Maybe next time." He fired again and said, "Didn't anyone ever tell you that your suit's too small?"

Unwrapping the smoking coat, he shoved the pistol into his belt and tossed the garment toward the marshal with his left hand. The coat skidded across the lawman's desk and onto the floor. Dr. Gambree frowned and motioned impatiently for Rand to toss him the keys. The iron circle with the dancing keys floated toward him, and Dr. Gambree caught them with a casual move of his hand. Strolling toward

Star McCallister's cell, spinning the key circle in his hand, without a downward glance he stepped around Kayler and over the unconscious young deputy lying on the floor.

Chapter Five

Marshal Rand knew Dr. Gambree was actually Star McCallister's younger brother, Blue—although he didn't realize such a person existed before Star shared the news in jail and told the lawman to contact his brother in Abilene. With the command came a payment of five hundred dollars and a promise of a matching amount upon escape. He knew of the plan to involve Kayler and make the gang's escape look like a lynching gone bad.

Kayler's men would be blamed and no one would know the difference. As marshal, he would gather a posse in the morning and go after the Kayler riders. By the time everyone figured out it wasn't a lynching, the gang would be well into the Nations and impossible to track, even if anyone wanted to try.

The youngest son of J. D. McCallister left Dodge at the age of six. Unlike Checker, Blue McCallister was taken by his mother, Georgia McCallister, who ran off with a farmer to a new life. Star refused to go and sought his father with the awful news. When Old Man McCallister became sober enough to understand the situation, he sent men to kill the farmer and bring his wife and child back. His small band of misfits, buffalo hunters, and outlaws didn't find them, for the farmer and his lover had planned their escape carefully.

The threesome ended up on a fine farm in western Nebraska with a new name not easily traced: Wilson. The Wilsons were formally married, even though she wasn't divorced; no one in the little community knew otherwise. Her son became Blue Wilson. Together, the Wilsons had three other children. As a young teenager, Blue Wilson was constantly in trouble, finally killing his new "father" with a knife when he was sixteen and leaving home with most of the family's savings.

He changed his name to Billy Frederick to avoid detection by the law. Three years later, U.S. Marshals were after him in Dakota Territory for defrauding an old couple out of their small ranch, then murdering them. After that, he changed his name back to Blue McCallister and sold easterners on fake gold mines, then changed it to William Frisco and sold his gun to a mining company.

After a close encounter with local law over a killing, he left the region and began calling himself Blue Gambree. It was a name he had noticed in a magazine and liked. This occurred about the same time that he came upon the wonder of patent medicines. He learned the business from a crafty peddler who went by "Dr. January," claimed his wares brought new life to all who used them, and enjoyed the effect spitting out biblical verses had on crowds. As Dr. January's assistant, Blue toured with him throughout the region. Blue augmented his meager income with robberies. At twenty, he was paid to kill a man for the first time and liked it.

Three years later, Dr. January disappeared and "Dr. Gambree" took his place. Killing remained a profitable sideline, but only under circumstances to his liking. According to Star, his younger brother toured from town to town, selling nostrums that would cure everything from thin blood and severe coughing, to rheumatism and baldness, to sores and a lackluster love life. His spiel was as smooth as the branded, syrupy, whiskey-laced medicines he sold, tying in the Bible and salvation along with quotations from Shakespeare for good measure.

Salome joined him within the last two years. She was wanted for murder and extortion—also under different names—in New York. The black-haired, well-endowed woman did fortune-telling and occasional whoring, but was better known for an exotic dance promoted as being handed down from Salome of biblical fame and had taken that name a year ago. Star said the woman was good with poison and not to eat or drink anything she offered. He said his younger brother often used her skill to handle killings for hire, instead of catching the victim alone and dispatching him with a gun or a knife.

Two years ago, Dr. Gambree came to Dodge and reintroduced himself to his older brother. Star McCallister reconciled with his younger sibling, or at least acknowledged his professional acumen. A Dodge City councilman had discovered McCallister's cattle-rustling operation through a friend, a Chicago cattle buyer staying in Dodge during the trail-drive season. They had threatened to go to the U.S. Marshal unless paid to remain quiet. The councilman died unexpectedly in his sleep and the cattle buyer was knifed to death coming out of a saloon by an unknown assailant.

Much was memorable about Star McCallister's younger brother—among them, long light brown hair, a sarcastic tongue, and flashy clothes—but the first thing Rand noticed were his light blue eyes. Behind wire-rimmed spectacles, Dr. Gambree's eyes were controlled heat; yet they were also ice, holding their target intensely and contemptuously. A hint of the cold violence that would follow the biting humor, if necessary, was there too. He reminded Rand of someone else, but the marshal hadn't been able to place that connection yet.

Dr. Gambree's black attire set off long honey-brown hair that settled on his thin shoulders and that would make any woman envious. It was not as light as his older brother's—and, physically, only their cold blue eyes were a match. Star had told Rand about his younger brother and where to get him as soon as he was imprisoned. Finding Dr. Gambree wasn't difficult; he was in Abilene with his patent-medicine wagon show, as Star knew, before heading for Kansas City for the winter.

After arriving in Dodge, Dr. Gambree went to Rand's home as planned and received Star's final details on the evening's breakout. More than the cunning Star McCallister or the indomitable John Checker, this slender man scared Marshal Rand. He knew Dr. Gambree was a killer the instant he saw him, even though he apparently didn't carry a gun or a knife—at least not any that were seen. Dr. Gambree was not a man who killed to defend himself or protect others, like John Checker; Dr. Gambree was a man who killed for profit and pleasure. Probably both, most of the time. A shiver ran up Rand's back as he watched the man in black head for Star McCallister's cell. He was suddenly aware that the gang was frozen to the front bars, silent and waiting like a pack of wolves who have just discovered a lone calf.

The only one to comment, though, was Joe Coffey, who stood with both hands gripping the bars and his copper-skinned face pushed between them. High cheekbones squeezed his eyes into narrow slits that rarely seemed to blink. The bars pushed away the long scar that dominated his face. A thin goatee set off a toothy smile as he spat, "Good evenin', boys, good of you to bring death. We was a-needin' it."

From the farthest cell, a thin voice made no attempt to hide its joy. "It's good to see you, Blue. The good marshal here told me you had arrived and the plan was under way."

"Came as fast as Rand's wire and my trusty wagon could bring me, complete with juggling, whoring, and throat cutting."

Star McCallister stopped unfolding his suitcoat, frowned, and shook his head. His eyelids fluttered uncontrollably for a brief moment; the impulse was a physical deficiency since childhood.

"Is the wagon closed for the night? Or do you still have to make one of those awful spiels?" Star asked.

"Oh, brother mine, I'll have you know the crowds have been wildly taken with my King Lear mixed with a Psalm or two," Dr. Gambree said as he slid the key into the lock hole. "It goes perfectly with Dr. Gambree's Blood Pills."

"Did you take care of the other Triple C cowboy?" Star asked impatiently.

"Looks a lot like this one, only he's sitting like a drunken fool in the alley," Dr. Gambree said with a wide, toothy sneer gone happy.

"If someone walked by, would they be suspicious?"

"Of course not—he looks like every other fool Texas cow nurser. Doesn't he, Rand?" Dr. Gambree said, and looked back at the marshal who agreed with a simple "Yeah."

Annoyed at the flippant response, Star changed the subject. "When do the new Triple C guards come?"

"Midnight, it appears."

"What do you mean 'appears'?" Star snapped. "Don't you know for sure?"

"Get off it, Star, all I know is what we heard at the saloon. Checker's friend was there, dancing with some whore. What difference does it make?"

"Details make the difference—in everything."

Dr. Gambree chuckled to himself, knowing his brother's penchant for absolute perfection, and said, "Hey, be careful what you say to me. I could leave you to a lynching rope—or our favorite half brother."

"Checker wouldn't let us be lynched. He'd go down fighting first," Star said. His expression was a mixture of amusement.

"Looks like two of his men did, instead," Dr. Gambree observed, and changed the subject. "How many of this sorry-lookin' bunch are going with you?"

"All of them. The only worm in the bunch was Seals. When we find him, he'll wish he'd died as a child."

Even in jail, Star looked like a distinguished gentleman, but his short, frail appearance was magnified by the stress of his situation and lack of sleep. Youngish in appearance, his face showed unusual beard stubble and his light-blue eyes were underlined with bags. But his mind was a strategy map in constant motion, rethinking and rechecking each piece of mental minutiae; there was no time for his younger brother's idiosyncrasies. Almost as an afterthought, Star held out his hand and Dr. Gambree shook it after the cell door swung open, squeaking on cranky hinges. Neither brother's eyes caught the other's.

"What about Checker?" Star suddenly asked, releasing his brother's hand.

"What *about* Checker?" Gambree repeated sarcastically.

Star crossed his arms and stared at his younger brother.

Dr. Gambree grinned and said, "I saw a tall man that looked a lot like dear old father this afternoon. Had to be him."

"And?"

"Hey, Checker wouldn't know me. What was I . . . six, when he was run out of town?" Dr. Gambree sneered and added with a half-smile, "Funny, isn't it, dearest brother of mine. Our bastard half brother ends up the one who looks like dear old dad. Our sweet whore of a mother probably got both of us behind the shed somewhere."

"Shut your mouth. You don't need to talk about her that way."

"Why not? She took me and not you." Dr. Gambree chuckled deep in his throat.

Star changed the subject. "Anybody recognize you?"

"Hell, nobody in this town would know me if I walked up and introduced myself. I was only a kid when your sweet mother took me with her farmer," Dr. Gambree said. "And nobody asked me about your late friends . . . ah, that cattle buyer—and that poor dear councilman either. But I didn't know you cared so much about me, brother mine." He paused and added with a smirk, "Believe me, I can handle John Checker."

"Well, *believe me*, you don't want to try," Star snapped. "He reminds me of the old man. I assume you were quiet in the alley and didn't wake him or that happy friend of his. You were quiet, weren't you?"

Dr. Gambree grunted his disgust at the question itself. When the two brothers stood together, Marshal Rand could see a bit more family resemblance beyond their eyes and light hair, but not much. Something about some of their mannerisms caught his mind. He hadn't known their late father, J. D. McCallister, leader of a vicious gang of thieves and murderers back when Dodge was a center of buffalo-hunting activity. Neither had told him about their blood relationship to John Checker, and Rand hadn't picked up the significance of their comments. He knew the former Texas Ranger only as a man to be careful around, real careful.

Rand had lived in Dodge City only three years, and Blue, had left the region as a small child, long before Rand arrived. Rand knew Star was involved in a cattle-rustling scheme almost from the start. As long as Star handled it as smoothly as he always did, there was no reason to endanger Star's generous payments for Rand's innocent-enough service. Besides, the cattle herds were stolen, and the drovers were killed, outside of his juridiction. That was a county problem or a U.S. Marshal's concern, not a town policeman's.

As the two brothers freed the gang, Rand tried to keep his eyes off his downed deputies and the two other dead men. Deputy Hazewell was dead; Deputy Atkins was unconscious. Rand stood quietly beside his desk and kept telling himself this was no different than taking money from McCallister and other south side owners. They paid him to keep the Texans from getting out of hand in their celebrating and keep the nice folks living on the North Side pacified. He was good at doing both, and well-compensated by the saloon owners. *Why should I let John Checker and his upstart Texas drovers change a good thing?* he asked himself. Besides, he had been afraid to deny Star anything—even when he was behind bars and waiting for the hangman's noose—much less his younger brother.

"Got horses for us outside?" Star asked as he brushed dust from his rumpled black business coat and slipped it on.

Dr. Gambree's ready sneer was reinforced as he snarled, "That would've been real smart, coming down the street with a bunch of horses. You think someone might have noticed?"

As the words darted from Gambree's mouth, Star's eyes became twin tiny furnaces. The normally placid-appearing man fought to regain control of himself. His upper lip trembled, and his taller brother stepped backward in reaction to the anger. The room tightened.

"Let's try it again. Are the horses where they're supposed to be?"

Dr. Gambree grinned an apology for his remark and said contritely, "Your horses are waiting two buildings north of the tracks, in the alley, next to that drugstore. Salome is holding them for you. I'm headed back to the wagon, and she'll return as soon as you ride out."

"Where'd you get them?"

"They're Kayler's."

"Did you have any trouble convincing him to keep his men out of town?"

"Nah. He was so full of himself—and so eager to show up Checker, it was easy," Dr. Gambree said, and glanced at Kayler's body, then back at Star.

"Well done, Doctor," Star said in a velvet voice, and his eyes released their hold on his brother, then fluttered for an instant. He couldn't resist adding, "Just the way I planned it."

Marshal Rand was surprised at the exchange. He never would have guessed Star would dominate his scary brother. When asked, Dr. Gambree reminded Star where Kayler's men were waiting so the gang wouldn't run into them on the way out. The two brothers completed the gang's release and the freed outlaws helped themselves to the rifle rack, then found and rebuckled their own gunbelts from the storage bin. There was little talk, only purposeful movement.

Star continued to fire questions at his brother concerning supplies, money, and John Checker. Star was miffed there weren't enough horses to make it look like a lynch mob had taken them away, only enough for the gang itself. Dr. Gambree snorted at the obsessiveness over such meaningless detail and said no one would know the difference. Star said Checker would, but Dr. Gambree ended that argument with the fact that it wouldn't matter by the time he did. Star reluctantly agreed.

Dr. Gambree also reported meeting with the manager of Star's saloon and working out the buyout arrangement Star wanted. The older McCallister brother didn't expect to return to Dodge but didn't want to give up his most valuable asset for nothing either; monthly payments would be sent to a post office box in Kansas City. Dr. Gambree was to share in the profits as his payment for the breakout.

Most of the gang were anxious to be gone from the jail but didn't want to state so directly to Star, not even Coffey or Iron-Head. Instead, they kept checking the cracks in the shuttered windows for any signs of discovery of their escape. The streets were empty, with only the haunting sounds of cowboy revelry in the distance. The fat-bellied Norwegian outlaw picked up Deputy Hazewell's shotgun lying on the floor beside the dead man. He broke it open and asked Marshal Rand if he had additional shells. Rand was jolted by the politeness of the request, opened the right-hand desk drawer, withdrew a box, and tossed them at the Norwegian.

Dispassionately, Rand watched him empty the box into his pockets, but he shivered as his mind jerked him back to the moment—a little over two weeks ago—when the former Texas Ranger John Checker advised him coldly, "Make no mistake about it, Rand. There will be justice today. With you or without you. It doesn't matter to me. But I'll bet it does to your city council. If that's not clear enough, call off your deputies or the town will be looking for a new marshal."

Rand shivered again. He remembered the scene far too well, with Shanghai Pierce's cowboys filling around him in the saloon and Checker standing there with his boot on McCallister's hand and a gun in his fist. He remembered McCallister pulling on his hand and Checker putting more weight on it. He saw again tears of pain trickling down the crooked saloonkeeper's cheeks.

"Now, see here . . . Ranger. I've done business with Star McCallister." Marshal Rand straightened his back as he spoke. "He runs a fine establishment. You've got the wrong man."

Rand's face reddened as he recalled his first reaction to Checker's challenge. Then came Checker's hard-edged challenge.

"Rand, you didn't want to help us earlier." Checker's eyes tore into the marshal's face. "Now I'm giving you another chance to act like a lawman. Put these two in jail and go with us to get our herd back. Star McCallister is their leader. I'm taking him with us. He'll stand trial for murder and rustling when we return."

McCallister started to say something, but the increased pressure from Checker's boot as the first word came out convinced him otherwise.

Marshal Jubal Rand ran his tongue along his upper lip and said, "Ranger, I ride with you. My deputies will put these two in jail. They'll stand for murder."

Marshal Rand took a long, deep breath to let the memory slip into the grayness of the room. They had arrested McCallister and his gang that day. Checker and his friends had even made them walk back from where the herd was grazing across the Arkansas River, waiting to be loaded on train cars headed east. He remembered McCallister spouting some wild words about his father and Checker. No one knew what he was talking about.

He had never seen the reserved McCallister as upset as he was that day. Far beyond the temper trantrum displayed here. It was like watching a pet dog go rabid before your eyes. Unlike his younger brother, Star's frail frame and youngish face never did look like a killer's. When they were alone, Rand told Star he thought the saloon owner was innocent. He recalled Star McCallister smiling and thanking him. Star's offer of a thousand in gold to help him escape had been an easy decision. He already had half of it carefully hidden at his house.

The towering Iron-Head Ed Wells, with an oversized mustache and matching wiry eyebrows on a square-jawed face, strutted up to Rand and said, "Mucho thanks, law daig. We'll put this hyar iron to good use. Yessir, John Checker's a dead man. Say, you got any tobac, law daig?"

Without warning, a feeling came over Rand that made him swallow to keep from saying or doing something he would regret; he was ashamed of himself. The outlaw's smile was lopsided and missing teeth, more like that of a jack-o'-lantern. Rand pointed at a box of Monogram cigars on top of the desk and the huge outlaw took it, shoving the container under his arm and walking away, chuckling. He handed one to a grinning Joe Coffey, who was strapping on a pistol belt over his fringed leggings. On the belt hung a holstered long-barreled Colt with walnut handles and an elkbone-handled knife in a beaded sheath. At his left wrist hung again the looped handle of an ever-present leather braided quirt.

Rand couldn't help thinking about John Checker and the Triple C drovers still in town. In his mind, he rehearsed his alibi. The dead Kayler and Triple C rider would make the breakout appear as if they had broken into the jail to lynch the gang. The Kayler riders would be blamed, and no one would listen to their pleas of innocence—innocence due only to the fact that they never got their hands on the rustlers, not from lack of intent.

His new wife would vouch that he was with her until he left for midnight duty. To make certain she wouldn't know otherwise, he had placed sleeping powders in a glass of whiskey for her at bedtime, courtesy of Dr. Gambree's medical supplies. She had insisted on his making love to her but had passed out before he could finish. He did anyway.

Withdrawing his pocket watch, Rand snapped open the lid and checked the time. He and his third deputy were due to relieve Atkins and Hazewell in two hours. After Star's gang left, he would return to his house and wait until it was time, wake up his wife, and head back. He looked down at himself and

91

studied the black coat he was wearing to keep anyone who might have been looking from knowing it was him. That and one of Dr. Gambree's hats. He was ashamed, and he bit his lower lip to fight off the drowning sensation.

"Where's my gun, Rand?" Star broke into the lawman's self-examination, and Rand was glad of it. This was not the time for reflection; he was in too deep to do anything else but go along. That seemed like the story of his life, just go along and everything will be all right.

"Right here, Star. I put it in my top drawer, special-like, for you."

"Yeah. More likely you figured on keeping it for yourself after they stretched my neck."

"Oh now, Star, oh no. I wouldn't . . . you know that," Rand said a little too loudly as he yanked open the drawer, withdrew the pearl-handled pistol, and handed it to Star.

The gang leader examined its cylinder, frowned, and asked for bullets. Rand urgently found a box in his drawer and watched Star methodically reload the weapon before returning it to his shoulder holster. He took a step, stopped, and spun back toward the desk. With a flourish, he picked up a wanted poster resting on the top of a stack of other notices. Rand knew what it was and swallowed.

" 'Wanted for robbery, murder and conspiracy. Blue Wilson, alias Billy Frederick, alias Blue McCallister,' " Star read aloud, waving the paper first toward his brother, then toward Rand. "At least it doesn't say medicine wagon, so they haven't got that close. What the hell do you have this around here for, Rand?"

Rand's face was whiter than the paper Star held. He had discovered the poster by accident after meeting with Dr. Gambree and going through his stack of warrants and posters seeking something on a now-forgotten cowboy that looked familiar to him. He had been fascinated to read the back trail of this killer and had forgotten to destroy it.

"I—I came a-across it t-this mornin', Star. I—I was gonna burn it 'n' forgot. H-honest."

Dr. Gambree stared at Star, then Rand, and grinned a toothy evil smile.

"Blue, pay the marshal the rest of his money. When does that second deputy come, Rand?" Star said, laying the paper back on the desk.

"Ah, about two hours. Midnight," Rand answered, knowing Star was fully aware of that. Immediately, he walked over to the desk and took the poster, folded the paper three times, and put it in his pocket.

"Yeah, good, you'd better get out of here as soon as we leave. You'll be fine if you stick to your story. Do you know it?"

"I know it," Rand answered, trying to hide his annoyance at being asked. He offered nothing more, and Star stared at him until he recited the story. "I will be a few minutes late, so my deputy, Eli Vincent, is here first. I will order him to check on the other Triple C guard, then go to Checker and report that Kayler and his men tried to break in and the gang got out. I will offer to lead a posse after you—after we arrest Kayler's men."

"Good, Marshal. Good man," Star said. "Just remember to head northeast—first. Blue, give him the money."

93

Dr. Gambree tossed an envelope filled with money on the desk, then whispered in Star's ear. The older brother's expression showed nothing, then he nodded agreement. Rand made no move to pick up the envelope; somehow, standing there seemed like the wise thing to do. The thought crossed his mind for the first time that they intended to kill him too.

My God! How could I be so stupid! he thought, and glanced down at his buttoned coat where the outline of his holstered pistol was distinct. The practical side of his brain realized they might notice his sudden concern, and he quickly looked up and around the room, avoiding eye contact with either brother. But the two brothers were engaged in last-minute discussions with the gang and hadn't noticed.

Star directed two men to check again through the shuttered front windows to make certain no one had become suspicious of the jail's night visitors. Both reported that the area was empty except for the dead Triple C sentry in the hotel alley. Star went to look for himself.

Satisfied, he gathered his rearmed men around him and said, "All right, everyone out the back. No talking. I want you walking by yourself. No bunching up. Let the guy in front of you get to the tracks before you start. Walk. I don't want somebody getting excited because they see you running around in the dark. People don't get scared of slow. Got it? If someone spots you, keep walking like nothing was wrong. Talk if you have to, but don't run and don't shoot. Everybody got it?"

His white teeth flashing interest, Coffey asked, "Boss, we're goin' after that damn Ranger and his Triple C drovers, right?"

The small gunman stood with his thumbs hooked over his gunbelt. A chew of tobacco occupied most of the right side of his mouth. A sweat-and-tobacco-juice-stained shirt was contained at his wrists by beaded leather cuffs, with the quirt handle lying across the left one. Coffey's hat rested on his back shoulders, held at his neck by a stampede thong tie. In the hatband was poised a red hawk feather. He looked only at Star.

Standing a few feet away from the group, Dr. Gambree grinned and said, "That's right, Star, are you going straight to the old soddy? I thought you'd want your dear half brother's head. He's the one to blame for all of this. Or do you want me to handle it? No charge. Sibling courtesy."

"Remember our sweet little half sister?" Star said.

His hard glare had a vacant, unbalanced look that made even Gambree take a step backward to remove himself from its intensity. The gang was struggling to understand the significance of Checker being referred to as a "half brother." Most thought it was just a way of joking and chuckled accordingly.

"Didn't you try to get between her legs—when we were kids?" Dr. Gambree's eyes sparkled. "An' Checker, he—"

"We're going to her place—first. I know how to hurt John Checker—worse than a bullet between the eyes," Star interrupted, his words coming like bullets. A shrill laugh followed, one that stopped every gang member.

A mixture of grunted agreement preceded their collective trek toward the back door. Then Dr. Gambree stopped and said, "I almost forgot what you

Cotton Smith

said, Star, Rand, where's that coat I tossed your way?"

Marshal Rand was stunned by the question. He had just found relief in their apparent leaving. He stood for an instant with his mouth open, unable to answer.

"If you'll wait a minute, Rand, I'll find an easier question for you," Dr. Gambree snapped, drew his pistol, and smoothly replaced the spent shells with new bullets.

"A-a-ah, h-h-here it is. O-o-on the floor."

"Good boy," Dr. Gambree answered, and grabbed the bloody coat from the frightened lawman. After wrapping the coat thickly around the gun and his hand, he pointed the gun at the head of the unconscious Deputy Atkins and fired. Muffled sound and straggling smoke followed. He strode through the bodies, assuring himself they weren't breathing and slipping a pistol into each dead man's hand.

Joe Coffey watched the killing and nodded approval. "I woulda used this, not the gun." He held up a large knife pulled from the sheath on his gunbelt.

"Already got one of those that way. But it's supposed to look like a jail break, peckerhead, not a damn knife fight," Dr. Gambree said, a bit annoyed. "Even the dumb citizens of Dodge might get suspicious if they're all cut. Why don't you stick to something you know, like rustling cattle—or spitting?"

Coffey flinched at the insult. He spat a brown stream of tobacco juice in Dr. Gambree's direction, but Dr. Gambree didn't notice. Star shook his head and motioned for the mulatto gunman to join the others. Coffey's intense yellow eyes showed that he

96

wanted to confront Dr. Gambree, but he followed orders without saying anything more.

"You can thank me later, Marshal," Dr. Gambree announced, and then growled to the rest of the gang gathering at the back door, "Hey, you boys, be sure to give my best to Amelia. Last time I saw her, she was ripe."

That brought chuckles from all of them except Coffey. Marshal Rand managed a thin grin too. But it was quickly cracking at the corners from disgust at what he had done.

Chewing on one of Rand's cigars, Iron-Head Ed Wells asked, "Aren't ya goin' with us, Blue?"

Dr. Gambree glanced at his brother before answering, "No, my friend. Salome an' I gotta bring the wagon. We're going the other way. I'll catch up with you at the soddy."

"You could leave it, Blue," Star said, "and ride with us."

"Nah, I'd be lost without that thing. Kinda like home. Hell, I'll probably beat you there—if yo-all take turns with Amelia."

That brought more laughter, and Star ordered the gang out the back door. The Norwegian asked if they were going to stop for something to eat first, and that kept the happy attitude in place until Star told them to be quiet. Without a glance back at the lawman, Dr. Gambree followed the gang out the back door and disappeared into the night. Rand stared at the closed door for minutes, then at the bodies strewn across the jail floor, gagged, and vomited on his desk.

Chapter Six

"Checker! It's Sonny. Wake up, we've got bad trouble!" Sonny Jones yelled hoarsely into the thick hotel door, pounding it with his thick-knuckled fist, streaked with blood.

It was ten minutes after eleven. Hooded eyes were bright with distress instead of their customary joy. His face and hands were blotched with blood; traces were on his blue flannel shirt and kerchief.

A balding businessman with a half-awake expression opened the door from his room on the other side of the hallway and stared angrily at the Triple C cowboy. Long, brushlike eyebrows swirled on his forehead, emphasizing the man's tall, well-oiled pompadour. The overly sweet, violet smell of the barbershop surrounded his self-important stance.

Sonny glanced at him and said, "Get back inside, mister, unless you like fightin' more than standin' around with your thumbs up your butt."

The businessman blinked like an oversized owl and immediately closed his door.

"Check—"

"I heard you. Get inside before you wake the whole hotel," Checker interrupted as he opened the door. "What's the matter? I didn't hear anything. Is another lynch mob stirring around somewhere?"

Sonny entered quickly; his spurs jingled a distinctive tune in the night's hush. A timid candle in its filmy glass holder on a small dresser was the only light in the room. Checker stood barefoot in his long-johns with a pistol in his fist. Shoulder length, black hair was tousled from sleep. Any other time Sonny would have laughed and made up a song about his friend's appearance, but not now. He was having trouble just holding himself together.

"John, somebody killed Harry. Slit his throat wide open and left him in the alley. It's awful-looking. He never saw what hit 'im until he was cut dead!" His words rushed out with a sad groan riding with them.

Yellow candlelight drew flickering lines down Sonny's broad face, over his flat nose and wirey mustache. He was a warrior with a laughing face and a quick wit. It wasn't like him to be rattled, but he was. He stood before Checker like a frightened girl and was not ashamed of it. He took a deep breath to help fill his mind with some sense of understanding.

Sonny paused to let the first part of his news sink in. Checker's lean face looked as if someone had punched him hard. The arrowhead-shaped scar on Checker's right cheek reddened. For once, he was easy to read. Shock pistol-whipped his face. He stared at Sonny like he was trying to get inside of his mind to determine what had happened and why. The unintended intensity was too much for Sonny and he blinked, then looked at his boots, muddy from running through the street.

"Where's Tex?" Checker finally asked.

Looking down at his boots, Sonny answered, "Kayler's bunch did it. Tex was with 'em. Kayler's dead in the jail. So's Tex. Two deputies too. The rest took Star and his gang out the back an' rode off. North."

"That can't be! I didn't hear anything. I couldn't be that sound a sleeper." Checker turned away and went to the window, pushed aside a faded purple curtain, and stared at the street below.

The former Ranger's mind wanted to have the awful news validated by seeing the event unfold again in front of him. But there was nothing outside to indicate such a terrible thing had ever happened. It was a night like all the others in Dodge. Two drunken cowboys were walking in the middle of the street. A buggy jigged around them and headed back to the respectable part of town after a night of revelry. He inhaled the bite of the growing tension within him and glanced at the jail. It, too, was dark. His gaze was pulled in the direction of the alley, as if he could see around the building itself.

Checker knew what he was going to see in that lonely place; a man who was no longer a man, no longer anything. It was a sight he'd faced too often, a sight he never got used to, nor wanted to. What was once a joyful human being was now deteriorating sand. He closed his mind to the pictures that wanted in, of the carefree Harry Clanahan, and then of the vain, but insecure, Tex. He felt nothing. He must find Star McCallister and his men and bring them back—before they were hanged. He must. Kayler's men must pay too; they were warned. But it didn't make any sense. It was all wrong, terribly wrong.

"You say Kayler an' Tex—and two deputies—are dead. How come we didn't hear any shots?" Checker returned to the same issue.

"Well, I don't know fer sure, John, but those bastards took Harry's new coat and wrapped it around a gun. That would've cut the noise pretty good, I reckon." As soon as Sonny made the observation, his emotions again took over. "His new suit coat! Found it there, all smoking—a-a-and powder-burned. Ruined it, those bastards did. I—I—I laid it over him when I came back. H-h-he was so proud of that suit. He hadn't taken it off since . . ."

"That might explain why we didn't hear the shooting—or at least one man's gun. But there'd be no reason for those deputies to keep quiet. Just the opposite," Checker said, buttoning the shirt and stuffing it into his pants. "You're sure it was a lynching? Something isn't right."

"You can look for yourself if you . . ."

"I'm sorry, Sonny, I wasn't doubting you," Checker said. "How long a lead do you think they have?"

After a moment, Sonny's eyes darted upward toward the candle from under long, black eyelashes, as if seeking solace in the flame. Instead of looking at Checker, he spoke toward the candle.

"Hard to tell. Not long, I reckon. Maybe an hour," Sonny said, his voice cracking with hurt. "They were gone when I got there. Had horses waiting across the tracks. Like I said, the tracks went north, but they could've cut back anywhere. Probably gonna string 'em up someplace out of town."

"An hour's enough time to hang any man."

"Yeah."

The tall lawman continued to stand motionless at the window, his right hand held the pistol and hung at his side. Sonny wasn't sure what he should do next or say. He wasn't sure if Checker was more upset about Harry being murdered or Star being lynched. Checker was a hard man to reach, except for a few. But Sonny had become one of those few. A strange friendship between an outlaw and the lawman who had once caught him. But that was long ago and another time; Checker trusted Sonny Jones, and he didn't trust many men and was feared by most. The former outlaw and former Ranger had become good friends, drawn together by each other's courage.

In Texas, more than a handful of men were frightened just to hear the name of John Checker, much less learn he was after them. One Triple C drover who knew him as the daring captain of a Texas Ranger company had told other riders during the drive that "Checker's a man who's seen trouble and trouble ran like hell to git away." It was widely rumored that Clay Allison had backed down when he and Checker met in El Paso once. Checker's was a reputation, like Clay Allison's, that stood with the scary legends of other pistol fighters Texas bred after the War of Northern Aggression.

Staring out the window at the quiet street, Checker rubbed his face as if it would bring clarity to his pounding head and spoke softly. "That silly Irishman . . . he was a good man. A good man. I was wrong about Tex." Checker stared at the wall. "I remember when . . . why . . ."

Nothing more came, and Checker shut his eyes for a moment. Sonny watched the hard-edged Ranger grieve within himself. Only the tenseness in Checker's face gave away the feelings hammering away at his mind, and they were only tortured reflections in the window's glass.

"John, I reckon we underrated Kayler. Didn't figure he had the gumption—or the savvy. He wasn't lucky, though. Neither was Tex or . . ."

Checker didn't answer. His shoulders rose and fell as he walked to a faded green sofa where his clothes were piled. Tossing his pistol onto the bed, he passed up his newly purchased dark suit and began pulling on a trail-worn pair of freshly laundered Levi's.

Sonny blurted, "I—I came early so Harry c-c-could go see that redheaded gal he's so crazy about. I didn't have nothin' else to do. Figured on lettin' Tex go too. Jackson would be along soon enough to keep me company." He bit his lower lip and forced a raw addition to the first thought. "John, if I'd come earlier . . ."

"Harry was a warrior, Sonny. He knew the risks. So did Tex, when he stopped to think," Checker replied harshly as he slipped his arms into a gray linen shirt with pinholes above the pocket where a Ranger badge had once been positioned.

"There's something else that doesn't fit, John. Tex's belly was cut open—with a knife. Ain't that strange?"

"Yeah, strange."

Sonny kept talking as Checker dressed and packed, restating that the gang and their captors had gone out the back door, across the railroad tracks, and had horses waiting in the alley beside McCarty's Drug Store. He was certain they headed north out of town, but he had stopped trying to trail them on foot when he reached Front Street itself. There were too many tracks for him to tell anything. As the former outlaw talked, Checker realized his friend had chased after the lynchers without any thought of the odds he would face if he caught up with them.

The corner of Checker's mouth curled upward as he told himself that it was typical of Sonny. He wouldn't ask his outlaw friend why he didn't shoot a warning shot; he already knew the answer. If the lynch mob had been close, it would have warned them before he had a chance to get closer. It was obvious Sonny fully intended on attacking by himself. And it was so much like him.

Checker picked up his gunbelt draped across the back of the chair and strapped it on. A reverse-draw holster and a Comanche scalp knife in a beaded sheath hung from the belt. The double row of cartridge loops—one for his rifle, the other for his pistol—were freshly filled. Two extra boxes of cartridges lay beside it. From the bed, he retrieved the black-handled, short-barreled Colt .45 with white, elkbone circular markings embedded on each side.

The trigger guard was half removed, leaving the part nearest the handle and the open area toward the barrel. If a man was good, Sonny knew, it was a life's breath quicker than a regular trigger guard, and that could be enough. Checker flicked open the cylinder shield and spun it. Satisfied, he returned the gun to its holster. Sonny watched him and instinctively looked down at his own pistol belt, then back at Checker.

"We can't track 'em at night," Sonny advised. "Well, I can't, anyway. I reckon you could track 'em in a blizzard at midnight." He tried to smile but couldn't.

Checker glanced at him, then at the small table beside the chair, where things from his pockets lay: a roll of money, a pocketknife, a watch, and a Bull Durham tobacco sack and papers. He picked up the cigarette makings and smoothly rolled a smoke. The pause had another purpose, letting his mind connect well with the task before him. An old habit for a man who had seen the terrors of the night too often. Without speaking, Sonny accepted Checker's offering of the sack and papers. A match snapped to life on the buckle of Checker's gunbelt. The glow surrounded his chiseled face for an instant before disappearing into soft smoke, then moving on to light Sonny's just completed cigarette.

Letting a trail of smoke cross his face, Checker finally answered, "Running men leave sign, even at night—if you look hard enough. We'll see it on the outskirts of town. If we can only tell which direction they went, we're that much closer come daylight. If it's a lynch mob, they're likely to head for trees real quick. If the gang escaped somehow, there's no telling which way they'll go. We can take two horses each to give us fresh mounts. Either way, we haven't got much time. Probably too late if it's a lynch mob."

"I know you can read track like a redskin, remember?" Sonny said. A small grin wandered across his mouth and vanished. "John, we can't just go off 'n' leave Harry like that. Not Tex either, even if he did go bad. We just can't. It could be days before we get back. I can't do that."

The statement hit Checker like the dawn of a new day. It hadn't even occurred to him. His thoughts had been only on catching up with the lynch mob—or the gang—whichever it turned out to be. His hunch was growing that Star had managed to pull off an escape. His face strained with signs of stopping himself from saying what his mind thought. He took a deep drag on the cigarette. It gave him time to think.

The tall Ranger looked at the man he had once chased and said, "You're right. I'll start after them alone. You and the boys take Harry and Tex out into the prairie. Find some trees and a little pond, or something. Bury them there. They'd both like that. Wait until dawn to wake the others. Jackson'll be along after a while, anyway. He can help you. Don't be in a hurry, though. They shouldn't be buried at night." His words had regained a familiar edge, that of a man used to being obeyed without question.

"I'll bring along some Irish whiskey—for a toast."

Checker was surprised at Sonny's immediate response and realized, for the first time, where his friend was focused. "Yeah, sure. There's an Irishman who rides with the Crossed Bow. Sings like an angel—I heard him in the Long Branch a couple of nights ago. Should be easy to find if he's still in town. You can ask the Irishman to ride along and sing something—Irish. Tell him I asked for the favor. Pay him if need be—I'll cover it."

"Maybe I'll do that myself—sing a song over their graves. Harry was always partial to my singing. Tex liked it, too. Leastwise, he always laughed."

Sonny's eyes brightened with the thought. He pulled the cigarette from his mouth and wanted to say something more but didn't. His whole body was so heavy with sorrow, he didn't think he could raise his arms. For once, he didn't want to fight, didn't even care about revenge. All he could think of was doing what was right for a dear dead friend, Harry Clanahan, and doing things right for Tex, too. He tossed the cigarette at the spittoon next to the door and missed. Sighing, he walked over, flipped the glowing butt into the container, and stood, bent over, staring into it.

"Should I ask that redheaded gal to go along?" That triggered two more questions exploding from his trembling mouth. "Did Harry have anybody waiting for him in Texas? Why didn't I ask him more about his family?" Sonny stood up, and his face contracted into watery shreds. A wild sob escaped from his soul.

"O-o-oh, w-w-we should've never come to Dodge. I—I—I shoulda never let him go on guard duty. H-h-he couldn't move good—an' I—I—I knew he wasn't thinking about anything but that gal. Y-y-yesterday, h-h-he showed me a brooch—in that jewelry store down the way. He wanted to get it for her. He asked me what I thought. John, he wanted to marry her. I never told him that she w-w-was . . ."

Checker placed a hand on Sonny's shivering shoulder and tried to comfort him. Sonny pulled away and yanked the old watch from his vest pocket. Pieces of hard candy and cartridges clattered on the floor. He didn't hear them. Frantically, he clicked open the face and stared at the crusty photograph of the young woman there like it should come alive.

"See that, John? That's what it's all about—having a woman who cares about you. A family. Kids. Not riding alone, wondering when a horse'll throw you an' break your neck . . . or some bullet finds you . . . an' nobody—nobody—will care that you're dead."

"It's never too late, Cole—Sonny."

"Oh yeah?" Sonny's eyes fiercely grabbed Checker's face. "I left her—to ride owlhoot. Now she's dead. S-she's dead, John—an' I wasn't there. Just like I wasn't there when Harry needed me."

Checker hung his head to his chin for a moment. The cigarette hung in the corner of his mouth, waiting for him to pay attention to it again. Stray thoughts of his own were whipped along by Sonny's breakdown. Checker had already decided he wouldn't return to Texas. There was nothing waiting for him there but a badge and more lonely nights in the saddle. No, he would move west and start over. His sister had invited him to stay with them. That was tempting—for a day or two. Finding Amelia had healed an inner black hole that he had ridden with for too many years. But there remained an emptiness within him that he rarely acknowledged, or even let out of its scarred corner. He, too, longed to find the comfort of a woman who would walk beside him on life's trail and make it good.

For no reason, the unmistakable scent of Sarah Ann Tremons filled him. She had lived within his mind since they met. Always there, waiting for him to return. He had known that feeling only once before, and that was prior to joining the Texas Rangers. Right this moment he wanted to race to the Tremons home and ask her to marry him, to ride away from this hell. But he couldn't, even if she would have him. He had nothing to give a fine woman like her, nothing but well-oiled guns, a fast horse, and a reputation as a man to be feared. She deserved a lot more than that. This was no time to be thinking of her, anyway.

He pushed his thoughts toward Star McCallister, his evil half brother. Was this really a lynching? Kayler's ego might well have urged him into this kind of scheme. Tex, too, for that matter. It made sense that they would have wrapped their guns to muffle the noise. That still left the question of why would Rand let them in? Certainly they didn't fight their way in. Any disturbance in the street would have been tantamount to a loud cry for help. Even though this side of town was soggy with night celebration, he would have heard the lawmen returning fire, outside or inside the jail. If they did.

Where would Star go if he had actually escaped? Into the Territories? North? West? Toward Kansas City? Why did it have to be this way? Why couldn't he have the peace he sought from reuniting with his sister? From being with Sarah Ann? Why did he always have to be pulled back to the gun? Should he let his half brother go? No—the answer came like a fist—he couldn't do that.

Another thought crowded its way into his mind: Was he hoping Star would be hanged and it would be over? Did that explain his deliberate manner at the moment? Down deep, did he want to deal with the lynch mob rather than his half brother? Was

Cotton Smith

there some kind of weird connection between them that went beyond blood? Or was he just preparing himself mentally for a renewed battle, one that would last until Star was behind bars again? No answers to any of those questions followed. Checker drew deeply on the cigarette, smashed it into the lamp's bowl, and looked up at his friend.

A grieving Sonny stood with his head down, arms at his sides. Sonny's shoulders rose and fell; he bit his lower lip and returned the watch to his pocket. His face slowly rose to meet Checker's. Sonny made no attempt to wipe the wetness that covered his cheeks. He didn't recognize that Checker was suspicious of the lynch mob scenario.

Checker's voice was soft and vulnerable. "Harry was my friend, too. Tex went against us, but he's still a friend, I reckon. You get the boys together to do what's right for them. Star's my half brother and my problem. I'll ride out to find what I can. He's either hanging by a rope or running. I'm not sure which I hope it is."

Struck by his own words, the former Ranger pulled the wad of money from his pocket and handed several bills toward Sonny. "I'd be obliged if you'd buy that brooch for Harry's girl and—tell her that he had it with him when he died. That he planned on giving it to her. And anything else you think he'd want you to tell her."

"You mean, like he wanted to marry her?"

"Looks like that was the way he planned it."

"A little fast, don't you think, John? Hell, she's nothing but a money poke, you know!" Sonny snapped. He hadn't taken Checker's money. His face had reddened.

110

"If she's as good a woman as Harry was a man, she'll appreciate the words. If not . . ."

"Don't say it, John," Sonny said, and accepted the currency. "It's the right thing to do."

"Is that enough?"

"Yes. I want to pay on it, too."

"Now, go find Jackson and Tyrel. You can bring Harry to my room. He can rest on my bed . . . until you and the boys are ready to take him . . . away. I'll head out after that."

"What about Tex?"

"Tex too. He's one of ours. I'd stay to help, but the sooner I'm on their trail the better."

"John, if you don't mind, I'd like to bring Harry to my room."

"Sure."

Sonny stared hard into Checker's face. It was the former Ranger's turn to blink. Sonny blurted, "I won't let you go after those murderin' bastards alone. After Harry an' Tex are buried, I'll ride into hell with you to get 'em, John Checker. Just leave me somethin' to follow. I ain't the tracker you are, *Ranger*. Well, I know my way to hell, but they may not be goin' by the same trail."

"Whoever killed Harry will die hard, I promise you that," Checker said. His voice remained soft, but the statement slid across the room like a razor.

"Just don't try to whip 'em all until I get there. I reckon the others will be comin' with me, for that matter."

"You're one to talk. Who was going to take on that whole bunch by himself—or do you want to tell me a different story?" Checker said.

"Yeah, guess I was. Didn't think much on it at the time."

"Harry Clanahan was a lucky man to have a friend like you."

With no more words to add, Checker slipped a small pouch hung from a rawhide thong over his head and neck. It would hang under his shirt. Unlike his Comanche warrior buckskin tunic, taken in battle, this pouch of wolf medicine had been a gift from an old Kwahadi war leader. The Kwahadi were the fiercest of the five Comanche warrior bands, known for their love of fighting. Ironically, the old man had become his great friend before passing to the Shadowland a year ago.

From the dresser drawer he lifted a folded envelope, holding a letter from Amelia that had brought him to Dodge, and shoved it into his shirt pocket. Next, he pulled the tunic over his head and settled it in place on his shoulders. A long-ago remembrance of hand-to-hand battle. The beadwork and elkbone designs were laced with smells of wood smoke and gunpowder. He placed his flat-brimmed Stetson on his head and patted Sonny on the arm, and they left the room silently. The businessman, awakened earlier, had regained his courage and was peeking out as Checker passed.

"What goes for my friend goes double for me," came Checker's jabbing reaction to the man's curiosity. "It's a bad night to be nosy."

This time the businessman didn't take the time to blink before closing the door. The harsh click of a bolt latching followed. Their spurs were the only sound, and they seemed out of place along the darkened hall. Neither felt entirely comfortable with this hotel or any hotel. Too many years riding alone on the land did that to a man. Something became changed for all time. Something vanished inside a man that would never return, leaving an uneasiness when inside for any length of time. The Comanches understood it was a spiritual connection to nature, but they were enemies.

Sonny was rarely in his room anyway; he liked dancing and singing with any saloon band that would let him. When Checker wasn't with Amelia's family, or with Sarah Ann, or watching the jail, he was in his room. Waiting for the gang's execution, especially that of his half brother, was chewing on his nerves more than he wanted to admit.

A reoccurring nightmare had awakened him minutes before Sonny knocked on his door. His friend's intrusion was a welcome diversion from a horrible dream of his late, evil father and Star. It always started with Old Man McCallister putting his arm around Checker and asking for forgiveness for not acknowledging his parental obligation. Then he grabbed Checker and held him while Star took Amelia and Sarah Ann away. When Checker tried to escape from the overwhelming grip, he discovered he was chained to a tree. He broke free, but his mother appeared and begged him not to harm Star because they were all one family. Usually it ended with him unable to find either woman.

Checker tugged on his hat brim and headed down the cramped stairway, like a man hoping to find trouble. Sonny was a step behind, his face unreadable except for drying tear stains, like war paint down his full cheeks. A step before they reached the front door, Jackson entered. His face was curdled with grief. For the first time, Checker thought the black cowboy looked like an old man. Jackson's eyes ran to Checker's for answers, and none came. Behind Jackson was Tyrel Bannon, wide-eyed and pale.

Chapter Seven

Through the night, a lone John Checker tracked the flirting trail of the Star McCallister gang. He was certain now they had escaped and weren't in the hands of any lynch mob. Too many trees stood naked to believe the other story. Besides, it was obvious the gang had robbed a general store from the looks of the broken door. He hadn't stopped to investigate, but he figured they got supplies and money there.

It would have been good to know how much food they were carrying, but that would have taken too long to determine. For the first few hours, his obsession was total and he lived only to find Star McCallister and return his half brother to justice. But that quickly changed, and he found it difficult to maintain his concentration as fatigue continued its unrelenting attack.

Thoughts raced through his mind in a loosely connected fashion as he followed the traces of the fast-moving riders in the hard ground. Sarah Ann. Sarah Ann. Followed by the wonderful sweetness he had discovered in Amelia's family. Did he love Sarah Ann? Was he wrong to want the same things his sister had found? Would Sarah Ann want the same things—with him? Could he walk away from the reputation as a man of the gun?

Then came bitterness renewed at seeing Star McCallister and all he stood for in Checker's mind. The loss of Triple C friends. The brutal murder of Clanahan—and probably Tex. Was it wrong to want to see his half brother hanged? How did Star escape? Were there men in town who were part of it? What was Kayler's role? Tex's? Where were Kayler's men now? Why hadn't he seen the escape coming, instead of worrying about a lynching? Why wasn't he on guard instead of his friends? Would Sonny come, or was he too distraught? Why was he certain Marshal Rand was involved?

His tenacity in tracking an adversary had never stopped at sundown. Night belonged to Checker, holding no mystery for him. When the moon and her star children took over the world, no blindness assaulted him as it did most others. Instead, he could actually feel his senses grow in the dark. He easily read the stories left in the land for the knowing few. Except for not being able to discern color or measure distance, he could see better at night than in daylight because there were few visual distractions.

He locked onto the faint scuffle marks in the earth and followed them like they were a line of bright paint, fighting fatigue and a mind that wouldn't cooperate. Twice, he caught himself napping in the saddle, and that was dangerous. But he could not stop. He would not stop. He had to keep going or the gang would disappear within the wild Indian Nations. He could not let that happen. He could not let J. D. McCallister's son go free.

"Star, you aren't going to get away with this," he muttered to himself. "I know it's your doing. You may be J. D. McCallister's *real* son, but that isn't going to help you now. You killed my friends. My friends, you son of a bitch. You're going to hang."

His black horse flipped its ears toward Checker to determine if the words concerned its performance. Noting the interest, he patted the neck of the mustang and said, "You're doing great, big fella. Doing great." He hadn't yet switched to the long-legged bay brought along on a lead rope. His black horse was easily swallowing the land and showed no signs of tiring, but the great animal rarely did.

Being alone again seemed right. Solitude brought a familiar comfort, even when edged with the tension of knowing death could be riding ahead of him. That, too, seemed the way it should be, for he was most alive when challenged. He had been a typical Ranger: young, unmarried, and invigorated by danger, open land, and fighting for Texas. But for Checker there had always been another dimension: a deadly intensity combined with extraordinary fighting skills. Few could match it. On either side of the law.

As a Ranger, he had been by himself most of the time and was the most dangerous that way. His tracking tenacity and battle courage had been the subject of many stories told by fellow Rangers. Each had a favorite, usually about a scene they had witnessed personally. Of course, they all loved the story of Checker tracking Mexican outlaws to the Rio Grande, throwing down his badge, and crossing after them. After killing two in the river, he brought the other three, all wounded, back across for hanging.

Another favorite was the time he fought and killed the Comanche Kwahadi war chief Blue Elk in hand-to-hand combat, receiving wounds to his cheek and shoulder from the powerful warrior's knife and tomahawk. Around the two deadly combatants, eighteen painted warriors watched in silence. They created a human amphitheater to watch great courage unfold on the grass-swept Staked Plain, the feared Llano Estacado, honored land of their ancestors, the wild land of wolf and wolf spider, tarantula and Kiowa, centipede and Comanche—and once, endless buffalo. Checker's Ranger company came galloping into view and the war party bolted, a wobbly Checker waving a bloody scalp at them. He had worn the war leader's tunic since.

Most of the stories were about Checker and a gun. None had seen better. Even so, no one knew how he had managed to bring in the Trimmel gang by himself. The three outlaws that rode in with him seemed relieved to be turned over to the authorities. The other three gang members had been left facedown in the hot prairie sand, stopped by Checker's bullets.

The most puzzling story had nothing to do with a gun. It was his purchase of a small house for a widow with two youngsters. He apparently barely knew her and had no particular caring for the woman or the children, nor any, ongoing relationship. He would only say that she reminded him of someone from a long time ago.

The most unbelievable story, however, was that he had been close friends with an elderly Kwahadi war chief, almost a father-son connection. Most said that was saloon talk. There was no way Checker would be friends with an Indian. Any Indian.

"Whoa, boy," Checker said. His black horse stopped immediately, but the trailing bay bumped into its rear. He swung down and looked for a handful of small rocks.

"Sonny, I'm headed this way. If you don't come, I'll understand. It's hard to ride away from death— but you have to." His words came like a night song as he stacked three stones on top of the other, with a fourth pointed in the direction to follow. If they came.

He wasn't counting on it; Sonny had been devastated by the death of their friends. Usually Checker wouldn't yield to those feelings even though they pounded at him. He rarely had since leaving Dodge as a boy. It always hurt too much. The emotional disconnection had helped make him a legendary lawman, but an empty one. This night was different. His reunion with his sister and her family had softened him in ways he didn't understand. It made him vulnerable to his feelings, and that was both uneasy and wonderful.

He couldn't stop the flow of his love toward them even if he wanted. Seeing them together made him realize how much he had missed. Sarah Ann Tremons came again to his thoughts, and he made no attempt to shut her out. He stood staring at the faint stars and let his tired mind find her arms and her lips. His black horse nudged him, and he shook off her soft scent and remounted.

"Look out, Star, we're gaining on you. You can't be more than two hours ahead. Good job, ol' hoss," he whispered to the black, and patted its wet neck.

Edginess grew with each passing hour, blossoming from lack of sleep, worry, and guilt. And at the far corners of his consciousness was something he usually had no trouble handling: fear. Certainly it was there before any fight. Only an insane man would be free of it. But he wouldn't admit to it, couldn't admit it. Now he was worried that he had something to really live for, something he could lose—and he wanted badly to keep it.

"No wonder most Rangers weren't married," he told himself.

He passed an old buffalo wallow, one of the few signs left that the great beast once reigned supreme on the plains. His thoughts eased toward his old friend and counselor, Stands-in-Thunder, and his fierce Kwahadi tribesmen. He hadn't thought of the dead war leader in a long time. Instinctively, his gaze went skyward, to the pale moon resting there. It certainly was no Comanche moon when the earth would whimper at the sight of merciless warriors riding with the fury of lightning and thunder.

But such were no more—or at least, Mother Moon no longer shined on the Comanches in Texas. Not since the buffalo were destroyed, the Comanche horse herds captured, and the souls of the Comanche locked away on reservations. Even the brilliant leader, Quanah Parker, finally surrendered. Now their fierceness was like the dirt popping up from his horses' hooves.

Isolated Comanche war parties continued to roam the Nations, along with savage bands of Kiowa and Southern Cheyenne, in search of yesterday. Never again, though, would Mother Earth be warmed by the joyous fighting spirit of *Noomah,* "The People," as the Comanche called themselves. Or *komantcia,* as their enemies, the Ute tribe, called them—"enemy who fights me all the time." Now their broken lives were littered about the Fort Sill reservation, where the U.S. government jammed the southern tribes and told them to forget the buffalo and learn the plow.

"I miss you, old friend," he muttered aloud, and surprised himself. His mind ran back to their first meeting.

Checker had come to the reservation in search of a half-breed wanted for murder. He and his men were reluctantly given permission by the Quaker agent in charge to search the lodges. With his men spreading out among the encampment, he approached a singular tipi alone. Set far apart from the others, the heavily painted sides of the lodge told of a great warrior inside, one with strong spiritual connection and known prowess in war. A guttural sputter greeted him, "Chek-err. Warrior of Tehannas." Alone, the tall Ranger paused, hitched his gunbelt for confidence, and continued walking toward the tipi.

A slump-shouldered Comanche elder appeared at the lodge's slitted entrance and immediately sat cross-legged on the ground in front of the tipi. He was naked except for a white man's suit coat and long breech clout. Gray-streaked hair lay unbraided across bent shoulders, the last vestige of a warrior's pride. Long wrinkles in his dull mahogany face, heavier on the right side than the left, made him look like God had squeezed him hard. Smoke from a white man's pipe swirled about his face like a wet morning fog.

"Yes, I'm John Checker. Who are you?" The Ranger's Comanche was stilted but understandable. He supported it with fluid sign language.

"I called Stands-in-Thunder."

"You are a great war leader," Checker said, and pointed to the painted achievement stories decorating the aging lodge.

"No more. Now I am rock."

Checker didn't know how to respond at first, but finally he said, "It is a bad time for all Comanche. I am sorry."

Stands-in-Thunder told Checker he was called *Tuhtseena Maa Tatsinuupi*, Wolf with Star, by Comanche warriors because he tracked them like a fierce wolf. The aging war leader said the wolf was Checker's *puhahante*, spirit helper, and that the mysterious beast gave him much wisdom when tracking—and much courage. This shadow guide would provide strong access to the spirit world and was strong *puha*, strong medicine. The Ranger should not take it for granted as the Comanche had done with their buffalo medicine. Checker hadn't believed this tale, but he saw no reason to be impolite to an old man trying to deal with the reservation's unrelenting annihilation of the Comanche way.

"I'm looking for a man who is wanted for murder in Texas," Checker explained. "I don't suppose he's in your lodge."

"You may look, Tehanna warrior. He was not there when I came out."

Checker laughed and shook his head indicating that it wouldn't be necessary.

Stands-in-Thunder took the pipe from his mouth and challenged, "Chek-ker at Palo Duro Canyon fight? Yellowlegs take heart of Comanche that day. Ancestors take my war medicine forever. Yellowlegs take Comanche horses, take Comanche pride. Put me behind walls and throw raw meat over like we were lions."

"I wasn't there," Checker said. "Glad I didn't have to fight against you—any time."

Stands-in-Thunder's smile cracked across his wrinkled face. "One of us would not be here today."

"I would have missed you."

Stands-in-Thunder's head came up and saw Checker's playful grin and burst into gravelly laughter. Checker followed with a chuckle of his own. Stands-in-Thunder told him that, as a young fiery warrior, the songs of spirits of long-departed ancestors had told him the days of the Comanche were over, but he had refused to listen then. Checker listened in silence, not knowing what to say.

Finally, he put his hand on the old man's shoulder and gave him a small leather pouch filled with tobacco. It was a spontaneous thing. Stands-in-Thunder had stared at the gift for a long moment before thanking him. Checker left soon afterward, and the half-breed was found in a nearby town a week later. But the chance meeting had pierced a blackness in each man, and Checker visited Stands-in-Thunder whenever he found an excuse to ride near the reservation. Each time, it was a happy story-telling, cigar-smoking, and whiskey-drinking occasion, mixed with the old man giving him counsel in a mixture of broken English, guttural Comanche, and fluid sign language.

In a strange way, Checker had found the father he never had—and Stands-in-Thunder, the sons he'd lost to war. Rangers and warriors who knew each man and his violent battles with the other side couldn't conceive of such a friendship. Checker always brought tobacco, whiskey, candy, and other small gifts his friend might enjoy. He was always careful, however, not to embarrass Stands-in-Thunder, thinking the old man had little to give in return. But that had never been a problem. Proudly, the old war leader had given him a white stone that sang, a small pouch of wolf medicine for him to wear, and a war club. The pouch hung under his shirt on a leather thong around his neck—more a remembrance of his Comanche friend than an indication he believed in the wolf as his spirit helper. He wasn't certain what had happened to the pebble or the weapon.

The bittersweet memory faded as he passed a long string of scattered buffalo skulls and bones. Like broken white china shoved along a shallow dune, driven there by winter winds. He had seen much worse. He'd ridden through plains in Texas so thick with the skeletal remains of bison that his horse couldn't move without stepping on bone or skull.

With renewed concentration, he could see each stone in the night-moist ground and he understood each story of riders who had passed recently, kicking the stones. It didn't appear to him that there were more riders than the gang itself, but it was difficult to know for certain. There could be a couple more, he admitted. He observed every black clump of grass and saw signs of their having been stepped on by hard-moving horses. He heard the frightened scurry of every tiny creature as he moved through the night. An owl slid past him overhead; he knew it without looking up, only hearing the rush of great wings as the bird searched for a mate.

The gang had chosen to take advantage of the opportunity that night offered to distance themselves from Dodge. They were riding fast and not worrying about covering their trail. His tracking was made easier by his discovery that three horses had knicks in their iron shoes. This assessment was the product of studying their waiting place in the alley. Most of the night, he read the gang's direction from the saddle, particularly catching the signs of distinctive hoof marks in the barren land. Sometimes he had to dismount and search for any slight indication of their direction, but the night was always helpful to him and the land was eager to talk about their passage.

Just outside of town, the gang made a feint to the northeast, then galloped hard to the west, turned again, and were now headed mostly south. They were headed for Indian Territory, he was certain of it, and he let his black horse lope without rein as he gained confidence in his judgment.

At the corners of his mind, shreds of his earlier nightmare returned. For an instant, his father's sinister stare appeared in the darkened crook of a gnarled tree to his right. Star McCallister's grinning face followed. He blinked it away and rolled his stiffened neck to clear away the hate. His late mother's face spun at him. A pained growl came from deep within. It hurt too much to think of her.

He had learned to crowd out those thoughts, and he did so once more.

His mind slipped to a recollection of the gang itself. He told himself it was good to know who he would be facing. There were eight, not counting Star—and he wouldn't fight if he could avoid it. That's why he had Ed Wells, the big, square-jawed brawler, and Joe Coffey, the scarred mulatto gunman. The two-gunned Ferguson was dangerous, because he got scared easily and could blurt into action no matter what the situation. It was hard to tell what O. F. Venner, the black rustler, would be like in a gunfight, but Checker figured he would do whatever Star asked of him.

Checker couldn't think of the name of the fat Norwegian. Wes Morton was a huge cowboy whose high-pitched voice didn't match his frame; he would be hard to handle if pushed into a corner, but he was no gunslinger—only a man who thought rustling cattle would be easier than working them. Then there was Tom Redmond, the ex-Confederate who used to ride with Sonny Jones on the Texas border, back when he was Cole Dillon. Sonny said the man was a vicious back-shooter. Checker had wounded one of the remaining outlaws in the shoulder when they took back the herd. It was the day he downed Waco, Star's main gunman. Tiller was the man's name, he recalled. The outlaw wore a high-crowned hat and a bandolier of rifle bullets over his shoulder and favored a Winchester. In fact, he didn't carry a handgun. If they turned to fight, Checker would die—but he didn't dwell on that fact. He was counting on their desire to escape to keep them running, at least until he came up with a plan, or his friends joined him. If they did. Like a smoldering fire, it wasn't a thought to kick into very hard.

Out of the corner of his eye, a deer in the cottonwoods to his right caught his attention. He shook his head to clear it of the nasty mind clutter and reminded himself of the need to remain alert. The last hour had been difficult for him, and he realized that most of the time he hadn't been paying much attention. He vowed to stay focused. It could mean the difference.

There hadn't been any signs of the gang doubling back, but that didn't mean they wouldn't. It would be like Star to leave someone behind to see if they were being followed.

A wolf howled four times in rapid succession. He sat straight up in the saddle. Four more came quickly behind the first. That was the sign of danger to a Comanche war party, a signal their medicine had gone bad. No warrior would advance after such a warning. He couldn't recall hearing such a repetition before. Over the years, usually while alone, he had grown accustomed to hearing the singular cries of the mysterious animal in the night. It was distinctively human-sounding. Comanches believed the wolf had the soul of a man and valued a connection to him highly.

Remembering his medicine pouch, he touched the small lump under his shirt and tunic. He hadn't thought about the spiritual connection until tonight, dismissing it as a simple, harmless belief by an old man he had grown fond of. Something told him this was different, and he was alert. But there was no thought of turning back. He whispered, "If you were ever right, Stands-in-Thunder, old friend, make it now."

Insecure shadows were slowly seeking cover as a pink sky swelled to red and began pulling a new day into view. His head was locked onto the land passing below him, catching the reassuring messages of the gang's direction. He had forgotten about leaving behind signs for Sonny and possibly others to follow. Suddenly an odd coldness struck his body and icy sweat pierced the palms of his hands. The gang was headed directly toward Amelia's homestead! My God, why? Horses! Then he saw tiny marks in the dirt that indicated one rider had left the group. The direction was toward a soft rise in the land ahead.

He guessed it to be a hundred yards away, but he knew the dark was not good for judging distance. There was no reason for Star to suspect anyone was following them so soon. Checker figured that meant there was every reason for the cunning outlaw to leave a man behind, just to be certain. He reined in the black as if he had lost the trail; the bay quickly trotted to a stop beside them.

Dismounting slowly, he kept the horses between himself and where he thought the outlaw might be waiting, holding the bay's lead rope and his reins in his right fist. Standing alongside the front of the black horse, leaving little of himself exposed, he peered over its neck and studied the innocent-appearing knoll ahead. Nothing indicated a problem, but he felt it inside. Someone was waiting. He ignored the ache in his stomach that was worry about Amelia and her family, for he had to deal with this first.

Kneeling, he ran his hand across the ground as if searching for sign, being careful to stay behind the animal's front legs, and tried to think what he should do. If he rode away, his back was an immediate target. He didn't like running away from a fight anyway; he had never seen it work well. Under his hat brim, he looked sideways to see if a glint of steel would tell him more. But whoever was there was hunkered down, waiting for him to pass and provide an easy target.

Rising slowly, Checker knew what he must do. It might not work, but it was better than waiting or running. Leading the horses alongside him, he walked methodically toward the knoll, as if he were tracking the gang on foot. His angle virtually hid him behind their bodies. If the outlaw fired now out of frustration, the bay would most likely be hit. Checker didn't like that thought, but it was better than his black horse going down—or himself.

After twenty yards, he stopped, kneeled, and repeated his search of the ground with his eyes cocked toward the knoll. Something moved! Just a glimmer—and to the left of where he thought the man might be. Weakening moonlight slithered off a gun barrel. The man was getting nervous. *Good enough*, Checker thought. *Let's give him the chance to make a big mistake.* Was it Ferguson, the rustler who was with Iron-Head Ed and Waco at the showdown in Star's saloon? The thick shape could be any one of several gang members, he decided. If it was Ferguson, he was likely to scare himself into shooting at anything he saw or thought he saw.

Rising again, Checker walked beside the tired horses, keeping his body aligned with the animals' necks. Even the bay seemed to understand the need for quiet, steady movement. The black's ears lay along its neck, sensing the danger its master had discovered. Checker eased them away from the knoll, walking slowly, like a man searching for trail sign. His direction was at an angle halfway closing the rest of the distance between him and the hidden outlaw. At the right moment, he turned the horses around, quickly switched sides to remain on their far side, and walked back toward the knoll. So far, the outlaw could only be frustrated by watching the man he was supposed to kill meander back and forth looking for sign.

If he had judged correctly, the knoll was only fifteen feet away, as he led the horses in an angle that would have him passing the hidden position if he continued in the same direction. But he had no intention of doing that. In one smooth motion, he released his hold on the reins; the black horse lowered its ears for a moment and stood silently, its leather touching the ground. He pointed the bay toward the knoll, released his hold on its lead rope, and slapped its withers hard.

The startled animal charged forward, and he lunged behind the galloping bay, drawing his Colt as he ran. In three strides he was standing next to the surprised outlaw, whose attention had been immediately distracted by the horse thundering past him. It was Ferguson.

"You've got a hard choice to make," Checker growled. "You can drop that gun or use it. Makes no difference to me. It's your life."

Wild-eyed, the outlaw swung his rifle toward Checker, and the former Ranger's pistol roared twice. The thin-framed outlaw's body jackknifed, and he fell backward into a sitting position. He stared at his shirt growing black from unleashed blood. His slender, unshaven face was pale; his eyes were blurred.

"Y-you killed me," Ferguson said in a frightened gurgle. He tried to reach for one of the cross-belted pistols at his waist, but Checker kicked his hand away from the gun butt.

"Just like you intended to do to me," Checker growled. For the first time, he realized the outlaw was a young man, probably not much older than Tyrel Bannon. He shouldn't feel sorry for the outlaw, but he did. "Sorry, Ferguson, you gave me no choice. Where's Star?"

"Yeah, I—I—I savvy that. Y-y-ya surprised me, comin' at me like that, is all. I—I t-thought you was lost. Didn't expect . . ."

A blood-filled laugh followed from the dying outlaw. Thin eyebrows arched high to match his response. "Y-you're too late, Ranger. He's burnin' down your sister's place an' tearin' 'em apart. Iron-Head was achin' to git at it. S-so was that half-nigger, half-Injun Coffey. H-he's a scarey b-bastard, ain't he? Star picked me to stay behind, said I was too young fer that stuff. Now, I—I—I'm dead, s-s-shot by John Checker hisself. I—I—I guess that counts fer somethin'."

Checker was no longer listening. Bile tore at his throat, and he spun and ran toward the waiting black horse. The dying outlaw lay on his back, held his spurting wounds with both hands, and gurgled, "H-he done plan on to takin' her youn'uns down into the Nations. G-gonna trade 'em to some Com-

ancheros he know'd. Heard him say it was better
than killin' y-you. Y-yessir, that's what he said. M-
mean son of a bitch that S-Star McCallister, ain't h-
h-he?"

Checker swung into the saddle and spurred the
black into a flat-eared run. He didn't hear Ferguson
add that Star's brother was worse. Grazing a few feet
away, the bay had perked up its head and immediately followed. The loose lead rope swung wildly
from side to side as the animal galloped to catch up
but soon dropped farther behind.

He cleared a rock-strewn knoll and his worst fears
were reinforced by long claws of smoke ripping into
the swollen red sky. Smoothly, he drew his Winchester from its saddle sheath and cocked it at a flat
run toward his sister's place. The bay was barely in
sight behind him. Through a gathering of small hills,
the former Ranger saw the burning homestead alone
in the corner of a long valley.

The aging elm in the front yard appeared more
snarled than ever, repulsed by the heat from the
nearby house. All of the buildings were disappearing into flame and black smoke, except the small
stone house for storing butter and milk. He saw no
one and reined in the heaving black horse and
yelled, "Amelia! Amelia! Orville! Johnny! Rebecca!"

Only the fire's cruel laughter reached his ears. His
black horse was trembling, wanting to run away
from this awful place as fast as it had brought its
master, but Checker kept reassuring the animal with
his voice as he nudged it closer to the burning structure. His eyes tried to rush inside but were turned
back by the sheer wall of flame devouring the front
of the house. He saw the yellow-and-red face of his

dead father laughing at him from among the lashing flames, and then it was gone. He yelled again, "Amelia! Amelia! Orville! Johnny! Rebecca! Oh, God, let someone answer me. Please, God, please!"

His horse wanted to bolt, and he realized it wasn't worth trying to search the area on his back, so he spun the animal around and returned to the elm. There, he dismounted and flipped the reins over a low branch. It was far enough away from the fire to allow the horse to settle somewhat. After slamming the rifle back into the boot, he returned to the task of finding someone alive.

But first he saw the lifeless body of Amelia's husband, Orville Hedrickson, by the west corner of the corral. Under the tall Swede was a shotgun, and two feet away was his worn pipe. He had tried to fight from behind a buckboard wagon, which stood as a silent testimony to the futility of his defense. A solitary horse danced toward him from the ripped-open gate. He stepped aside to let it run free and away from this burning hell. Eight hens scooted away from biting flames; he hadn't seen them before. Where was Amelia? Where were the children?

They must still be inside! He pulled the Comanche tunic up around his mouth to serve as some protection and ran toward what had once been a window and was now a roaring invitation of flame. Three strides from the building, he heard a soft moan—or thought he did. There! It came again, and he stopped at the window and turned around. He choked from the thickening smoke as hot air rammed into his throat and lashed at his eyes.

He saw nothing. A faint voice told him, "My Johnny and my Rebecca aren't there. They've taken them. They've taken my Johnny and my Rebecca."

A tall woman, bloody and half naked, stood from behind a stone well near the front porch. Her hand held the will to keep her from falling. Her body trembled and her eyes did not see him, or anything else. Her mind had stopped from the horrors of the night. Checker was shocked and, for a moment, didn't move. It was Amelia—only this graceful woman was almost beyond recognition. It was like seeing his dying mother again. Her face was purple and swollen. Her filthy dress was shredded, leaving her breasts exposed. Parts of her arms and legs were blood-raw from being dragged. The side of her head was a knot of blood; a swath of her hair was gone, yanked from her scalp.

As her dulled eyes focused, she recognized him and cried out, "Oh, John, I thought you would come. I prayed you would come." He heard, somewhere in his mind, the promise he had made to her when they were forced apart as children: "I'll come back." "Say you promise." "I promise."

He ran over and took her into his arms. She was beyond sobbing, beyond caring. It was obvious she had been dragged and beaten. He held her close and tried to comfort her. Her sounds were like those of a dying animal, wheezing its last fears.

After a few moments, he brushed aside the blood-clotted strands of hair stuck to her swollen face and said, "Amelia, I am here. No one can hurt you anymore. I am here."

She stared at him and slowly opened her hand. In the blood-streaked palm was a button, the one she had taken from his shirt years ago when they were separated. Checker's mind went to their reunion, when he had at last returned to Dodge with the Triple C trail herd. He was walking again with Amelia on a tour of her home. Framed pictures of family atop a cabinet in the corner of the bedroom caught his eye. One was of Amelia's family, taken before Rebecca was born. Another was the same as the one in his pocket watch, only larger.

Without a word, she stepped to the cabinet and picked up two small items displayed among the photographs. A thimble. A button.

"Remember these?" she asked, the corners of her eyes wetting. "This was Mother's . . . and this . . ."

"Yeah, you took it off my only shirt." He smiled at her, then wiped his finger across his nose. "I can't believe you kept it."

"That's all I had, Johnny. That . . . and your promise."

"I was mighty slow getting around to keeping it, wasn't I?"

"Your little sister . . . says yes. I say—you're here now . . . and that's what counts," she said, and gave him a long hug.

With a clinched-teeth moan, Checker shook away the memory and squeezed her hand shut over the button. The former Ranger had seen more than his share of scalped men and women and murdered children, the victims of renegade Mexican bandits and wild Kiowa war parties. It still didn't prepare him for this sight. He cried.

"S-h-h-h-h, my little Johnny, it will be all right," Amelia cooed, and patted his arm, and then passed out.

Lifting her beaten body in his arms, he carried her to the tree where his horse was tied. Behind him, the blackened remains of buildings gasped and relinquished their souls to the morning sky. Flames zigzagged across the open yard, angrily seeking grass and weeds because nothing else remained for them to destroy. Mother Earth let them play until only a few gasping flickers remained. Checker wrapped his sister in the blanket from his saddle, washed her face and arms with water from his canteen. She was unconscious, but her fist held tightly to the button and he made no attempt to take it from her.

Fevered exhaustion stalked his body. His mind was erupting with hate. He wanted revenge. Savage revenge. He wanted to catch up with Star McCallister and torture him like he'd seen Comanches and Kiowas do to their enemies. He wanted to face all of the McCallister gang and kill them. One at a time. Sleep took him, but the nightmare returned, slamming him awake again. He shivered in spite of the hot morning sun, gazed at his unmoving sister. How much time had passed, he didn't comprehend.

An emptiness burned at his soul, imitating the flames that had destroyed the Hedricksons' home. A red sun tore through the powerless clouds and took its place high in the sky. Warmth dried the brown grass, patted the earth, and encouraged whisperings from charred remains of the destroyed homestead. He listened and heard them tell memories of a family growing and loving. He looked over at his battered sister, then squeezed his eyes shut to keep her battered face away.

From over the broken hills, he saw the silhouettes of three riders pushing hard toward them. He struggled to his feet and yanked his Winchester from the saddle boot, cocked it, and waited for the midday sun to reveal their identities.

Chapter Eight

Sonny Jones studied John Checker's strained face as they rode into the blackened horror of the Hedricksons' homestead. Jackson and Bannon were flanked on each side of him. Sonny tried to find his friend in Checker's gaze, but it was the stare of a man Sonny didn't know. On a lead rope in Sonny's hand was the Ranger's bay. The horse had stopped to graze after losing ground to Checker's hard-running black horse.

With readied rifles across their saddles and morning light to guide them, they knew it was an escaped gang, not a lynch mob, they sought. Their minds were too filled with sorrow and fatigue to wonder how the breakout had been done. Their sweated horses expressed displeasure at entering this terrible place. Ears peaked, nostrils widened, and an easy lope became a side-stepping stutter as their riders tried to calm them.

Cotton Smith

At the heels of young Bannon's horse, Dan Mitchell's dog, Captain, trotted on its three legs; its thick nose was low to the ground in a study of its own. The three men were bone-tired, their minds walking with friends buried at dawn. Their clothes were damp from the earlier rain, but drying quickly as the afternoon's breezes pushed against them. Stunned reaction to the burned-out dream was painted on their weary faces.

The stench of black destruction swelled their minds, and each man steeled himself to the jagged glass of feelings that tore at their insides. All three had been to this home before at a bittersweet celebration after their herd was recovered and Star McCallister and his gang arrested. All three had met Amelia Hedrickson, her husband, and their two children. All three had seen the strong connection between John Checker and his long-separated sister. All three knew Star McCallister was their half brother. Now they must compare those memories to the aching sight of wretched black skeletons that had once been home, barn, and shed, a family's place of laughter and love.

Overhead, a red ball of a sun watched as unmoving as the former Ranger standing before them. Checker's eyes were narrow slits of hate; his body was as rigid as the burned-out corner post of the home standing far behind him. It was a stranger that waited, and Sonny sensed the danger without understanding.

"John, you all right?" Sonny asked. His gaze swept the valley and returned to the Ranger. His friend was the only danger he could see. Checker didn't respond.

Returning his rifle to its boot, Jackson dismounted first. He handed his reins to Bannon and headed toward Amelia, carrying saddlebags and a canteen. It was his nature to be methodical and practical. And caring. His long gray coat carried streaks of drying rain as well as red spots of clay from flying hooves. His knowledge of medicine was more than trail savvy; it had also been gleaned from a prized medical book he'd found somewhere.

Sonny whispered, "Wait." But it was too late.

"Don't touch her! Stand where you are!" Checker snapped. The Winchester in his hands rose with his command and the heavy cock of the hammer broke into the gray midday. "What do you want here?"

The Triple C cowboys froze in disbelief. Bannon glanced at Sonny and saw his hand slide into the carbine's trigger guard. The young farmer frowned, disbelieving what he saw. Sonny and Checker were good friends. Jackson was cut by the former Ranger's remark. It was the first time Checker had ever rejected him like others did a black man. He'd always thought of the tall Ranger as a friend. They were not as close as he and Sonny, but they were definitely friends who had ridden together through adversity. He tried to hide the hurt, blinking it away, but Sonny saw it and so did young Bannon, who felt helpless and wondered if he was having a bad dream.

"Easy, John, it's Sonny. And Jackson an' Tyrel. We came to help," Sonny said, sitting in his saddle.

He'd seen men snap from far less; maybe Checker had gone mad. He could understand that. Only a blurry half day back they had buried two friends under a wide cottonwood and stared at eternity in

139

the cold, broken hole they dug for them. Tug and
Randy Reilman had taken Dan Mitchell back to Dr.
Tremons, along with Minnie Oliver, who sobbed the
entire time and wore her new brooch. Sonny hadn't
found the Irish cowboy, hadn't looked for him actually, and had done the singing himself. He sang
the song of "Breenon on the Moor," the Irish high-
wayman who rode the land Harry Clanahan loved.
It was Harry's favorite song—or, at least, the favorite one that Sonny sang—and the only Irish song he
knew.

They had been riding hard since that painful cer-
emony, leaving behind them a chaotic town. When
they left, the marshal was gathering a posse of
mostly townsmen to go after the Kayler riders. Most
Texas drovers refused to go, and many were already
talking about heading home to Texas since justice
had been done. Sonny had exchanged only a few
words with Marshal Rand, who wanted to know
where Checker was. Sonny told him he had gone
fishing for a few days, and the lawman wasn't sure
what to think of the comment.

Sonny pushed back his rain-pounded derby, and
his sweating forehead glistened at its introduction to
the day. His trail clothes were clammy from their
ride through the rain earlier. Their heavy dampness
made him feel even more tired than he was. This
was the longest day and night he could remember.
Even when the herd was stolen hadn't seemed this
awful, this bleak. There was only one other time that
matched its agony, exceeded it really, and he would
not let his mind return to that moment.

He spoke slowly. "Put the gun down, John. We're
your friends, you know that. We've been ridin' since

dawn to catch up to help you. John, it's Sonny."

Checker blinked and blinked again, shook his head, and looked at the three friends like he was seeing them for the first time. He frowned and said in a hesitant voice, "W-when did you get here? D-did you see where Star went? I—I w-was too late. Star took the k-kids. He took the kids, Sonny." He glared at the rifle in his hands and seemed confused by its being there. He let the weapon slip from his grasp and clunk on the ground, splattering mud on his boots and pants.

His last words were a jab to the stomach of each rider. Air hissed through Sonny's clinched teeth in reaction to the awful news. But their kidnapping seemed better to his frazzled mind than what he imagined might have happened. He had already seen the body of their father by what remained of their corral. Bannon bit his lower lip and remembered the fun of playing with little Johnny and Rebecca. He squeezed shut his eyes hard to keep wetness from entering them. Jackson's wide shoulders rose and fell, and a prayer spun from his mouth as if from a man out of breath.

"It's all right, John. You've been through a lot. How is . . . Amelia?" Sonny finally responded. His hand remained in position on the Winchester.

"I—I don't know. They dragged her. D-dragged her by the hair until it came out. I—I think she's sleeping. Jackson, you know more about caring for folks than I do—will you mind taking a look? I'd appreciate it."

Jackson glanced at Sonny, who nodded, and the black man went quickly to Amelia. Jackson realized that Checker's earlier response had nothing to do with him at all. A soft smile came to his face, as usual, and the corners of his eyes crinkled in pleasure, in spite of the situation. He kneeled beside the unconscious woman, laid his cold pipe on the sticky ground, and carefully arranged his saddlebags so he could reach into them easily.

Before examining her, he said, "Tyrel, there's some starter kindling here in my saddlebags. See if you can get a small fire going. I'm going to need some hot water. Checker needs, we all need, some hot coffee—and food."

"Good idea," Sonny said without dismounting.

No one was aware that he continued to hold his rifle at the ready. He'd seen too many men break to be satisfied yet. He'd seen the same signs in himself a long time back. The haunting memory of three men who happened to say the wrong thing to him at the wrong time, after he lost the woman he loved, would creep into the corner of his mind if he wasn't vigilant. John Checker was a man on the same edge. He would wait a few minutes before dismounting—or putting away his rifle.

In response to Jackson's order, Bannon nodded and swung down from his horse. He was happy to get down. The sorrel horse, from his trail string, hadn't been ridden for a while and was eager to let him know it remembered the days when it ran free. Most of the morning, the animal had alternated between crow-hopping, jog-trotting, and a peculiar sideways canter.

Only a tight rein kept it from bursting ahead of the other two riders. The performance had provided a bit of levity on a ride that carried only sorrow. But he wasn't happy about being the object of that laughter, even if it helped Sonny and Jackson get over burying their friends. When it was raining, he was distracted by keeping his slicker over his new Winchester sitting proudly in the saddle boot. He didn't want even one drop to get to the stock. Of course, the pounding rain wasn't agreeable, nor was the bottom of his slicker. As soon as the rain stopped, he wiped off the wooden base with his chaps and nearly fell off when the sorrel jumped sideways at some imagined peril.

Taking care not to get a boot caught in the stirrup, he spoke quietly to the frisky animal as he dismounted. "Easy now, Red. Don't make me look foolish. I mean it now, you stand—like the other horses. I'll hit you right in the nose, you hear me? I will."

The sorrel turned its whole body toward him, pawed the ground, but finally dropped its head. He was relieved. *I don't need anything else right now*, he thought to himself. *I just don't. It isn't right.* To his left, Captain waited with a wagging tail and came to him as soon as the farm boy stepped down. Bannon gave the dog a cursory scratching but was distracted by the awful sight around them.

His young face was tight with the shock of the burned-out homestead, the news of the kidnapped children, and the earlier scene of the dead young outlaw they assumed Checker had shot. The outlaw reminded him of himself and this terrible place brought images of his own home in Texas, and he didn't like that connection right now.

He tried not to think of his mother or his sister looking like Amelia Hedrickson, or what might happen to Johnny and Rebecca. He squinted again to keep his mind from trying to tell him all the possibilities. Yet he was instantly homesick. Oh, so homesick. He wanted to see his mother and his sister. Now. He wanted to be away from all this sadness. Too many friends of his had been ripped away from life. He wanted to be home. He could see his mother and his sister waiting to hug him and bring him inside.

Holding the reins of both horses in his left hand, Bannon accepted the sack of dried kindling and rolled prairie grass from Jackson, along with two stick matches. It was a preparedness kit most trail-savvy men carried. Bannon was embarrassed he hadn't thought to carry one himself. Captain nuzzled Bannon's leg, and he scratched its ears. Captain wanted more attention, but the farm boy was distracted with his new assignment.

Swinging the kindling sack in his hand, Bannon walked toward the scattered brush settled around a clump of greasewood twenty yards south of the remains of the house. Untouched by the fire, it should yield mostly dried-out wood, he thought. Captain bounded along with him, eager for a new adventure. Bannon marveled to the ugly dog how odd it seemed to be making a fire when all around them had been a disastrous inferno. Captain's sad eyes seemed to understand, and Bannon patted its head and ruffled its ears.

He felt the heavy weight at his hip and glanced down to see his new Colt resting in its holster. Every time he saw the weapon, he smiled. It was a beautiful gun. He reloaded both weapons when the rain stopped, after seeing both Sonny and Jackson do so. It made him proud to slip fresh bullets into the chamber. Of course, the sorrel caused him to drop several because it wouldn't settle into a nice lope. He hated that horse, he decided, and it hated him.

Captain wandered farther, disappearing on the back side of a hollow log. The dog's alertness indicated more than casual exploration. A frightened sage hen fluttered to safety on heavy wings.

"Good job, Cap. We shoulda had 'im fer breakfast. You best be careful, tho," Bannon said, mostly to himself. "There likely be skunk about." With that lame warning, he found a likely spot and began preparing a fire. But his mind was on the dog, and he looked up several times before being relieved to see him reappear from the mangled swirl of brown buffalo grass, weed, and bush.

"Silly dog," he muttered. "Ya need to stay closer to home, boy. That's whar I'd like to be, fer sure." With that, he hollered, "Captain, come here, boy!"

Captain's ears saluted and the animal went into its distinctive three-legged lope toward the farm boy. Bounding into him, Bannon laughed as he tried to hold off the dog's slobbery greeting to his face. He scratched its ears again, and along its back. Captain arched its body and welcomed the touching.

Across the open ranch yard, Jackson kneeled beside the unconscious Amelia. Lifting Checker's blanket, Jackson saw her exposed breasts and immediately replaced the covering. He felt Checker's penetrating gaze somewhere behind him but didn't glance around. From his weathered saddlebags, he took a clean gray shirt, unfolded it carefully, and slid it under the blanket. After covering Amelia's bosom, Jackson began examining her battered body.

Her left arm was definitely broken; he could see the bone pushing against her pale skin, laced with

145

streaks of purple and red. Her face was rubbed raw in places from being dragged. He untied his bandanna and used it to make a sling to hold the arm in place, next to her body. It would have to do until they could get her to a doctor in Dodge. She was barely breathing, so her arm was the least of his concerns. Unless he was greatly mistaken, she was bleeding internally, and that he could do nothing about except pray.

"O Lord, give this fine woman the strength to overcome this awful thing they've done to her," he muttered to himself. "And, Lord, you stay right alongside John Checker, too. He's going do some things he shouldn't if you don't. Amen." He hitched his stiff shoulders and added, "Oh, and Lord, you take care of those little children—until we can get to them. You can do that, Lord, I know you can. Amen—again."

He was certain her nose was broken and several teeth were loose. It was his experience that most teeth would reset themselves in time. There wasn't anything he could do about it either, anyway. Her once-angular nose was barely discernible on a face bloated with purple and red welts. Her right eye was swollen and pushing tightly against the eyelid. Bile hit his throat like a bullet, and he turned his head away to keep from vomiting on her if the reaction kept coming. It didn't. Slowly, he took a deep breath and then another, until he was strong enough to resume the examination. Slowly, he cleaned the ugly wound where her hair-lock had been, removing the mud, clotted blood, and tiny pieces of cloth.

"It's bad, isn't it, Jackson?" Checker's question

was soft and stilted, like that of a man who really didn't want it answered.

"John, we're going to have to get her back to town quick as we can," Jackson said. "There's not much I can do." He turned to face Checker with the news.

Checker listened without any comment. Jackson waited momentarily, then went back to Amelia. Swallowing away his bitter anguish at her condition, he straightened her nose, staring at it from the left and then the right until satisfied it had been restored to the proper position. He took a folded handkerchief from his coat pocket and wet it with canteen water. He wouldn't wait for hot water; he felt the need to do something, anything, now. Gently, he washed away dried blood on her face and arms, then her stomach. He didn't look at her bosom to see if it carried remains of her beating. He cleaned the lower portions of her skinned legs, but he didn't feel he should examine her thighs—it just wouldn't be proper. But he knew what had happened there. Carefully, he rewashed her face and laid the damp cloth across her injured eye.

A small jar of ointment, purchased yesterday from Dr. Gambree's wagon, was drawn from his saddlebags. He rubbed its yellow, greasy mixture on ugly cuts, purple bruises, and raw skin. Jackson's expression changed with the examination of each new wound. He applied a thick covering to the torn hole on her head. Checker watched him as if in a trance, saying nothing.

Sonny eased out of the saddle, looped the reins across the closest branch. The bay's lead rope was slipped into place next to it. Without comment, he casually strolled over to Checker's dropped rifle and

147

loosened the kerchief around his neck. After wiping the gun clean, he returned it to Checker's saddle boot and retied the dirty scarf around his neck. He returned to his own horse to take off the saddlebags carrying food. He cursed to himself at the tightness of the wet knots holding them in place and finally resorted to his knife to pry them apart. Placing the separated saddlebags over his right shoulder, he walked over to Checker, who was standing rigidly watching Jackson care for his sister.

"John, why don't you go see if that wagon by the corral is all right. Looks good from here. We're going to need it to carry your sister back to town. There's three of their horses grazing over yonder by the long grass. See 'em? Must've run off when Star left with the others. We'd best round them up too. Gonna need some hosses that'll take a hitch." He smiled thinly at Checker when he finished.

"S-Sonny, I'm going to kill Star. I'm going to kill him real slow. I'm going to make him wish he were dead long before he is," Checker stammered in response.

Sonny's glance caught the same expression he had seen riding in. It was that of an evil man, a man he didn't know. Checker walked stiffly toward the corral a few steps, and Sonny watched his friend's face soften. Checker's eyes glazed over with anguish as he again saw Amelia's downed husband. In two strides, he changed into an old man with crinkled crow's-feet at the corners of his bleary eyes and a sunken mouth line that couldn't smile. His body sagged with despair. Sonny had never seen the formidable Checker like this. Not after the herd was stolen and their friends killed, or even after Clana-han and Tex had their throats cut.

Sonny didn't respond to Checker's statement. There was no reason to. His friend was in shock and probably had no idea what he was saying or even who he was talking to. It was Sonny's turn to be strong.

"Look for some harness, John. Maybe the fire didn't get it all. Do you know where Mr. Hedrickson kept it?" Sonny said, trying to get Checker to focus on what needed to be done.

"I—I have to go after him, S-Sonny. Star took Johnny—and little Rebecca. He took her kids, Sonny. He killed Orville. I was too late, Sonny. I—I was too late to help them. I should have known he would come here. M-my God, h-he's her brother, Sonny. H-her brother. How could he do this?" Checker's face was blistered with anguish that wanted out.

Sonny understood his friend's condition. That had been the way he felt last night, trying to come to grips with the loss of Harry Clanahan. He had said his goodbyes this morning. Now his mind was tired but clear. Clear enough, anyway, to make him want to see McCallister's bunch hang—or die in front of his guns. He realized Star McCallister had a good lead, the better part of a day, and was obviously headed into the Nations. Star was moving with the Hedricksons' horses and that would slow him down some, even if the gang used them for relief mounts. But that lead would expand to two days before the foursome could start their pursuit after going to Dodge with Amelia. Enough of a lead to disappear, especially if it rained.

But their first obligation was to get Amelia back

to town and a doctor's care. He could tell from Jackson's expression that she was as bad as she looked. This bitter dilemma only made his decision more firm: He would follow Star McCallister now. Alone. With Checker's bay and his own tired horse, he would ride as far as he could before sleeping, then continue. The others could take Amelia to town and follow later. He would leave signs for them to follow.

Sonny glanced at Jackson, who was finishing with Amelia, then walked over to Checker, who hadn't moved and seemed bewildered. The former border outlaw wasn't certain how his friend would react to his suggestion, but it was the only way that made sense.

"S-Sonny . . . I have to go after them. I'm their uncle. T-the boy's named after me, Sonny, h-he is," Checker said, took a deep breath, and closed his eyes. "S-Sonny . . . Amelia was depending on me an', an' I—I wasn't here."

"I know, my friend," Sonny said. "I know. We'll get them back. I promise." He decided not to tell him. Yet.

"I promised her I'd come back an' . . . s-she kept a button of mine an . . ."

"Why don't you go look for some harness, John, and we'll talk about it later. If there isn't anything left, we'll rig up something. I'll get some grub working. Won't be anything like Dodge, but it'll fill ya up. After coffee and something to eat, you can start back with her." Sonny spoke with far more confidence than he felt. "Jackson's horse will take to the harness, good as any farm hoss, I reckon, if the Hedricksons' won't. Hell, I think every hoss in his string'll do it. Never seen the like."

Checker stared at him without speaking for an instant, then muttered, "I—I'll find the harness, Sonny."

Sonny watched him slowly walk away. He decided not to tell Checker the town was in an uproar this morning and the marshal was rounding up a posse to go after the lynch mob. Satisfied that Checker was, at least, tracking on the assignment, Sonny returned to Jackson, who was tending to Amelia's head again.

"I'm riding out after we eat. We can't lose their trail—and we will if we take her back to town," Sonny announced. "There's more rain comin', too, I can feel it."

"What about . . ."

"Checker? I'll tell him—after we get that wagon ready. You can carry her back in that."

Sonny leaned over, past Jackson, and gently brushed a lock of Amelia's hair away from her battered face. Her eyes fluttered open, and she looked at him for a sweet moment, then closed them. Jackson watched without speaking. Sonny's eyes studied her momentarily, then he realized what he was doing and glanced quickly at Jackson.

"Thought it was stuck there," Sonny coughed and blurted. He stood up straight again.

Without comment, the black cowboy placed the blanket carefully around her neck and shoulders and pointed to his saddlebags. "There's some extra jerky in there. Corn dodgers, too. I'll get 'em for you. Better take both our canteens, too. Better ask Checker for his field glasses—you might need them."

"Thanks. I'll ride Checker's bay first off and lead mine. It's about played out for now."

"Yeah," Jackson said, and added, "You know Checker won't like this, Sonny."

"No, he won't." Sonny grinned. "But he'll know I'm right, might even say so, when his mind gets right. I can leave piled-up rocks as good as he can. If we lose their trail now . . ."

Finished with tending to Amelia, Jackson stood and shook his head to the incomplete statement. "She might not make it, Sonny. I think she's all torn up inside. There's nothing more I can do."

Both glanced at Checker, then at each other. The tall Ranger had gone over to a mound of black ruins that had been a shed. Bending over, he was searching through its remains with a long branch. His manner was slow, mechanical. Without speaking, each man knew the other's thought: Checker might go crazy if she died. Jackson separated the food from his saddlebags: wrapped-up salt pork for cooking, along with some hard biscuits. The rest of his trail rations he laid aside for Sonny.

"I figure your pony'll pull the wagon, don't you?" Sonny asked as he placed Jackson's trail food into his own saddlebags and withdrew a small pouch of ground coffee beans.

"Better than the rest, I suppose," Jackson answered, and emptied the rest of the supplies in his saddlebags for Sonny. "We'll need a second. I'm thinkin' that brown—behind the gray—looks like he'd give us a steady head." Jackson pointed in the direction of the grazing Hedrickson horses.

Sonny started to ask how Jackson could judge whether a horse would pull a wagon or not by just looking at it, but decided if anyone could, it would be the black cowboy. There was something else on his mind he wanted to share more.

"Been chewing on the idea of Tyrel going with me," Sonny said as casually as he could. "He's young, but he's savvy. Good with a gun if need be. Likes my singing, too. What do you think?"

Jackson took a deep breath before answering. "Why don't I go instead?"

"You think Ty can handle Checker? What if there's a problem with Amelia on the way to town?"

"Promise me you won't let him get into trouble."

Sonny's grin came slowly. "I do believe you worry about that boy too much. I've seen him handle himself."

"Just ride careful."

"That's why I said what I said." Jackson stood and changed the subject. "My coffeepot's right here. You got a frying pan, or do you want to use mine?"

"I've got one," Sonny said, and patted the bags.

"When did you wash it last?" Jackson asked, a smile drifting to the corner of his mouth.

Sonny chuckled and said, "Well, we crossed the Red, didn't we?"

Jackson's eyes lit with delight. He needed the relief from tending to Amelia Hedrickson. Sonny sighed, and the picture of a laughing Harry Clanahan wandered into his thoughts. It was a day of too many burials, but he would take it upon himself to bury Amelia's husband after Jackson and Checker left for town. That would take time too, but they couldn't leave him. Sonny's gaze took in the lifeless shape by the corral, then shifted to the scarred remains of the house. There might be items that were destroyed, he realized, but he decided they would have to come back to sift through the remains.

Getting after Star quickly was more important. Once he traded those kids away to Comancheros, it would be difficult to find them. If he left them somewhere, they wouldn't last long in the Nations. Not a small boy and a little girl. He looked at the sky, shook his head, and headed toward Bannon's sputtering fire. Jackson followed with his hands filled with food.

Bannon was becoming frustrated at the slow acceleration of his fire. Captain nuzzled against his forearm, seeking more attention. Bannon told him to wait. Most of his sticks were wet, and their addition to the trembling flame brought sputtering and disappointing smoke. As he worked, his mind returned to home. But thinking of his mother made him feel guilty about having been with a woman in Dodge. What would his mother think if she knew?

The sensation of that moment lingered close, and his manhood tingled with the memory. He decided his report about town experiences would include only receiving the guns, shopping, and the trial. Maybe he would include the medicine wagon and its performers. That thought brought Salome, the dark-haired beauty, from the shadows of yesterday. He stared off into the sky, and she performed her enchanting dance for him alone, inviting him closer and closer.

"How's that fire coming?" Sonny blurted, and Bannon jerked back into today.

Sonny put his hand on Bannon's shoulder as the farm boy squatted beside it, feeding the small flame with moist twigs and small sticks with renewed frenzy. "After we eat, I'm going on—after Mc-Callister. You want to go with me?"

Bannon looked up, surprise in his eyes and pleasure at being asked at the corners of his mouth. The honor drove away any thoughts of homesickness. "Sure, sure, Sonny. But what about Mrs. Hedrickson—an' Jackson, an' Checker?"

"Jackson and John will take her into town and then follow us. I don't want to give that bastard Star too much of a lead. That's rough country he's heading into. Maybe we can catch up to 'em before they get rid of the kids—or before they're looking for us."

"Just you 'n' me?" Bannon asked as Jackson joined them at the fire.

"Yeah, if we're lucky, we can track 'em and keep an eye on 'em—until Jackson and John join us."

"Count me in, Sonny."

Captain barked excitedly, as if he knew an adventure was about to begin and wanted in on it.

"Good. I'll tell Jackson," Sonny responded, and walked away.

Without hesitation, Bannon looked down at the dog and said, "Now, Sonny 'n' me, we gotta go after some bad men, Cap—an' you gotta stay with Jackson 'n' Checker. You got that?"

Captain attempted to lick his face and succeeded. Bannon left the wetness on his cheek and nose. "Hey now, I mean it, Cap. You can't go along with Sonny 'n' me. You jes' can't." He scratched the dog's ears and returned to his fire tending.

Finishing what he could do for Amelia, Jackson did a quick count in his head. That still meant the outlaws outnumbered them two to one. More, actually. And that didn't count whoever had helped them escape. Four to one against Sonny and Bannon. He picked up a larger piece of wood and placed it on the fire; it sizzled its acceptance, and sparks splattered the air. He would talk with the farm boy about being careful, and he wished he hadn't suggested his going.

"I'm going to tell John," Sonny said, striding past him. "Wish me luck."

"Don't forget to ask about his field glasses. That'll help make him think."

"His thinking is what I'm worried about."

Chapter Nine

"What do you think, Doc? Will she be all right? Doc?"

John Checker's urgent questioning was a fast-drawn gun. His words slammed against Dr. Tremons as he stepped into the shadowed hotel hallway. An unconscious Amelia Hedrickson lay in Checker's darkened room behind the just-closed door.

Dr. Tremons looked at the anxious Checker, pushed his spectacles into place out of habit, and tried his best to smile. Checker's fearful expression shoved away what little optimism the doctor felt. He coughed to give his optimism time to return before speaking, but the fragile sense had vanished. He moistened the first two fingers of his right hand and stroked a wayward lock of hair back in place within a thinning, gray pompadour. Another habit he displayed with irritating consistency. At times, it was difficult to watch him talk, especially when he got nervous enough to repeat the task like it was a punctuation mark after every sentence.

"She is a strong woman, Checker, you know that. But she's been badly hurt. Inside where I can't see. There are doctors in Kansas City that should look at her. They're better than me." Dr. Tremons's face mirrored Checker's anxiety even when he tried to mask his own.

"Are you saying I need to get her to Kansas City?"

"No, I don't think she could handle a trip like that. The next few days will be critical." He repeated the finger-wetting and again stroked the same strands of hair, which had no intention of staying where he wanted them to.

"All right, what should I do?" Checker's voice was hoarse and demanding. He resisted the temptation to grab the doctor's hand and hold it away from his scalp.

"Pray. You do know how to pray, don't you, John Checker?" Dr. Tremons snapped, irritated by Checker's insistence. His fingers froze in place inches in front of the trim mustache that set off his mouth. His square jaw pushed forward in defiance.

Checker's eyes studied the doctor's face for an instant, then he blinked and said, "I'm sorry, Doc, I was way out of line. Here you leave your home to come and help me—and I act like a damn fool. I'm sorry. My head's not doing much clear thinking right now."

"Don't think nothin' of it. I understand how you're feeling, son. Believe me, I've been there too," Dr. Tremons said as gently as he ever spoke, and he finished wetting his fingers and stroking the wild hair lock. "You know, you coulda brought your sister to the house instead of here—at this cowboy hotel."

"Well, I . . ."

"I know. You were jes' a-worried I wouldn't want another patient at my house," Dr. Tremons growled. "Well, I can see why, with a hellfire stubborn one like that thar cowman friend o' yours."

Inside, Checker was fighting to keep hatred from taking control. It had been that way since he carried Amelia from the wagon and into the hotel. He had dozed during the return trip, letting Jackson handle the wagon at the black man's insistence. The respite had helped clear his head. At least it did until he lifted her mangled body from the wagon bed.

The sensation of that moment was absolute in its temporary corrosion of his mind. He had never had such a crippling feeling before, like someone had ripped away his soul and left only the rage of his father. After all this time, he had finally been reunited with his sister, only to have her destroyed by their half brother. The only thing that mattered was to find Star and kill him, to kill all of his gang of thugs. There was no justice; there was nothing.

Even as Checker talked with Dr. Tremons, he was racked with the anguish of seeing her so badly mauled; with guilt about not anticipating that Star would do this savage thing; with sorrow about her children being taken away and his not knowing if they would ever be found again; and with frustration about not being able to go after him right away. Sonny's plan to split up made sense, but it didn't make things any easier. Yet how could a brother leave his sister at a time like this? His mind sizzled with conflicting emotions as he tried to concentrate on the grizzled doctor's blunt assessment of Amelia's condition.

The four Triple C men had buried Oliver Hedrickson within a grove of trees west of their homestead. Checker had made that decision in spite of Sonny's insistence that he and Bannon could do it. His sister would want it that way. He had asked Sonny to sing something, and the former outlaw had struggled through a rendition of "The Sweet By and By." The words always came out different each time he sang anything except "Dixie." At the former Ranger's urging, Jackson had also recited the Twenty-third Psalm.

Three of Hedrickson's horses, left behind by the gang, were easily roped. Bannon had ridden out on one of the recaptured animals and led his own contrary mount. Jackson hitched the quiet sorrel to the wagon, along with his own brown horse. The recaptured gray mare and Checker's black horse were tied to the back. A milk cow wandered into them while they were eating and was allowed to continue being free.

Checker's concentration reemerged to hear Dr. Tremons say, "You look like hell warmed over, Checker. You need sleep."

"I'm all right. Got some on the way. Jackson handled the team while I slept."

"Good for him. But you need more than a few winks—if you're going to be in shape to get them kids back. Star an' his rats will be waitin' for ya. Don't forget I was a fightin' man long before I took up fixin' folks. I didn't get this hyar gimpy leg from a barn dance." Dr. Tremons pointed at his stiffened leg, and for a moment Checker thought he was going to retell the story of how he took a musket bullet during the battle of Gettysburg.

"Yeah, I . . . ah, Sonny Jones, you remember him, and Tyrel stayed on their trail. Jackson and I will catch up with them as fast as we can." Checker spoke quickly to cut off the possibility of the recitation of that battle story. He'd heard it nearly every time they had been together. The old doctor seemed to need to convince the former Ranger that he, too, was a warrior.

Frowning, Dr. Tremons blurted, "Of course I remember him. Damn happiest man I ever met. No excuse for that kind of happy."

Checker's lopsided grin was agreement, and he added, "Yeah, he's also the toughest I've—"

"Yeah, all of you are, are . . . like brothers—of the gun," Dr. Tremons snapped. "Yessir, brothers of the gun, that's what you are."

Checker's eyes caught Dr. Tremons's gaze momentarily, then bounced away to examine the wall's lone lamp. Nothing in him wanted to be courteous, wanted small talk, even wanted to talk. His mind was black. Instinctively, he placed his right hand on the butt of the Colt resting on his hip. But Dr. Tremons wasn't finished.

"You best git to goin', John Checker. You've done all you can for your sis—I mean it, son. Sarah Ann and I will watch over her. It does no damn good for you to be here when that oily bastard has her kids. Lord A'mighty, I don't even want to come down on that thinkin'. When she wakes up, the best medicine she could have would be them kids at her side. Wish I could be ridin' with ya."

161

Cotton Smith

Checker's shoulders rose and fell in a long breath that carried heavy frustration. He had forgotten how windy the doctor could be. Next, he would hear about Chickamauga and how his division fought hand to hand there. He didn't need this. Inside the room, he knew Sarah Ann was tending to his sister. Not daring to admit it even to himself, he hoped to get just a glimpse of her before she left.

Checker hesitated, letting his frayed mind absorb the advice, before answering. "I appreciate all your help, Doc. I've already talked to the hotel manager, and he's gonna have one of the maids look in on her. Best I can do—for now."

"You'll do no sech thing, Checker," Dr. Tremons spat. "Me 'n' sis, we'll care for her. Dammit, man, where's your head? Or don't ya want me doctorin' your sister?"

Checker's mouth turned into a half-grin before responding. "Doc, I can't expect you to—"

"Tarnation 'n' blazes, ya can too! I won't have it no other way—an' I know Sis, ah, Sarah Ann, is a-gonna feel the same way. You're our friend, son. Our friend."

"I don't know how to thank you, Doc—"

"You can thank me by gettin' those kids back."

"Jackson's at the livery now getting fresh horses. I'll trail my black. Couldn't leave him behind. We'll get supplies at our chuck wagon. I want to catch up with Sonny 'n' Bannon by tomorrow."

Dr. Tremons glanced at the wall lamp, licked his fingers, and pushed the lock back before speaking. "Just don't be wearin' out your horseflesh, son—or yourselves. I remember during the War we got ourselves pinned down 'cause our mounts were played out an' . . ."

"May I go in and see her, Doc?" Checker couldn't wait any longer.

"Yeah, but you let her sleep. That's the best for her. I mean it, now. I'm gonna head downstairs for a short whiskey or two."

Without watching him leave, Checker entered the hotel room, quietly opening and closing the door behind him. He stood and swallowed away the turmoil that was assembling inside him. A solitary table lamp was trying its best to return the sun to the stark gray room. The former Ranger's eyes ran across his sleeping sister to Sarah Ann Tremons's face. She was standing on the far side of Amelia's bed.

The lamp's glow caressed her face, accenting high cheekbones and a perky nose. Her long auburn hair was tied in a tight bun, but the yellow light found places to dance anyway. She smiled at Checker and made him forget for the moment where he was and what had happened. Her firm jaw and bright eyes were definitely those of her father, making her appear both sassy and determined at the same time. The energy between Checker and the doctor's daughter was immediate and unrelenting.

"She is sleeping, John," she said, her eyes asking him questions he wanted to answer. "That's best for now."

"Thank you for coming," Checker said. He looked as wild as the Texas he once fought for, but the evil force of his father was back in its place deep within his mind. Checker's face broke into a warm smile, in spite of the situation.

"You knew I would, John."

"I hoped you would."

He walked over to the bed and stood looking at his sister. Her swollen face was turning shades of purple. The side of her head was bandaged, but he could see, in his mind, the awful bloody mess where her hair had been pulled out of her head when they had dragged her. He bit his lower lip to keep anger from taking command. At the corner of his eyes, moisture gathered, awaiting release. Sarah Ann looked at him like someone watches a wild animal at a stream. Then, without her consciously realizing it, she was by his side, with only the rushed whisper of layers of petticoats to give her movement away to either of them. For John Checker, the heady rush of her scent, of clean linen and lye soap, like the smell of fresh clothes hanging in the sunshine, of some soft mysterious ginger taste to his mind, reinforced her closeness and made it difficult to think at all. The only thing that mattered was having her next to him.

How could he be thinking so foolishly at a time like this? With his sister dying in front of him? And what did he have to offer a woman like Amelia? He was nothing more than a man with a gun. No serious money, no property, no future. She was just being nice to him because of what he and his friends had gone through, his mind whispered to his heart.

Sarah Ann stepped closer to him and said, "John, Amelia is holding something in her fist. She's holding it so tight that I didn't try to remove it. Do you know what it is?"

Instinctively, he looked down at Amelia's right hand, covered by blankets. "Y-yes, it's a button.

From my shirt, from the shirt I wore when we were separated—as k-kids."

"I don't understand. Please tell me." She took his hand in hers and led him away from the bed and toward the corner where a small table stood, adorned with a skinny white cloth, a porcelain bowl, a matching pitcher with a chunk gone from its lip, and the lamp.

Blinking back the emotion remembering brought with it, he told her about their separation and his sister making him promise to return, asking for a remembrance of him to keep until he did. Sarah Ann continued to hold his right hand, and reached for the other. Her fingers caressed his as he spoke. He explained how she had pulled a button from his shirt to be that keepsake, because he had nothing else to leave with her. She had kept the button in a special place along with a thimble of their mother's. He guessed she had grabbed the button before Star's men found her.

Quietly, he told her about feeling so good about finding his sister and her family, and tried to put words around his seeing her torn apart and his guilt for not being there to stop Star's men. He told her about Star being his half brother and their father rejecting his mother. He told her about being separated from Amelia and finding her again after so many years had passed. The words poured out, and more wetness bubbled close to the corner of his eyes.

"I am so sorry about your sister—and those poor kids," Sarah Ann said, tears streaking down her face. The strained bodice of her dress pressed aggressively against his chest; firm, fleshy mounds drove hot blood through his head and heart. Her eyes waltzed from that point up to his own eyes. "But you can't blame yourself for this. No one could have seen this coming. Not even you, John Checker. And I can't blame myself for wanting to kiss you—now."

Checker's eyes never left her face. Looking up at him, she said nothing. She wrapped her arms around his neck and her warm, open mouth sought his. He drew her into an even tighter embrace and hungrily returned their first intimacy. They kissed again, longer and still longer, their aroused tongues seeking the other's pent-up desire.

Her face inches from his, she whispered like the world was watching. "John . . . I'm sorry to be so . . . so forward. But I had to let you know how I felt. If I could, I'd keep you here. Safe. With me. But I know I can't. I've been saying that over and over to myself. I know you must go after those terrible men."

He kissed her lips gently. A tear escaped and rolled down her crimson cheek, and she added, "Just tell me you're going to be careful. And that you'll come back. To me, John. It seems like I've known you all my life. Isn't that crazy? I . . . know that I want to be with you. Always. Please."

"I want to be with you, Sarah Ann. There's so much I want to tell you," Checker responded. "The moment I saw you, I wanted to spend the rest of my life with you. I knew it. I dared not wish for it . . . but I couldn't stop. I couldn't. All I could think of was being close to you."

"That isn't all you want to do!" she responded, her eyes twinkling, then casting themselves on the bulge in his pants.

He laughed. "That's true. Keeps a man mighty warm at night, just thinking."

Their mouths found each other again and the room became the world for an instant. Reluctantly, they stepped back from each other, but their hands held each other's fast.

"I must go," he said. "I don't know when I'll be back."

"I'll be here." She squeezed his hands, released them, and said, "Waiting for you—and your sister will be right beside me. We'll take good care of her. Now, you go and bring those wonderful children back."

His spurs jingled as he half-stumbled away, and she said, "Wait a minute, darling, please."

He turned back and was surprised when she reached for his shirt. With a hard pull, a button popped free. She stared at the tiny circle in her hand, a loose thread still clinging to the holes, then closed her fist over it.

"It worked before," she said, and smiled. "Remember you promised. You said you'd come back to me."

He nodded, tried his best to smile, and resumed his hurried retreat through the door and into the hallway, without another word. His eyes were fierce and black; his jaw set hard to control emotions that wanted him to run back to her. He didn't see her reopen the door and watch him disappear down the steps into the hotel's lobby. He didn't see her open her fist and look again at the tiny button there. He didn't see her face fill with tears. He didn't see her whisper, "I love you."

As he walked down the hotel stairway, Checker tried to force his mind away from what had just happened. His spurs spun against the descending stairs, and everything in him wanted to turn around and take Sarah Ann away from all this anguish. But that could not be. He knew it. His mind also crackled with hate for Star McCallister for placing him in that position—a desperate hate that sought expression.

On the bottom step, his mind tracked back to Shanghai Pierce, the brash Texas cattle baron, and his men leaving town shortly after the gang's capture. They helped capture the gang, but Pierce was eager to get back to Texas. The tall former lawman liked this unpredictable cattle baron, known for controlling more open grazing pasture—and for owning more cattle—on only a handful of actually owned acres of Texas land. Pierce had won riches and lost riches in moving beef across the plains. He was respected by every man in Texas—and feared. Pierce's help—and his men—would have been good to have right now, he thought.

He and his Triple C friends would be outnumbered by Star and his outlaws, but there wasn't anything he could do about it. He wasn't interested in asking any of the Texas cowhands remaining in Dodge to come along. This wasn't a time to have men around him that he didn't know. More men with guns only helped if they were men good with guns—and judgment. Besides, a large group of riders would make it easy for Star to know they were coming.

It would have to be Sonny and Tyrel, Checker and Jackson. Randy Reilman, the foulmouthed wrangler, and Tug, their cook, would need to remain with the Triple C string of horses and their chuck wagon. Neither was good with guns anyway. Checker smiled grimly when he acknowledged to himself that both would want to go with him. If Mitchell were strong enough to ride in the wagon, they could start for Texas if they wanted to. He doubted they would.

Across from the lobby, he saw Dr. Tremons sitting at a table in the hotel restaurant. In the other direction, a muttonchop-sideburned clerk, behind the lobby registration desk, checked receipts with the inconsistent glow from a sputtering lamp in need of oil. Checker glanced at the hotel clerk, who was pretending not to be watching. The former Ranger pulled a small sack of gold coins from his pocket and tossed it in the direction of the clerk. The action gave him time to calm himself.

"Here, this will pay for my sister's keep—and then some. We'll settle up when I get back."

"That's not really necessary, Mr. Ch—"

"Just make sure she gets everything she needs. Everything. Whatever the Tremonses say. I'll take care of any difference when I return. Savvy?"

"Y-yessir, Mr. Checker. You can count on me."

"Good."

Checker resumed his walk into the adjacent restaurant to thank Dr. Tremons again before leaving. Evening lamps were merrily playing with each other and the half-filled room of patrons. In the northern corner, the feisty doctor sat at a table and was talking to a narrow-faced man with a handlebar mustache, closely cropped hair, and a new, wide-brimmed hat. His gray business suit was decorated with a badge that caught the lamplight and announced its presence to the room.

It was Marshal Jubal Rand, with a drink in his hand and a cigar in his mouth. He and his town posse had returned in the afternoon with six dazed Kayler riders under arrest. The Circle J cowboys were now in the jail to await trial for murder. Word around town, spread mostly by the marshal, was that they had hurriedly buried the outlaws after killing them. The lawman was obviously waiting for the Ranger. He watched Checker advance, laid the drink on the table, took the cigar in his hand, and announced with confidence.

"Checker, I heard about your sister's trouble. It's outside my jurisdiction, but I'll raise another posse tomorrow and go after them, whoever they are."

"You forgot one thing, Rand. I tracked Star and his bunch right from your jail last night. I know who attacked my sister. So do you—you were in on it." Checker growled. The man's presence tore at the scab of smoldering anger within him.

Rand pulled himself to his full height and tried to sound authoritative, annoyed at himself that he couldn't keep his voice from trembling. He dropped the cigar and leaned to pick it up as he spoke. "Our town won't tolerate vigilante law. We've got the lynchers. They'll tell us where the bodies of the outlaws are soon enough. Whoever did this terrible thing to your sister's family will be brought to justice, too, I assure you."

Checker's hard gaze sought the marshal's eyes, and Rand avoided the connection, returning the cigar to his mouth and puffing fiercely. The former Ranger snapped, "Rand, leave the lying for the fools who'll listen. You're talking to me. There wasn't any lynching. You let Star and his men out—after you murdered my friends. How much did he pay you,

Rand? Two hundred dollars? Five hundred? A thousand?"

"What?" Rand's face was a split between fear and fierceness. The forgotten cigar tumbled down his vest and onto the floor again. "You can't talk to me that way. T-that's—"

"You've got two choices," Checker interrupted. "You can tell the mayor you're leaving town and be gone when we get back with Star. Or you can stay. It doesn't matter to me. Either way, I'm coming after you. You're going to pay for Harry and Tex." His hard face reminded Dr. Tremons of someone he had known a long time ago and couldn't quite recall who or where.

"Are you threatening an officer of the law?" Rand said, his voice pressing against his emotions. The cigar lay at his feet. "Dr. Tremons, you're a witness to this criminal act. Checker, you're under arrest."

The doctor poured himself another drink and pointed at the cigar. "Ya need to decide whether you're gonna smoke that thing or play with it."

Checker folded his arms and said, "Get out of my sight, Rand, before I think about it more. Dodge deserves better than you." The statement was a razor.

In a swift motion, Checker reached for the badge on the man's coat lapel and ripped it loose. Rand jerked in reaction, but his arms only rose halfway and stopped. Checker looked at the badge and handed it back. Mechanically, Rand's open hand rose to accept it. The marshal's eyes were unable to look away from the small piece.

"Don't wear this, Rand. I've known too many good men who were lawmen. You disgrace their memory," Checker said. "Oh, let those riders of Kayler's go, too. You're real good at letting prisoners out. Unless they were in on the killing of my friends. If they were, hold them until we return. I imagine, though, they didn't do anything except be in the wrong place. They might have wanted to hang Star— but that's not a crime, is it? You can count me in that group."

Rand tried to swallow, but his dry mouth wouldn't cooperate by generating any saliva. He looked at his boots, then at the smoking cigar, and wished he hadn't come into the hotel. He didn't want to pick up the smoke again, but he couldn't get his foot to squash it. The pistol at his hip seemed a long distance away. He tried to look around the room to see if anyone was watching, but he couldn't see around the tall man standing in front of him.

"T-that's another threat," he managed to blurt out.

"No, that's a promise, Rand. You are going to pay for this. Run or stay, I'm coming."

Rand tried to think of something to say but couldn't.

His shoulders rose and fell, and he put the half-empty whiskey glass on the table and rushed out. Dr. Tremons's chuckle nipped at his heels. Checker didn't pay any attention to the lawman's exit, and instead turned to Dr. Tremons and thanked him as if Rand had never been there.

"Never did think much of that man. Heard tell he was on the take jes' about everywhere in town," Dr. Tremons said, and grimaced as he swallowed the fiery whiskey.

"Doc, thank you again for everything. I know Amelia's in good hands. Just wish I could do this different," Checker responded without commenting on Rand.

"Well, sure, son—but how far can you get tonight?"

"Far as good horses can take us—and no sleep."

"You remember what I said, now."

Checker gritted his teeth and responded, "I will, Doc. It won't be Gettysburg. Count on it."

"I sure would like to be ridin' with you, son. If it weren't for this hyar leg, I . . ."

"Well, I'd like to have you with me, that's for sure. Man of your experience and all," Checker said. "But I need you more here."

They shook hands, and Checker couldn't remember feeling so tired, so defeated. Dr. Tremons asked him if he wanted whiskey, and Checker declined. It would only make him sleepier than he already was.

"Be seein' you, Doc," Checker said, and turned away.

"We'll keep her safe," Dr. Tremons said. Water filled the corners of his eyes, betraying his carefully hidden emotions. Checker didn't hear him whisper, "Ride with God, son."

Outside the hotel, Checker drew a tobacco pouch and papers from his shirt pocket and rolled a cigarette, trying to gather his thoughts before seeing to Jackson's supply gathering. Captain lay waiting beside the hotel; the dog had reluctantly left Bannon at the homestead, and only after much encouragement by both the farm boy and Jackson. The three-legged cur rose and wagged its tail at Checker's arrival.

After scratching the ugly animal behind its ears, Checker took a folded envelope from his shirt pocket, addressed to "Mister John Checker . . . Texas Rangers . . . Fort Worth, Texas." It had been the last thing he took when he and Sonny left the hotel. He was drawn to the letter like it would give the answers to restoring his sister's health, bringing her husband back to life, and returning her children. He read again the wrinkled letter Amelia had sent him over a year ago, the letter that had brought him to Dodge, the one he had read every night on the trail. As cigarette smoke worked across his face, he reverently absorbed each precious page one more time, knowing he could recite many of the sentences by heart. His mind wandered over memories sweet and bad; most were vague images—only a few burned brightly in the darkness of years past.

It was Dodge City's time of the buffalo hunter. His father visited their tent, the only home he could remember. A red-faced J. D. McCallister tore open the tent flap and roared into their tiny shelter, "Where is that little bastard? I'm gonna whip his ass for what he did to my boy. Git out of the way, woman! Git out of the way—or I'll slap you silly."

He was wildly angry because the young John Checker had just whipped his oldest son, Star. Younger than Checker, Star had teased him about living in a tent and about his mother being a whore. Checker twisted the boy's arm behind his back until he whimpered an apology. He vaguely recalled Star's younger brother, about six years old, trying to poke out his eyes with a stick when he was holding Star. When he grabbed the stick, both McCallister boys ran away crying.

For a bright moment, he saw his father's face and realized much of it was his own. Anger rattled through Checker as the memory continued. His mother stepped between J. D. McCallister and himself. He shook his head to wipe away her battered face and the ripped-open dress that followed—and the whipping his father gave him. That was the last time the evil man came to their tent. A few years later, Checker's mother died of whooping cough. He was fourteen; his sister, eight. Pictures of that awful time, when neighbors took his sister in and he was sent away for trying to kill his father, haunted him when he read the letter, but still he couldn't resist.

Actually, Checker was more like Old Man McCallister in looks and manner than Star, but the elder McCallister refused to ever acknowledge him and Amelia as his offspring and had nothing to do with them. Checker felt his presence within him at times and struggled with that feeling. Or was it a longing for the father and family he did not have?

Captain made a strange sound in its throat, spun toward the tie rack, and ran toward the slump-shouldered man dismounting there. Checker moved his hand toward his holstered pistol in the same motion as he tossed the cigarette to the ground. Dan Mitchell, the wounded Triple C trail boss, was holding a Winchester like it was a part of him. His once-tan complexion was pale under a weather-challenged broad hat. A jutted-out chin and gray beard stubble made him look older than he was. Around dark eyes, a web of squint lines flowed across a face anchored by big ears and a lopsided grimace, made more so by a chaw of tobacco jammed against the side of his mouth. His familiar wide orange scarf and dark cloth vest were partly covered by a leather coat that had seen too much prairie too often.

At first glance, he looked the same, yet he didn't. He squatted uneasily to meet the enthusiastic greeting of his trail dog. Immediately, Checker headed for the tough cattleman, torn between being happy to see him and knowing Mitchell had no business being here. The gunshot wounds he'd taken during the cattle rustling were serious; he was lucky to be alive, thanks to young Bannon bringing him quickly to town.

"Dan, what are you doing out of bed?"

"I'm goin' with you to get them bastirds. Done heard all 'bout it. 'Twerent' no lynchin' atall. Star done went'n' figgered how to git hisse'f out an' a-runnin'. Doc's got himself a loud voice. Came soon as I could git my britches on," Mitchell explained, rising from the dog. His eyes sparkled with resolve. His chin pushed forward, a sign he had made a decision. Captain happily ran circles around the man like a cat chasing a mouse. The movement caused Mitchell to teeter for a moment, then catch himself.

"You're a helluva friend, Dan—but you can't go," Checker said, rolling the made smoke in his fingers before meeting Mitchell's gaze.

"Who says? Jes' cuz you was a Ranger don't give ya no ri't to tell folks where they kin go," Mitchell exploded. " 'Sides, Doc said it'd be jes' fine." His leathery face blinked red, then returned to its pale shade. He straightened his back and swelled his chest.

Checker caught himself smiling in spite of the situation. "Oh, really? Well, Doctor Tremons is in there right now. You want me to go ask him?"

Mitchell squeezed his face into rejection of the idea and said, "Naw, but he don't know ever'thin'.

Checker, they killed my men. My friends. They near killed your sister—and did kill her husband. They took her kids. You insult the hell out of me if you think I'm gonna lay in some damn soft bed while you go after 'em."

"Dan, there's nobody I'd rather have with me. But you can barely walk and you know it," Checker said. "We'll be riding fast and hard."

"I weren't askin' to go on no picnic."

Checker replaced the letter in his shirt pocket and built another cigarette. He stepped closer to his wound-weakened friend, using the match to light his cigarette as an excuse to get reaffirmation about Mitchell's condition. Yellow flame spread across the trail boss's face and uncovered the pain he was trying to keep hidden. Checker knew it had taken nearly all of Mitchell's strength just to get dressed and here.

"Dan, I need someone I can trust to watch over my sister while I'm gone. Someone who can use a gun, if need be," Checker said, drawing on the cigarette and letting its first string of smoke meander across his forehead and slide around the brim of his hat.

Mitchell's body sagged like it had been propped up with an invisible stake. His face followed suit. As long as he denied the reality of his body's condition, he was strong enough. When he acknowledged it, the terrible weakness resumed control. He weaved, then caught himself.

"Dan, whoever helped Star might still be in town. Likely, I'd say."

Mitchell's face and body perked up at the possibility of being able to help in some way. "Ya reckon they might try somethin'—with your sis? Damn. Well, you kin count on me, even if'n I cain't ride."

Captain pawed Mitchell's right leg, and the trail boss scratched its ears, then told the dog to sit. The dog obeyed immediately, content to wait.

"I know that, Dan," Checker said, and nodded. "I'll tell Randy and Tug to be on the alert too. Watch Rand. He was in on it. I told him he was going to pay."

"So that's why he came a-boltin' outta thar a few minutes back. Looked like the boy had seen hell itself."

"He had."

"Jes' Jackson a-goin' with ya?" Mitchell asked. "Why don't ya git Pierce or some other Texas boys to go with ya?"

"Pierce already left. An' I don't want anyone we don't know. Our best chance is to get close without them knowing. So the fewer the better. If they know we're coming, they might . . ." He didn't want to finish the sentence.

Mitchell placed his right hand on Checker's shoulder, and the former Ranger could feel the weakness of his body trembling through it. "Ride careful, John. I never seed nobody ridin' with so much hate—fer you. Star McCallister'll know you're a-comin'. He wants you."

"I'm counting on him not expecting us to be so quick on his trail. Sonny and Tyrel are only hours behind him."

"Yeah, but they ain't you."

Chapter Ten

"Sonny! Over thar, is that them? See?" Tyrel Bannon's excited voice cracked from miles of riding in silence.

"Yeah, I see," Sonny Jones replied. Dusk was heavy upon the two men, and so was weariness. The first glimmer had straightened him in the saddle, with young Bannon's question hitting like a ricocheted bullet. "Ease up until we get a closer look. We're gaining on 'em—but I don't . . ."

He didn't finish the statement, but focused instead on the flickering fire barely visible in the murky gray horizon. As he tried to make out what they were riding toward, he yanked his Winchester free from its scabbard. The *crack-crack* of its cocking was a formidable sound in the early-evening air. Bannon followed his older friend's action and pulled free his new rifle, admiring its cold steel and polished walnut stock and slowly levering the gun into a readied state.

They were two days out of Dodge City and gaining on Star McCallister's gang, or so Sonny figured. Until spotting the fire, both men had been lost themselves in their own thoughts as they rode across treeless, windswept Kansas plains. Except for an occasional song bursting out of Sonny. They had run through every conversation topic either man was interested in: women, horses, guns, dogs, cattle, ropes, weather, Star McCallister and his gang, the attack on Amelia and Oliver, even John Checker and Jackson. Neither wanted to bring up the children and what might happen to them.

Once-crowded cattle trails were ghostlike in their silence, since the Texas herds had evaporated for the year. Glimpses of shod horse hooves led them southeast toward Indian Territory. During daylight, they stopped only to switch to their second horses, relieve themselves, and leave three-stone markers for Checker and Jackson. Their tracking ended each night when sundown finally played its last red streak and they could no longer read the trail.

"Ty, I don't think this can be Star. It just can't be," Sonny advised, laying the rifle across his saddle. "I put them a long day ahead of us, but I sure could be wrong."

"Maybe they done decided on holdin' up to rest," Bannon said.

"They wouldn't do it out here—where God and man can see 'em for miles. But let's ride careful until we can put a brand on it."

As Sonny spoke, silhouettes of longhorns grazing on brown buffalo grass began to take shape and he released the tension with a long exhalation and chuckled. "It's a trail herd, Ty. Small one. Should be friendly enough."

"Didn't reckon anybody pushed beef this late."

"Yeah. Run the risk of bad weather and no grass, that's for sure. Maybe they like getting holed up in Dodge for the winter."

"They must be payin' mighty high wages, then."

Sonny laughed, out loud this time, then uncocked and returned the Winchester to its scabbard, and hummed a song he'd heard in one of the dance halls. Bannon frowned at having to put his own handsome weapon away, but carefully laid the hammer back in place and slid the gun into the leather sheath under his right leg.

"Tyrel, we're gonna have to stop. You know I can't track at night. Only man I know can do that is John Checker. Must have some wolf in him or something. Never seen the like."

"I reckon you're doin' real fine, 'ceptin' for that one piece back thar a ways. Anybody could've done that. Had me fooled, that's fer sure."

Sonny smiled and said, "Could be, Ty. Anyway, we might as well be with some company for the evening. Reckon your ears'd take to another man's voice for a spell. Or is my singing hypnotic?"

"If they've got somethin' to eat, I'll listen to anything, even your singin'," Bannon answered, inhaling and exhaling deeply to let the tiredness know relief from the saddle was coming.

Sonny smiled at the demonstration, feeling the same weariness his young companion expressed, and yelled out, "Ho, the camp! Two riders looking

for a hot cup of coffee and somebody else to talk
to!"

He motioned for Bannon to halt his horse until
they were invited to proceed. They waited, and the
land was silent. A trickle of muffled sounds of scuffling and short, urgent words reached their ears.
They could see shapes of men moving but couldn't
make them out clearly. Sonny thought it was a herd
of no more than a thousand.

"Come on in, but keep your hands where we can
see 'em," came the brittle response.

Sonny glanced at Bannon and said, "I'll bet these
boys had a run-in with McCallister's bunch." He
turned back and yelled again: "We hear ya. We're
coming in easy. Ain't looking for trouble, just some
beans an' coffee." To Bannon, he muttered, "Tyrel,
keep your hand a long way from that fancy new
Colt. These boys seem jumpier than most."

"I hear ya. Hope they got somethin' to eat."

They rode into the dull golden light of the camp,
each trailing a relief mount. Two men sat around the
fire, their stoic faces cut into strange shapes by the
fire's uneven light. Sonny could see each had a rifle
in his lap, not a customary campfire tool for drovers.
From the darkness, a lanky man with a half-grown
beard and wearing a filthy long coat over worn
batwing chaps stepped forward. He switched a Winchester to his left hand and held out his right.

"We ain't got much—but never seed the day when
the Bar Four turned a man away from the fire," he
said grimly, his square face sad, not hostile. Sonny
shook his hand, then Bannon followed the greeting.

"Jeff, go check to see if they got any friends waitin'," the lanky leader ordered, and a stocky cow-

hand in a floppy, wide-brimmed hat jumped up from his place beside the fire and headed into the darkness.

"Looks like you boys are expecting trouble," Sonny said, looking around.

"Already had it. My handle's Buchanan," the man said. "Yo-all come over hyar 'n' help yourself. Got plenty of beans an' hot coffee. Maybe a few biscuits left. Sam, did you eat down all them sourdoughs we had?"

The heaviest man at the fire shook his head negatively and looked at the man next to him and said quietly, "I didn't, honest."

"That's mighty nice of you, Buchanan," Sonny said. "I'm Sonny Jones. This here's Tyrel Bannon. We ride for the Triple C."

Bannon nodded and hungrily eyed the pot of beans and the plate half filled with fresh sourdough biscuits. They hadn't eaten since morning, and that was a cold breakfast of corn dodgers and beef jerky in the saddle.

"You boys headed home?" Buchanan asked, and poured a cup of coffee for Sonny and another for Bannon, then handed them tin plates and forks. "He'p yourselves. It's tasty. Ol' Jeb makes a fine biscuit, if'n I do say so myse'f."

"No, we're trailing a bunch of rustlers. Man-killers. They busted out of jail—in Dodge. Killed two of our friends and took two little kids with 'em."

Buchanan eyed Sonny intensely, then poured himself a cup. He stared at the hot liquid, took a long swallow, and growled, "You boys lawmen?"

"No, no," Sonny replied, and tried to keep a slight smile from edging onto his face. Briefly, he told the

Cotton Smith

gathered men about the Star McCallister gang and what they had done. Every man at the fire looked stunned. Sonny noticed the drover return from checking out their story.

"Lan, you kin come out now," Buchanan said out of the corner of his mouth, and a long-coated, bespectacled man carrying a shotgun appeared from the darkness. Buchanan made no attempt to explain their action. He pulled a tobacco sack from his shirt pocket, rolled a cigarette, and lit it.

"This bunch you're a-chasin' came in easy enough, saying they had hosses for sale. Seein' them kids with 'em kinda threw us off, I reckon," Buchanan said, letting the first inhaled smoke follow his words. "Our trail boss, Mr. Vander, told 'em we weren't carryin' much cash money—an' our remuda was in plenty good shape."

One of the cowboys blurted, "They done kilt Mr. Vander! Shot him in the haid. A mean little feller done it. Long scar across his face like this. Wore Injun pants. Kinda looked like one, sorta. The head man, who tolt him to do it, had yeller hair—kinda like yurn." He was staring at Bannon.

Another asked, "You related to that feller?"

With a heaping spoonful of beans just deposited in his mouth, Bannon looked surprised at the question but chewed fast to be able to answer. Sonny answered for him, "No, he isn't. No law against yellow hair, is there?"

"No, I reckon not. My wife's got yeller hair. I didn't mean nothin' by it. Jes' askin', that's all. Oh yeah, an' a big feller, biggest I ever saw, done busted Emmett's nose real bad. No reason we could figger. Jes' wanted to. Emmett's a-sleepin' yonder."

Nodding his understanding without paying much attention, Bannon took a big bite of a biscuit and smiled at the taste. He spoke for the first time: "Them are mighty fine biscuits, mister. Mighty fine."

Buchanan gritted his teeth and said, "We done buried Mr. Vander back along the trail. They took most o' our food an' the cash box. Outnumbered us two to one. We ain't gun-savvy nohow, jes' cowmen. What we got left fer grub, they jes' didn't come across. Jeb has a strong habit o' hidin' things so us drovers don't git into it. Took four steers, too—fer eatin', I reckon. Leastwise, they didn't take the herd. Told us to be right thankful 'bout it all. I've been headin' up the outfit since. Only one that's been to Dodge a'fer."

The heavyset man stood and brushed himself off, surprisingly gentle in his ways. He spoke shyly, his face barely crossing the campfire: "Beggin' no offense, mister—but are you two all's that's going after 'em? There had to be eight, all carryin' serious iron."

Sonny took a swallow of coffee. Bannon's mouth was full of beans, and he was quite uninterested in talking. Pushing his derby hat back on his forehead, Sonny smiled and said, "No offense taken. Two more riders are coming behind us. They had to take care of the woman first. She's my friend's sister. John Checker's his name. Former Texas Ranger."

"Checker? John Checker?" Buchanan asked. His tone was disbelieving. "What's he doing in Dodge? Last I heard, he were down 'round the border. Heller with a gun, accordin' to the windies I've heard tell."

"Well, he's that, for damn sure," Sonny answered, and filled a plate with beans for himself. "He came to Dodge to see his sister and her family. Hadn't seen her in a long time, since they were kids."

"Damn, I almost pity them owlhoots," Buchanan spat. "Havin' Checker after 'em. I hear tell he jes' don't stop."

"Yeah, well, I reckon that's so," Sonny said, and swung his right boot across the other.

Buchanan sipped his coffee and smoked without speaking more, then observed, "Bannon, is it? I reckon you're gonna bust wide open if'n you eat any more of them beans."

Sonny laughed the loudest and said, "He may look a tad green, Buchanan, but he saved our bacon with the McCallister bunch. Kept Checker out of trouble, too. Right handy with that iron himself."

Bannon blushed at the attention and finally said, "I'm sorry, mister. Shoulda know'd my manners better'n that. Sonny, here, ain't much o' a cook." That brought more laughter from men who needed a reason to laugh.

"Say, you don't have any books or sech you'd be willin' to part with?" the bespectacled cowman asked, breaking open his shotgun and removing the shells. "Done got all the cans memorized."

Bannon smiled smugly and said, "Not with me. My good friend, Jackson, has ten or twelve books. He's a fine reader, you know. He kin ree-cite words from the Bible without a-lookin'."

"Well, unless your Jackson is hidin' out among them rocks, he's not gonna do me much good, now is he?"

Sonny glanced at Bannon, resuming his attack on a biscuit, and chuckled. "My young friend here has finally met an educated man—and he's right taken

by it—and he should be. Jackson's one steady hand.
As good with a horse as any I been around."

"I take it neither o' you got any readin'."

Sonny laughed, and Bannon bit his lower lip.
Sonny chuckled and said, "We did get a tad carried
away there. Well, I got a newspaper in my warbag.
You're welcome to it."

"Why, thank you, sir. That'll do jes' fine."

"I reckon Jackson'll be along in the next day or
so—he's riding with Checker," Sonny said. "You can
ask him about a book yourself. Although I figure
he'll be slow to part with any."

"Well, don't hurt to ask."

Bannon glanced at Sonny, then blurted, "He's a
colored man."

"Well, then, I should be able to tell him from this
Ranger fella yo-all are so high on," the bespectacled
man said.

From the fire came a muttered "I wouldn't ride
with no nigger—an' I sure wouldn't take anythin'
from one. Bound to be filthy. Maybe we oughta
shoot this one fer what the other'n did to the boss."
It was Jeff, the one who had been sent to check their
back trail.

Bannon tensed. Sonny crossed his arms and widened his stance. His spurs announced the adjustment. Sonny's words were like the cocking of a
buffalo gun. Hard. Brittle. Terrifying. "You know,
mister, I'd be real careful about where I tossed my
words. You've just called my friend something I
don't like. You'd best back up and start again."

His face crimson with fury, Bannon added,
"Count me in, mister."

Waving his arms in both directions, Buchanan

stepped between Sonny and the fire. His face was bunched with concern. "Hey now! None o' us need this kind of pawin' an' bellerin'. Jeff, you done keep your mouth shut about coloreds, you hear? Or I have a strong feelin' these boys'll shut it for you. You got that?"

His face streaked by the fire, Jeff looked like a man trying to decide how to answer the question. He didn't want to appear to be a coward, but he didn't want to die, either. He glanced at the rifle at his feet and looked up. Sonny's hooded eyes caught his face and wouldn't let go.

Walking toward the coffeepot, the bespectacled cowboy paused and said, "Jeff, ya might want to sit yourse'f down on the fact these two fellers are actually tryin' to catch up with that bunch that buffaloed us. Think about it, Jeff. Say you're sorry."

Sonny's hands hadn't moved. Across his flat face was the hint of a smile, like he hoped the man would press the challenge. Bannon was sure of it. He'd seen that look before. Sonny was baiting the man by keeping his hands away from his Colt. Looking closely, he could see Sonny's fists tighten and release. Bannon even wondered if Sonny was singing to himself. That would be like him, the farm boy thought. It was easy to misread Sonny Jones. Sitting there on a log, Jeff was close to making that mistake.

Bannon knew what the cowboy saw. Here was this thick-shaped, iron-mustached man with an old derby hat and old shotgun chaps, with his shirttail hanging out under his vest. Here was this happy-go-lucky cowboy with vest pockets jammed with everything imaginable and then some. How could Sonny possibly be dangerous? He wondered if he should tell them Sonny was as deadly with a gun as Checker, that he loved to fight. He remembered Jackson telling him there were men who looked dangerous and were, and men who didn't look dangerous and weren't, and then there were men who didn't look dangerous but they were. That was Sonny Jones. Checker was the other kind: He looked dangerous—and he was. Both were deadly when crossed.

Bannon decided to warn the camp about his friend. As he opened his mouth, Jeff lowered his gaze, shuffled his spurred boots against the ground, and began to stir the fire with a stick.

"I—I didn't mean nuthin'. Sorry, I jes' . . ."

Buchanan couldn't wait. "Jeff's sorry, mister. He runs off at the mouth, ever so. He's sorry. All right?"

Sonny didn't say anything. Instead, he walked around the yellowed campfire and stood in front of Jeff. The two men on either side of him moved away. Bannon was surprised at the mobility of the fat drover, who seemed to bounce from log to log. His eyes caught Buchanan's, and the worried new trail boss raised his shoulders in question about what was happening. Bannon shook his head slightly to indicate Sonny wasn't going to do anything, and hoped he was right.

"Put down that stick and look at me, Jeff," Sonny said. His voice was surprisingly soft. Slowly, Jeff looked up at him. His eyes were fearful.

"Today, you almost died. All because you said something stupid," Sonny said. His voice was low and even. "We won't say any more about it. You an' me. I'd like some coffee—how about you?"

Sonny stepped away and sought the coffeepot

without waiting for Jeff's response. The cowboy's face was shedding relief, and he jumped up. A wet spot covered much of his groin, but he didn't notice or didn't care. He walked over to Sonny and quietly offered his thanks. Sonny smiled like nothing had happened, picked up two tin cups, and poured coffee for both.

"Say, how are them women in Dodge, anyway?" the fat drover broke the tension.

Bannon beamed and began telling them in detail about the medicine wagon and Salome, then about "Thunder Alice." Only she became a much younger, much thinner woman with the telling. Sonny grinned and shook his head, and Buchanan chuckled. Slap-dark soon hit camp, but they talked on about women, horses, ropes, whiskey, cattle, and the weather. Soon the topic was the gang and the Indian Nations where they were headed. None of the Bar 4 drovers had seen children with the gang, and decided they had been held back purposely. Sleep came easy to all of them, and at false dawn they rode in opposite directions.

At midday, Sonny, Bannon, and Captain crossed the line into Indian Territory. The land was changing into rolling hills and thick woodlands. It felt like they had entered another world. Autumn rode ahead of them, bringing gold to the cottonwoods, scrub oak, and willows, adding crimson to the alder, redbud, and arrowpoint leaves, laying down a blaze of color in the draws and along the streambeds. The vast wilderness hid many outlaw gangs retreating from raids in Kansas and Missouri. War parties of Kiowas and Comanches struck without warning, in stark contrast to the civilized tribes of Cherokees,

Creeks, Seminoles, Choctaws, and Chickasaws who occupied the Territory legally.

The horse-killing distances made it impossible for lawmen to patrol this uncharted territory, even if they wanted to. Each civilized tribe had a mounted police force, but their authority was limited to other Indians. Only the most daring federal marshals would enter the Nations in search of fugitives, and only the best would leave alive.

For the first time, Bannon wondered if they should be looking for signs of the children's bodies as they rode. He shook off the idea, for it was too gruesome to think about. He asked Sonny what he thought had happened at the jail. It was the first time he had dared to. The former outlaw said he wasn't sure but guessed Kayler and his bunch tried to break out the gang to hang them, and somehow they got guns and broke free. It was the only thing that made sense to him, but Checker thought it was a Star McCallister plan. Bannon wanted to talk more about it, but Sonny was concentrating on the faint tracks too much to care for any more discussion on the matter. The happy-go-lucky cowboy was ever stern-faced, frequently using the field glasses Checker had given him, to evaluate the land ahead.

Along the fingered creeks, spongy bottomland was laced with autumn-brown canebrakes and blackjack and trees filled with roosting birds. Wildlife were everywhere, bursting into flight as they passed. Turkey, deer, grouse, and plover were to behold by even the most casual observer. Sonny finally relented and let Bannon bring down several birds for eating. The thought of fresh meat overcame his concern about the sound carrying to the outlaws and warning them. Bannon's observation that the Indians hunted with firearms all the time helped Sonny with the decision. The downed grouse made an excellent supper, with enough left over for breakfast the next morning.

They were up and riding again before daylight, but Sonny was having trouble staying with the trail in the uneven light. He yanked Checker's field glasses from his saddlebags and studied the land ahead without satisfaction. The day was gray, and the gathering clouds let it be known they intended to drench the land this day.

"Hold up, Tyrel, I can't read this," Sonny said, and jumped down.

He walked his horse and the lead-rope-trailing second mount to the western side of where he thought the gang headed. It wasn't a trail, only hard clay with scattered rock and buffalo grass. He squatted low and studied the ground, hoping the rising sun would cast a shadow off faint imprints.

"Yeah, they came through here. There's flat spots. Only a horse or a man leave flat spots." Sonny was pleased about his discovery. "Guessed right for a change. They're headed down through that arroyo."

He picked up three small rocks and stacked them one on top of the other and swung back on his horse. Immediately, he began to sing one of his favorite songs, "Camptown Ladies," only with his own words: "Star McCallister rode through here, do dah, do dah . . . Star McCallister rode through here, do dah do dah."

Bannon smiled, but he didn't think it was funny. The thought of getting caught out in the open in a heavy thunderstorm wasn't, either.

"It's gonna rain today, Sonny. Look at them clouds. What are we gonna do then?"

Sonny's only answer was to smile like he had a secret as they rode past high-arched bluffs in charge of the surrounding land. A hawk saluted as it flew across their path in search of breakfast. Bannon watched the winged hunter sail into the storm-filled horizon and suddenly asked, "Sonny, can you read?"

The former outlaw pursed his lips and slowly drawled, "You know, that there's a question I wouldn't be asking to just everybody you meet, Tyrel. Some might take real offense."

Bannon gulped and quickly added, "Oh, Sonny, I didn't mean nuthin' by it. I was just thinkin' about last night 'n'—"

"I know you didn't," Sonny interrupted. "Yeah, I can read some. Write a bit, too. My mother was quite a stickler for those things. Now, I can't handle words like Jackson. He works them real smooth."

"He's been learnin' me."

Sonny turned in the saddle and said, "That's great, Tyrel, that's great. Right now, though, it'd be a bigger help if you can read sign. You didn't learn that from John Checker by any chance, did you?"

Bannon blushed and stuttered, "W-well, no, but I kin follow a deer 'bout anywhere. You kin ask Billy Joe or any o' my friends at home."

"Good enough. Just think about these boys as a bunch of deer, then," Sonny said. "Because I need your help. Reading sign just isn't my strong suit. We've got to catch them today. If this storm hits, we're gonna lose 'em, I'm afraid. You keep a close watch or I'll have us riding in Alaska."

193

Sonny grinned and Bannon did too, but the thought of catching up with the gang was ice to his mind. Sonny kicked his horse into a lope, moving as fast as he dared while still following the gang's trail. There were no words as the happy-go-lucky cowboy's demeanor disappeared into an intense scowl. At noon, they stopped, switched horses, ate a cold biscuit and a piece of jerky, and washed it down with tepid canteen water. After drinking lightly, Sonny poured water into his derby and gave it to his horse, refilled the hat, and gave it to the other mount. Bannon smiled at the exchange and did the same with his horses. Minutes later, they were riding again.

Black clouds bullied the sky into retreat. Sonny knew well a heavy rain would eliminate any trace of the McCallister gang and they would be left guessing. He tried not to think about it and brought the field glasses to his eyes every few minutes like the hand of a clock. A glimpse of the gang was possible, he thought. They were that close. He could feel it.

However, the farm boy was bothered more, at the moment, by the raw spots on the inside of his knees where the knots of his new chaps rubbed him when pushed against the saddle. Every hour or so, he would stand in the stirrups and pull on his chaps to get the knots away from his legs. He wondered if any other man had such a problem. If Sonny noticed, he didn't say anything about Bannon's occasional saddle dance.

They crossed an older trail of unshod pony tracks, headed east. Likely a Kiowa war party or Comanche, Sonny observed without further comment. Bannon's back crawled with the thought, but he kept his concern to himself. They rode on and saw no more tracks other than the gang's occasional marks in the earth. Bannon decided there was actually comfort in that. Hours passed, and both men were lost in their thoughts.

When they came to the remains of a campfire beside a long-empty lean-to, Sonny jumped down to examine it more closely. He handed the reins of his horse to Bannon; his second mount, on a lead rope tied to the saddle horn, stood quietly beside the stout gelding. Sonny ran his fingers through the ashes of the dead fire, then looked around. The ashes were warm. A raven on an overhanging branch scolded them for interrupting his supper.

Bannon waved the bird away. "Git outta here, bird. We're busy. Whoever lived thar didn't take to folks much, did he?"

"It's still warm, Tyrel. We're gaining on the bastards. Even I can tell that," Sonny said. "We've got to close in before the rain gets us. That's our only chance." Sonny's right fist opened and closed several times to emphasize the significance of his statement.

Bannon glanced at Sonny to see if he was kidding. The look on his face was clearly not. Bannon wondered what Sonny intended to do if they did catch up. Two against that whole gang isn't exactly a fair fight. At the same time, both saw the tiny footprints trailing away from the encampment toward a brushwood thicket fifteen feet away. Alongside the children's steps were the imprints of man-sized boots. There were no returning prints. Why were they taking the kids over here? Bile jumped into Sonny's throat as he rose and followed the footprints where they disappeared into the thick undergrowth. He glanced at Bannon, and the farm boy's pale face told him that he, too, had seen the same trail—and had the same worry.

Chapter Eleven

Sonny took a deep breath, pushed aside the thick, waist-high bushes that cut off their path, swatted an overhanging vine away from his face, and entered the thicket's inner space. Nothing. Then he saw two dark circles in the earth near a tree. He walked over, touched one with his finger, and smelled it. Urine! His emotions slammed into him, and he chuckled. How could a man be so pleased to know a child was peeing!

At the base of the tree were hoofprints and a scuffling of footprints that explained why there were no return tracks. Sonny read it as one outlaw riding into the thicket from the far side with two horses and the two men lifting the children into separate saddles and heading south again without returning to the camp area. The feeling was almost as good as finding the children themselves. He returned to the open and told Bannon what he had seen. The farm boy bit his lower lip and turned away.

What if there had been two small bodies there? Sonny's mind spit back the thought in revulsion, and he shook his head to help it along. But the question wouldn't leave as they loped through layered hillside dotted with timber and underbrush. Yet he couldn't bring the thought into spoken words. Most of the farmboy's thinking was about women, particularly Salome, or going home or eating a big hot meal. Sonny glanced at Bannon and wondered if he had seen the tracks of unshod ponies they had just crossed again. No signs of trailing travois poles. It was definitely a war party. From the boy's faint smile, he guessed Bannon hadn't.

Tyrel Bannon started the conversation with Sonny again, and it wasn't about any of the things Sonny was chewing on. His question wasn't about finding the children dead, or catching up with the gang, or what they would do if the rain took away the trail, or even horses, or cattle, or fighting. It was about women.

"You ever wonder 'bout settlin' down, Sonny? You know, marryin' an' havin' kids," Bannon asked, feeling the rhythm of his horse pounding through his body, almost like walking on air somehow.

Sonny glanced over at the young farmboy, took off his derby, and let the dusk air cool his forehead. "I reckon that day has passed me by, Tyrel."

He patted his vest pocket, bulging with his watch and other items. Bannon knew the significance of the gesture, because he'd seen the cracked photograph in Sonny's pocket watch. He didn't know anything about the young woman that stared back but didn't think it was something he should ask about. Besides, he was more interested in feelings stirring within him.

"How do you know when it's—she's the right one?"

Sonny inhaled and let the breath come out slowly. "Well, ol' Harry thought he'd found her. I reckon ol' John Checker has been roped, even though he doesn't know it yet." He laughed and began singing: "Oh, come along boys an' listen to my tale, I'll tell you my troubles on the Old Chisholm Trail. Coma ti yi yippy yippy yea. Gonna tell you 'bout a woman that I left behind. Coma ti yi yippy yippy yea."

"What do you think of Salome?" Bannon asked, his words colliding with the song.

"Who?" Sonny asked, swallowing the last of his made-up verse.

"Salome. You know, the gal with the medicine show in Dodge."

With a wipe of his hand across his mouth, Sonny kept the smile that was emerging from going anywhere. "Ah, I really don't know her, Tyrel."

Immediately, Bannon began describing her, turning their casual visual connection into a significant meeting. Sonny listened closely and said, "Can't tell you much about women, Tyrel. I can't read that trail either."

Bannon looked at Sonny and waited for more. He could feel his neck heating up from his admission of his fascination for Salome. Daydreams had placed her in the same situation as he had experienced with Thunder Alice, and they were wonderful dreams.

Returning the derby to his head and tucking his loose shirttail into his pants, Sonny continued,

"Now, you take a woman like John's sister, Mrs. Hedrickson. That's a fine lady, Tyrel, the kind a man could join hands with and take on the world. Yessir, that's what you should be looking for, Tyrel. Somebody like her."

"Uh-huh," Bannon responded, but his mind was on Salome's dancing.

They rode through a wide arroyo and under a massive overhanging rock ledge that protruded from the northern slope like an ugly nose with flaring nostrils. Below its base ran a heavy slide of rock that spilled onto most of the arroyo's floor. Spiked slabs jutted from the massive eruption like beard stubble on a giant face. Iron-shod horses had passed recently, leaving white marks on the bigger rocks in the stone carpet. Splitting the basin into two more or less equal parts was a struggling creek that sought its way out of the incline—or was the remnant of a larger body of water that had long ago created the arroyo.

Bannon studied the stone frame as they rode under it, assessing its length. Fifty feet, easily, and twenty wide. He imagined the invisible hand of God had pushed the slab into the hillside, just for the fun of it. A bent pine tree grew out of the rock slide fifteen feet from its base. Skinny and possessing only a handful of gnarled branches, the hardy plant impressed the farm boy with its tenacity.

"Good spot for an ambush, huh," Sonny said without taking his eyes off the pockmarked trail.

Bannon shot another glance at the ledge and its surroundings, seeing it from a different perspective. He hadn't thought of it being a place where they could be killed. For the first time, he noticed Sonny was riding with his Winchester across his lap.

"Yeah, guess so," he muttered, looked down at the pistol at his hip, shivered, and then drew his rifle from its saddle quiver and laid it on his upper thighs in dutiful imitation of his more experienced friend's preparedness.

As they rode out of the arroyo and returned to a prairie laced with occasional trees, the sky smeared into an ominous gray and yellow. From the north, black storm clouds brazenly shouldered their way through the shivering horizon. Silently, Sonny asked God to hold off the rain until they found the gang. He marveled to himself; it was the first time he had prayed since his beloved Mary died. He glanced over at Bannon to see if the farm boy noticed, but Bannon had untied the rolled-up long coat behind his saddle and was busy putting it on. The coat belonged to Dan Mitchell, but Tug, the hard-of-hearing trail cook, lent it to the farm boy after the burial of Harry and Tex. Sonny thought the idea made sense and did the same with his drover's coat.

"Tyrel, it's going to rain—soon—and it's going to be mean," Sonny declared. His field glasses constantly studied the land ahead as they moved. "Not more than a handful of minutes until it hits, I reckon."

"Wal, I hope she holds off. Can't hardly follow them boys as it is."

"Let's keep at it as long as we can," Sonny said. "If it's bad, we'll have to stop. We could ride right past 'em and never know it."

"Whar we gonna go—when she hits?"

Still looking through the field glasses, Sonny said,

Cotton Smith

"Only place I can think of is that overhang we just passed."

"Yeah, whar it'd be a good spot for an ambush. It ain't much." Bannon looked at the threatening sky and asked, "Shall we do 'er now?"

"Let's ride a little farther. I know we're getting close. Maybe we can see where they're going to camp during the storm. Tyrel, we can't lose them now. I know we're damn close."

Rumbling signaled that Sonny's assessment was acurate, and the first drops of rain splattered on the land and on the two riders. Only minutes were required for the domineering clouds to make a decision, and the sky soon emptied itself in a cold, hard rain that made it difficult for the two men to even see each other. Both rode hunched over as the storm changed their world into a sheet of water. They were soaked instantly, and their horses moved uneasily with ears flat and heads down. Breath-smoke from animals and men was battered into submission by the watery avalanche.

Bannon was unhappy his new hat was drowning and its wide brim melting around his face. His Winchester was getting soaked, too, but Sonny hadn't put his rifle away, so he shrugged and continued to look to his older friend for unspoken counsel. Sonny had already wrapped one side of his opened coat over the weapon's breech to keep the bullets dry. Bannon's brittle fingers numbly worked the buttons of his coat to loosen it so he could do the same. Sonny rode without talking, staring into the field glasses, holding them with one hand; his other held the reins, lying on top of his half-wrapped rifle. Lightning crashed on a naked hill far ahead of them and brought an instant of ugly yellow glow to everything.

"Yes!" Sonny muttered, and reined his horse. "There they are! There they are! Look, Tyrel!"

Sonny pointed toward a thickly timbered creekline directly south of them and handed Bannon the field glasses. The farm boy had never used binoculars before. He fiddled with the sight adjustment several times before being satisfied with their clarity. Frowning, he took them away from his face, wiped the rain from the lenses with an already soaked coat sleeve, looked again, and whined.

"I don't see nuthin', Sonny. Whar'd you say they be?"

"What! Give me those!" Sonny exclaimed, and yanked the glasses from Bannon's wet hands. The former border outlaw urgently put them to his eyes and said, "I'll show . . ."

His words ended before resuming again. "They're gone, dammit, they're gone. I saw them there. I did."

"Maybe they done rode over a hill or somethin'."

The roar of the storm filled the silence between them. Sonny's chin lay against his chest. Tyrel shrugged his shoulders, as if it would remove the soaking, and started to say something. Sonny spoke first.

"You go on back to that overhang, Tyrel. Take my backup horse, too." The pounding water stung Sonny's tired face and swished away his words as fast as they came from his mouth.

"Whar ya goin'?"

"Up there. I'll catch you in an hour or so."

"I'm goin' with ya, then," Bannon yelled over the roaring storm.

Sonny smiled. "No, Tyrel. I promised Jackson I'd be careful. Besides, one man is more likely to ride without being seen in this mess. Maybe I can find where they've camped. Got a feeling they were headed for shelter somewhere up there. But maybe they're just heading into the trees."

"Ya won't be attackin' them yurnse'f, will ya?"

Sonny kicked his horse and yelled, "Go on, Tyrel. Wait for me there."

Bannon watched his friend disappear into the wall of rain, then eased the horses in the other direction. A half hour later, he stopped under the stone ledge. Only a few feet away, the rain continued to pound the earth. Watching it pour made the rocky space seem even drier than it was. The two backup horses stood close to his gelding, moving their rumps to get fully under the ledge's protection. He stared at the world of rain and wondered if he would ever get home again. He dismounted, holding the reins and lead ropes of their four horses with both hands along with his rifle.

Sonny's backup horse moved away and got its lead rope wrapped around Bannon's rifle barrel as the farm boy stepped down. The harder he pulled on the reins, the more the horse backed up. Exasperated, he let go of the Winchester, allowing it to release itself from the entanglement and fall to the ground. The clatter was louder than he expected, and he immediately hunched down and searched the darkness for any response.

Satisfied there was no immediate danger, he began loose-wrapping the reins of each main horse to boulders, then he half-hitched the lead ropes of the secondary mounts to other large rocks. Sonny's second horse bit at Bannon's sorrel and the red horse kicked back. Bannon yanked hard on the lead rope of Sonny's horse and threatened to put the animal out in the rain. Then he tied it as far from the other as he could without letting it get wet.

He couldn't remember feeling this worn out, even on the trail drive. Somewhere in the distance, a weary red sun had completely given up and sunk into the earth to await another day. A knife-cut of a moon was slowly crawling up through the storm to its rightful place. No stars had yet gathered the confidence to join it. With the sun's demise, nightfall joined the rain in total control. Breath-frost from Bannon and the horses soon became a part of their shallow reprieve from the storm, settling around them like low-hanging clouds.

After laying his rifle against the rock slide, Bannon poured canteen water into his hat for his horse. He frowned at the horse's eagerness to drink, pushing out the crown of his hat as far as it would go. But he repeated the process for his sorrel without attempting to reshape his derby, then for Sonny's second mount. All accepted the liquid with loud slurping, and he worried someone would hear it. He frowned at the distortion to his new hat, now soaked inside and out, then returned it to his head, yanking hard on the front brim. He smiled when he decided it looked like the way John Checker wore his hat.

White wisps of breath-frost surrounded the farm boy's face, and he rolled his shoulders to stimulate more warmth. He shivered and stamped his feet. Would it ever stop raining? Suddenly he thought of the Hedrickson children out in the storm and gasped out loud. His knees buckled, and he fell to the rocky ground. His stomach growled its displeasure at his not eating. It was actually a welcome distraction from the depression settling within him. He resisted getting up as long as he could, then stood and went to the saddlebags and retrieved a piece of beef jerky and a corn dodger. While he ate, he studied the lone pine tree struggling for its life on the rock slide and wondered why it had picked that spot to live.

At the edge of the rock shelf, a curtain of rain closed off the world. His gaze kept returning to the scrawny tree and thinking it was likely the only dry wood in miles. No, he told himself, he shouldn't cut down that tree. It had fought a gallant battle to live in spite of the heavy demands of the sliding rock. He shivered, and pulled Mitchell's soaked long coat around him in an attempt to bring warmth that wasn't to be found in the wet darkness.

He couldn't remember feeling so alone. *I should've stayed with Sonny*, he told himself. *No, Sonny was right. One man wouldn't be seen in this storm. Two might. Does he really expect to find them? Would he come back if he did?*

He glanced again at the tree. It would make a nice fire—and a fire would sure be good right now. He shivered again. His clothes were drenched, and his fine new hat looked like Jackson's old one now. He had been looking forward to showing it off to his mother and sister when he returned to Texas, along with his new shiny guns. That seemed so far away. What were they doing right now? His mother had sent him a long letter that was waiting when he got to Dodge City. With Jackson's urging, he had written her back. It wasn't long, though, just a scrawled page. Jackson assured him that his mother would be thrilled to receive it.

Aw-cheww! he sneezed, and the sound echoed faintly within the protective rock area. "That's it!" he said aloud. He wouldn't be any good to Sonny if he caught a cold. A fire was a must. He walked over to the quiet horses and found a large skinning knife in Sonny's saddlebags. A half hour later, the branches of the pine tree were crackling and sputtering as the fresh wood found flame. He watched the rainbow of the small fire swirl before him. Occasionally, he waved his arms to drive away the fat smoke. It wasn't providing as much warmth as he imagined it would, but even the appearance of heat was comforting.

An hour more passed with no sign of Sonny, and Bannon decided to clean his new Winchester and pistol. He reloaded them with fresh cartridges and studied each weapon proudly. Satisfied with his examination, he laid the rifle against the slope, holstered the pistol, and shut his eyes. Just for a minute. The small fire felt good to his body. Daydreaming about home came easy. Soon he was introducing Salome to his mother and sister. Salome was wearing a skintight glittery dress that showed off her memorable figure. She smiled at him and asked to go on a picnic, just the two of them.

As they left, arm in arm, he saw his mother at the steps of their small home and heard her calling sweetly to him, "Tyrel . . . Tyrel . . ."

He was in that sweet halfway place where reality turns into dreams of something else. A hand touched his shoulder and shook it lightly. He opened his eyes. Clattering hooves on the ground rock was the only sound he heard. Standing before him were the silhouettes of two men. Frosty breath-smoke surrounded their faces and made them ghostlike. Behind the two dark shadows, a full regiment of stars had joined the glowing sliver of a moon, proclaiming the end of the rainstorm. *They must be after my mother!* Bannon jumped and reached for his holstered pistol. The hand stopped his arm and said, "It's all right, Tyrel. It's me, Jackson."

Bannon shook his head to clear away the wisps of his mind's night renewal and saw his friends for the first time. Jackson smiled. Checker looked agitated. Both were exhausted and drenched, their gum ponchos still slickened from the earlier rain. His tiny fire barely touched their hard faces in the darkness. But the night couldn't hide the fact that the powerful frame of Checker's black was streaked with white sweat and mud and its breathing was labored. Long strings of breath-smoke roped its face and neck. Each stride was more difficult than the last as the powerful animal trembled from exhaustion. Even the sense of the creek's refreshing water nearby wasn't enough to raise its drooping ears and neck.

Seemingly unaware of his horse's worn condition, Checker's first words were taut. "Where's Sonny?"

Bannon told them what had happened, that Sonny had seen the gang during the storm, that he told him to wait here while he looked for their camp, and that he would return. Checker listened without speaking. Since leaving Dodge, his mind had swirled with worry about finding the children and about Amelia recovering; with sadness about Clanahan, Tex, and Orville Hedrickson and their homestead; with guilt about not being there to help any of them; with warm thoughts of Sarah Ann; with questions about how the gang had managed to escape; and with an ever-bubbling hate of his half brother for what he had done. Thoughts of revenge drove him onward, spurred by the anger of being caught off guard and it costing lives of people he cared about. He tried not to let his thoughts wrap around Amelia's children in the hands of Star. He couldn't handle that.

The tall Ranger turned back to his black horse, loosened the cinch, and removed the saddle. He was barely aware that it was night, pushing through the storm with only a momentary stop at the lean-to, at Jackson's insistence. As soon as the rain subsided, they were riding again, using Sonny's rockpiles as their only guide.

Switching to his backup mount would give the black much-needed rest. He knew the horse had been ridden too hard and hated the result. As the leather was removed, the black horse wobbled and lay down, too tired even to move to the creek to drink. Startled at the reaction, he dropped the saddle, went to the rain-swollen creek, and brought back a hatful of water to the horse, pouring it slowly into the animal's mouth and lagging tongue. Minutes later, the black horse stood and shook itself so hard Checker thought the animal would lose its balance. Slowly, the horse wandered toward the creek, dragging its reins.

Checker's own breathing was labored and heavy. "We're gaining on them. We're gaining on them," he muttered, and returned to saddling his second horse. But the once-sturdy bay was worn from a hard ride yesterday and the yesterdays before that.

The animal's back trembled at the weight of the heavy saddle.

Jackson watched and said to Bannon, "I'll be right back, Tyrel." He was leading two tired horses himself. The tall, thick-framed, black cowboy pushed back his rain-battered hat to let the night breezes give him comfort and followed that with an adjustment of his wire-rimmed spectacles. His long gray coat and batwing chaps were soaked and splattered with mud from loping through the maze of creeks and timber. One pocket showed the outline of a book; the other, the unmistakable shape of a pistol. The gentle smile usually on his dark round face was replaced with a tight scowl, and an unlit pipe, too wet for smoking, was stuck in the corner of his mouth.

"John, we need to wait here for Sonny." The words came softly from Jackson, but they hit Checker like a hammer.

"What the hell are you talking about, Jackson?" the former Ranger snarled. "He might be catchin' up to those bastards right now!"

"This isn't about tracking now, John," Jackson said. "If they see us coming, you'll never see those kids alive again. Do you hear me, John? It isn't good enough for us to get close to them. We've got to get to the kids before they know we're there. John? Are you listening to me? We're not chasing a gang of rustlers; we're trying to save two wonderful kids. Star did this to hurt you. If he even thinks you're close, what do you think he'll do then?"

Checker stood without moving or speaking. His gaze was fixed on Jackson, and the intensity was excruciating. The soaked brim of his hat dipped low on his face, stopping at his eyes. Jackson took a deep breath and continued, "Besides that, we can't ride any further with these horses. They're played out, John."

"Well, maybe I'll just go on and you can come along whenever you've got a sweet mind to," Checker said, and resumed sliding the leather cinch into its girth ring. Behind him, the moon hooked onto his rain-soaked black hat and encouraged the stars to come closer to watch.

Without responding, Jackson stepped to Checker's left and knelt beside the bay. With an experienced hand, he fingered hocks, knees, and fetlocks, shaking his head whenever he found swelling around stiffening joints. He stood and rubbed the ears of the animal's lowered head and said, "If you ride this horse now, John, you'll lame it for good."

"Then I'll leather my black again." Checker's face was contorted and red. His eyes spat anger. "He's watered up—and he'll take me anywhere I ask."

"You've already asked too much of that fine horse," Jackson said. "He shouldn't even be drinking. He's too hot, needs to walk and cool down first. He'll end up with a knotted belly and be dead before morning."

"He's a lot tougher than you think."

"I know that horse well. He's a beautiful animal. Strong as an ox and can run like the wind. More sand than any horse I've seen in a long time. But you've run him into the ground, John. If you try to saddle that black, I swear I'll shoot him right here, so you won't punish him to death. I will, John."

Checker stared at him but said nothing. He had never heard his quiet friend speak this way before.

"Maybe my friends aren't as tough as I thought." A snarl contorted Checker's chiseled face into something sinister. At the fire, Bannon watched, not knowing what to say or do. His instinct drew his right hand close to the pistol holstered just under his opened coat.

Jackson swallowed away the fear that was seeking support in his mind and said, "I don't deserve that, John—and you know it."

"I *don't* know it. I only know there are two little kids out there somewhere—and my friend, Sonny." Checker waved toward the southeast. "And if we don't get there in time, I . . ." He couldn't finish the sentence. His brittle face looked like crushed paper as he fought to keep his emotions under control.

"John, we're going to find them in time, if we're smart about it. They don't come any better than Sonny. He'll return *here* just as soon as he can. He knows they can't know he's close. Give him time, John. That's what he wanted Tyrel to do." Jackson withheld his own queasy feelings about their friend being so close to a possible gunfight or ambush. It wasn't the time to share that uneasiness.

"Jackson, that's the only family I have—and I didn't know I even had family until we got to Dodge. What if they . . . they torture those kids? Let me take one of Tyrel's horses. What about that? That'd be all right, wouldn't it?" Checker's nearly frantic questions sought understanding from his friend.

Jackson had never seen the tall Ranger so frazzled. This was the man who had stared down death in fights with outlaws, Indians, and Mexican bandits all across the wildness of Texas. But now he had something to lose—and desperately didn't want to. Jackson knew that look; he'd seen it in the face of his gentle father after he had managed to sneak his mother and their young son away from slavery and into freedom. Later, he would learn the meek-appearing man had killed the slavemaster with his bare hands when they escaped.

"John, we're close. But there's no trail to follow. The only reason we found this was because of Sonny's rock signals—and Tyrel's fire. If this had been Star, the kids would have been in terrible danger the way we came in," Jackson said, removing the unlit pipe from his mouth as he spoke. He stuck his finger in the bowl to assess its dampness, frowned, and continued. "This is different than tracking, John, and you know it. If they see us . . . Star can't think we're anywhere close. When Sonny comes, we'll know what needs to be done next—and not until then."

"What if he didn't find them?"

"If he hasn't, we're going to have to pick up the trail again—and that'll take good horses. They will leave easy tracks in this soggy stuff from wherever they start. We just have to find that place. Now we have to do the tough job, John—we have to wait."

Checker stared at Jackson, trying to absorb his reasoning and bring salve to his frantic mind. Jackson continued, speaking in that soft, easy way of his.

"Why don't you an' Tyrel see if you can fix us something to eat. Hot coffee would taste mighty good. Maybe we'll have it ready when Sonny returns. I'll take care of our horses. All right?" Jackson's voice was smooth and reassuring.

Jackson's mind stutter-stepped on the unthinkable

213

possibility that his Ranger friend had snapped. His hand froze inches from the handgun in his coat pocket. He glanced at Bannon and nodded for the farm boy to help. Bannon wasn't sure what was going on or what was wanted of him, but he slowly came toward them.

"Tyrel, give John a hand with breakfast, will ya? I've got a sack of kindling in my bags. That'll help your fire until some wood dries out."

Bannon thought immediately of the scrawny pine tree on the rock slide and said, "I already done burned the onliest tree close by an' dry."

Jackson looked at Bannon, then at the tiny fire, and said gently, "That's fine, Tyrel. Find some small sticks and branches along the creek, something that'll dry out easily. Come on, now."

Without waiting for a response, he took out his pocketknife and began examining the hooves of the three close horses, removing mud and rock, and checking for bruises, loosened shoes, and sore tendons. Checker stared at him, and Jackson wasn't sure if the former Ranger had heard him or not. Then Checker spun and fiercely yanked the saddlebags from his saddle perched on the soaked ground. Jackson gave himself the luxury of a long breath to let the tension escape and headed for the black horse to check its condition.

He heard Bannon chatting loudly as he walked toward Checker and could barely make them out in the heavy shadows.

"How'd you be a-findin' me—us? I couldn't see more'n my hand. Thought it were gonna be like that Noah feller."

Checker smiled grimly and took a sack of kindling

from his saddlebags. "I know, Tyrel. We stopped in a lean-to until the worst of it was over. Pretty easy, thanks to your rock piles—and, at the last, your fire."

"Sonny done that, John. He were ri't steady with it."

"I know."

"Ya figger anybody else done saw my—this fire?"

"No, I don't think so. Under that ledge it reflected our way, but it wouldn't be seen anywhere to the south."

Satisfied, Bannon told him about finding the kids' tracks at the lean-to and what they were doing. Checker smiled and thanked him for the story. Bannon grinned and went about finding small sticks, twigs, and one large branch to add to Jackson's tinder pile. With practiced care, Checker nurtured Bannon's small fire, anticipating heavy smoke from the wet firewood but expecting the rock shelf to keep it from entering the night sky. His mind was dull, like the night itself, now cleansed of dust and heat by the rain. His movements were rigid and mechanical. Somewhere to the south, his friend was where he should be and it made his gut ache with worry. He rolled his shoulders to keep away the anxiousness and tried to concentrate on the fire.

Chapter Twelve

A midnight meal was fried salt pork, along with wild onions, a cut-up potato, hardtack, and plenty of strong coffee. It was the first hot meal in days for all of them. They ate quietly, chewing on both food and thought, and relishing relief from riding as much as the tasty meal. A glance at the cooking fire showed Checker had set aside a filled plate for Sonny. It was a symbol both of patience and of frustration. None spoke of the gnawing uneasiness about waiting for his return.

A coffee cup in his hand, Checker suddenly stood in one smooth motion, like a coiled snake striking. The ease of his movement was not lost on Jackson. But Bannon was more interested in consuming the rest of his breakfast. Tension again pulled the tired black cowboy to an unspoken edginess. Checker stood beside the soft coals of their cooking fire.

Yellow glow worked its way up his lean frame,

dancing along the double-rowed double cartridge belt with a row for rifle bullets and a second one for pistol loads. Timid light reflected from the black-handled Colt holstered in a reverse-draw rig, something no cowhand would wear. Jackson studied the white elkbone circular mark embedded on each grip like he had never seen it before. He remembered hearing that the symbol was powerful Comanche medicine and the wild story that Checker was, somehow, blessed by a magicial shaman and couldn't be killed, except by blood kin. When he first heard it, the tale just seemed like a typical Texas windy; now it struck a strange chord within him that Jackson wished he could shake off.

Here stood a man Jackson had known, before their trail drive together, only from tales told around a campfire. A gun warrior bred by the bitter Reconstruction in Texas and honed by battle with wild marauders, using the Rio Grande for sanctuary. Here was one of those rare men who turned back a wildness threatening the state's very soul. John Checker, Captain, Texas Ranger. That's all any Texan needed to hear to follow him.

Checker pushed the wet, wide-brimmed hat back to let the early-morning light favor pale-blue eyes that tore into a man's soul. What glow remained from their fire didn't reach his tanned Roman face and hawkish nose. A small shadow lingered at the arrowhead-shaped scar on his high cheekbone, making it appear larger. His long black hair brushed against his Comanche tunic as he swallowed the hot liquid in his cup. Darkness hid his weariness but not the heaviness under his eyes.

His voice gravelly but soft, Checker said, "You've

been a good friend, Jackson, and I've been acting like some wild-eyed fool. That's the way to get us all killed. Those kids, too."

Relief washed across Jackson's fire-streaked face and he muttered a reaction that sounded more like a prayer. Bannon watched the tall Ranger, then looked at Jackson, not understanding. With that, Checker walked away. His boots made a soft slushing sound as he went through rain puddles without noticing. The sound blended with the jingle of his spurs to give the night a distinctive music. At the edge of their makeshift camp, he stood alone, rolled a smoke, licked the loose flap, and closed it with his fingers. His hands shook slightly, but he didn't notice. He snapped a match to life on his belt buckle and inhaled and released the smoke, letting it crawl toward the moon, matching with his own breath-smoke from the cold night. He couldn't remember feeling so emotionally spent.

After a few minutes, he took a watch from his vest pocket and popped open the silver lid. On the inside of the watch cover was a tiny cracked photograph of a woman with two small children, a boy and a younger girl. He studied the images closely, wiping dust away with his fingers. His mother, his little sister Amelia, and himself. Why did it seem like they were three people he didn't know? Worry over Amelia's children had torn open the scab that contained those memories. He looked up to see Jackson walking toward him, carefully stepping around the puddles. Pipe smoke encircled the black man's face.

"John, I just wanted you to know you weren't the only man riding with hate in his belly—and worried sick about those kids. But you can't become Star

McCallister in going after him. Then you'll lose everything."

Checker drew again on his cigarette. Jackson turned to go, and Checker placed his hand on the cowboy's shoulder to stop him and said, "Thanks, for pulling me back—from that."

"All of us have been close to hell a time or two."

Jackson reported that Checker's bay showed some puffiness in its knees but should be able to ride tomorrow. He said the right front leg of Checker's black horse was tender and shouldn't be ridden for a couple of days. The black cowboy said his own sorrel showed signs of collicking. He planned to keep the horse up and moving until he was sure the intestinal trouble was over. He thought his second horse was all right, although weary. After assessing the horses, Jackson turned his concern to Sonny. It was time to let his own worry out.

He took the pipe from his mouth and said, "John, you don't think Sonny will charge into McCallister's bunch alone, do you?" Breath-smoke danced in front of his question.

Checker studied his friend's worried face and said, "No, I don't. Sonny may be as wild as a cut snake, but he'll be smart about those kids."

Jackson smiled his relief. "If you need me, I'll be down with the horses."

Checker nodded his thanks, and Jackson headed for the hobbled horses. A wolf's long throaty howl pulled him away. He listened, but no additional cries came. It was a good sign, he thought, and he remembered Stands-in-Thunder's solemn admonition that Checker's spirit guide would always be there to help him. Other night sounds were comforting. Night wind was caressing the land to encourage that it get over the storm's thunderous pounding. Stands-in-Thunder would have said it was spirits talking and a wise man should listen.

His eyes surveyed their small camp. Jackson was walking his black horse along the creek bed, avoiding the muddiest sections of the bank, and Bannon was sleeping. *How could things go so wrong so fast?* he asked silently. For an instant, he wished Amelia had not sent him the letter; then he wouldn't be here, feeling such awful pain. He touched the folded letter in his pocket under his poncho and tunic. Star McCallister wouldn't have needed to do what he did either, and none of this would have happened. Clanahan and Tex would be alive.

But not the other Triple C drovers, he reminded himself. Star's attack on them—and the herd— would have been successful. And he wouldn't have met Sarah Ann Tremons. His eyes caught the supplies next to a flat rock, and that pulled him away from his mind walk. Tin plates, cups, utensils, a sack of foodstuffs, a can of tomatoes, a half-empty bottle of vinegar, and a potato had been relaid on the canvas tarp for repacking and to keep them safe from any ground moisture.

Both backup horses had taken turns carrying the pack. Like a magnet, he was drawn to a neatly wrapped package apart from the others. He knew what it contained: new clothes for Johnny and Rebecca. Jackson had bought them before he got the horses. Checker hadn't thought much about the thoughtful gesture until now. Probably because he couldn't deal with the questions that would follow: What if they didn't find the children? Or what if they were too late? What if Sonny needed them right now?

He knew his half brother was using the children to cripple him emotionally. There was another motive, he knew: to get him so riled that he would make a mistake in following Star and ride into an easy killing. "Jackson knew it too," he muttered. "The children might already be dead," he said to himself, and shivered. It was the first time he had allowed himself to visualize the thought. His mind jerked back to the time he'd seen two white children jammed into stakes, the result of a Kiowa war party tired of their crying or worried it would give away their position. Checker staggered and fought off the nausea that followed.

Attempting to walk away from his anguish, he went to the arranged gear that had been methodically placed by Jackson. He lifted the brown-paper-wrapped package and opened it. A shirt for Johnny, and trousers. Socks, too. A soft blue gingham dress for Rebecca, with a white collar. Checker thought it looked more like a dress to wear to Sunday meetings than on a hard ride in the Nations. Fresh undergarments for both. Curled in the corner was a string of blue ribbon for Rebecca's hair. Checker fingered the strip of colored cloth, then coiled it in a tight circle and placed it in his pants pocket. With that, he carefully closed the package and returned it.

Smoke from his cigarette walked across his face and disappeared into the night. A sigh escaped his mouth, and he looked down. At his feet was a whitish pebble, nearly flat and mostly round. He squatted, gently picked it up, and rubbed the stone in his fingers. It was slick from the rain. The tiny stone was much like the one his old friend, Stands-in-Thunder, had given him as a gift. Stones are the oldest and wisest of beings, the aging Kwahadi war chief had told him. Certain men, if they were very fortunate, could hear them and learn from their special wisdom.

Stands-in-Thunder said the stone he had given to Checker had sung to him before great victories. Checker never placed much significance in the gift or the story and had lost it. He tossed this pebble away, stamped out the spent cigarette with his boot, then changed his mind and sought the tiny rock again, finding it stuck in a web of dead grass at the cusp of the rocky terrain. This time he shoved it into his pocket. He was feeling close to his Comanche friend, and he laughed to himself about their first meeting—an awkward encounter, with both men trying to express things that were not in them to do. His mind returned to the bittersweet friendship.

With a wry smile, Stands-in-Thunder had touched the Kwahadi warrior's tunic worn by Checker. The young Ranger had forgotten about it and suddenly felt ashamed, like he was rubbing in the white man's victory. In sign language, the old war chief said, "Great warrior, this one who fought you. His name I will say no longer in respect. Many coups. Strong *puha*. Many horses. Remembered fight. You honor him with wearing."

Checker was surprised at the response and said, in sign language, "Yes. Great warrior. I carry other memories." He pointed to the arrowhead-shaped scar on his cheek and patted his left shoulder.

The brittle leader smiled and said in a mixture of broken English, Comanche phrasing, and sign,

"Come. Eat. Smoke pipe. Laugh and tell story. It is good we meet before Shadowland. We no fight, you and me. We learn from other."

"I would like that."

Once Stands-in-Thunder told Checker that the darkness of his evil father was within him and the young Ranger must be wary, because he could become his father.

"You fight your father, Wolf with Star."

"I have no father, Stands-in-Thunder," Checker said, his eyes narrowing to keep away signs of his emotion. "He pushed us away. He killed my mother. I have only my sister. I have letters from her. I have not been able to write back. I don't know why."

Stands-in-Thunder watched his young friend in silence, then said, "Hear my words, Wolf with Star. In each battle, you fight your father. Yet he is within you. You must be of care. He will destroy you if he can. Ask the wolf to guide you. He will."

The old Kwahadi war leader had died last spring. Checker cried when he learned of it. He had only vague recollections of galloping wildly to his grave in a narrow slit of a rock wall, covered by shale and silt. At least they had managed to bury him off the reservation in the old Comanche way, he had observed bitterly. Since no horse was left in the grave, as was the custom with a great warrior, Checker killed his own mount and left it by the grave. Stands-in-Thunder would have a mount to ride into the Shadowland. Then he walked to the nearest town, carrying his saddle, and got very drunk.

"Maybe, old friend, it's time I asked my brother, the wolf, for help as you so often advised me,"

Checker said, and touched the medicine pouch under his clothing.

After removing two strips of jerky from their packed food, he headed for an open area he had spotted, away from their camp. He stepped carefully over rocks and around rain-soaked bushes, all the while trying to remember the words that Stands-in-Thunder had suggested. Whisperings of the land encouraged him to come closer. At a small gathering of cottonwoods fifty feet from the rock ledge, Checker found a branch, broke off a short piece, and drew a circle in the soggy earth with it.

He placed the jerky within the circle, sprinkled shreds of tobacco around the drawn edges, then added powder from a pulled-apart cartridge. The pebble was placed in its center. He drew his knife and cut himself across the palm of his left hand, raising a red line that began to bleed. Kneeling over the pebble, he slowly made a small, uneven circle with drops of blood, squeezing his hand to control the expulsion. His shoulders rose and fell as he stepped into the larger stick-drawn circle. Slowly, he held his arms out straight and spoke into the night, letting the drying blood crawl down his arm.

"Grandfather Above, my lodge is a circle. May you accept my gifts and the blood of a Kwahadi warrior in hearing me. I stand in the center of my lodge and seek now the help of my spirit brother. I stand within a sacred place and ask that you guide me to my sister's children in time. O brother Wolf, I need your eyes. I need your strength. I need your courage. I need your patience. Please help me, O brother Wolf, find my sister's children and destroy my enemies. I will always return the blessings you

224

have given me with gifts for your kindness."

It was the prayer his old friend, Stands-in-Thunder, had often suggested to him. The last part was his own addition. His raspy voice delivered his plea with no answer, and it evolved into a silent prayer to the white man's God. It was the first time he could remember praying since a child. When he was finished, Checker retrieved the pebble, tied a thin rawhide strip around it, and laced it to his left wrist, just as he had seen many Comanche warriors add their spirit medicine. It was powerful medicine, he knew. He could feel its rhythm of life within him.

From the creek, Jackson watched his friend in silence, then picked up the sound of someone coming toward them. Was he imagining things? No, there it was again.

"John! Tyrel! Somebody's coming!" Jackson declared, and grabbed his Winchester, which was lying over the drying saddle gear. Checker jerked himself back from his reverie and Bannon from his nap. They quickly spread out with readied rifles, sliding easily into the darkest shadow pockets. But they had barely settled themselves when Sonny's distinctive thick shape appeared at the crest of the southern arroyo trail, paused, and whispered, "Tyrel?"

"I be ri't hyar, Sonny—and so do John an' Jackson. We bin a-waitin' fer ya. Got some hot feed, too."

A wide smile cracked Sonny's face in two as he loped into camp and swung down, splashing water as he reined in his horse.

"I found 'em, boys, they're holed up in an old soddy about three miles from here. Must be a hideout they used from time to time," Sonny said excitedly. "Damnedest place you'll ever see. Back in those heavy trees. Got a hidden trail, and the entrance is covered by thorny bushes. But once you're past them, she opens up into a wide path, like riding through a tunnel. Wide enough for a wagon or a small herd of horses. Watch your face, though—they're thorny as all get out."

Bannon proudly reminded him of the food waiting. "We done saved some eats, Sonny. It sure tasted fine."

"Thanks, but we need to get back there," Sonny said. "I'll grab some coffee while yo-all saddle up. Those boys are hunkered in an' sleeping. Lots of whiskey on top of lots of rain. If we're lucky, we can get close before they know what's up."

Checker grabbed Sonny's hand and the gesture became a hardy embrace, then they pounded each other on the back. Checker was first to speak. "My friend, you're getting good at finding these boys. You'd make a good lawman."

Sonny studied the former Ranger's face to determine whether he was joking or not, and decided he wasn't. "Thanks. Had a lot of practice—on the wrong side of that star." He paused. "John?"

"Yeah?"

"There's something real strange at that soddy."

"Are the kids all right?"

"Don't know for sure, but I think so," Sonny assured him and continued. "Didn't try to get close. But that medicine wagon from town, it's there. Must've come before the storm hit. Really surprised me."

"Are you sure it's . . ."

"Yeah. It's Dr. Gambree's wagon, no doubt about it. What do you make of that?"

"Well, now we know how Star got out of jail," Checker responded, and turned to get his saddle. "Well, it must be a planned rendezvous—and the doctor went straight for it. He would've had most of the night's head start, an' there's probably a faster way."

"Not goin', ah, to your sister's place would be faster." The sentence came out like it didn't want to.

Checker winced and asked, "Mind if I ride your bay? Both of mine are down for a spell. I wasn't too careful coming after you."

"Now, why doesn't that surprise me, Ranger?" Sonny chuckled. "Sure, this ol' hoss is fine. Winded a mite, but fine. We haven't far to go anyway."

Bannon's eyes sparkled, and he asked, "Is Salome with them, Sonny? I'm sure she doesn't realize they're bad men, you know. She wouldn't—"

"Tyrel, if she's there, she's in on it," Sonny snapped, walked toward the dying fire, and grabbed a piece of fried salt pork with his fingers and gingerly placed it in his mouth. It was hot, and he inhaled quickly to cool it down, then chased it with a gulp of hot coffee from a tin cup Checker had given him.

"You're just jealous she likes me!"

Checker and Jackson stopped their saddling and stared at the young man. He glanced at each one sheepishly, then back at Sonny, who was eating another slice of meat. "Oh, I'm sorry, Sonny. I didn't mean that. I, ah, I reckon she'd be real taken with you—if'n she saw ya. I jes'—"

"There's two theories about women," Sonny interrupted, "and both of them are wrong."

After readying their horses, they each grabbed extra boxes of ammunition and jerky. A half hour later, they reined up beside a thickly timbered creekline off to the right of the trail. It was swollen from the rain and overflowing its banks. They moved their uneasy horses into the fat stream and across it. Only Bannon mentioned that the water was cold. Jackson nodded and motioned for him to be quiet.

The night had slipped into a dull gray place when even the stars had gone to sleep. It was difficult for Sonny to see even when he knew where to go. Only an undernourished moon gave them any light. Sonny stopped in front of a twisted wall of underbrush and saplings, butted up against huge shadow caves of dense greasewood, cottonwood, and willow trees. No one had ridden through there, Bannon thought, and he decided his older friend had gotten lost. Checker knew it was only a coincidence that a wolf howled as they approached the unlikely entrance. Still, he silently thanked his spirit helper and the old Kwahadi war leader who had been his friend.

"I—I don't reckon nobody's been through hyar," Bannon finally got up the nerve to state as the bushes whirled about his face and shoulders.

"Reckon that's what they want you to think, Tyrel. Most folks wouldn't see there's a trail's here even in broad daylight. I rode past it the first time—and I was watching their marks," Sonny answered excitedly, then added, "You'd best walk 'em through."

A fat jay scolded him from an overhanging branch, and Bannon knew it was a warning not to ride into this creepy place. Sonny observed that someone had added to the brush to make it appear unlikely as a trailhead. Leading his horse, Sonny told them to follow him and pushed his way into the horse-high bushes, disappearing into the swollen forest. Jackson followed. Checker's horse didn't care much for the idea and balked, jamming its forefeet into the ground. The Ranger coaxed, then cursed, the animal to follow him. Gradually, the horse relented and walked through the bushes like it had never had any doubt about going there. Bringing up the rear, Bannon watched the area, wondering if they were all a little crazed from the storm.

Ghostly shadows waited along the tree-lined passage. Shards of moonlight sliced the riders into stripes of gray and black. The farmboy's eyes widened, but he said nothing. Inside the dense cluster of trees, they startled a sleeping deer and her fawn. The two animals slid to another resting place deeper in the woods. But the opening was, indeed, actually wide enough for the wagon to pass through, and the rain hadn't washed away completely the deep tracks indicating that someone had done just that. Horses' hooves made soft gulping sounds as they slopped through the muddy trail.

A shallow creek served as the true mother of this wilderness, changing direction as far as the eye could see, especially now that its banks were flooded. They stopped to let their horses drink where the bottom was rocky. Checker jumped down to study the trail. Bannon noticed the horses were edgy, taking only short drinks before raising their heads to look around. He decided against dismounting. Bannon couldn't remember being in a more forlorn place in his life. Certainly not at home, where a person could see across the plains into tomorrow, or even on the long journey along the Western Trail into Kansas.

Tangled underbrush and unyielding timber in the broken hills gave him a sense of foreboding that made him shiver. *Are we headed toward the end of the world?* he wondered to himself as they resumed. He looked at the three older riders, but each was focused on the trail and clearly in no mood to discuss feelings. A wolf signaled its presence. A forgotten, cold breeze sang a song of loneliness. Bannon wished Sonny would counter it with one of his happy songs. But Sonny showed no signs of being bothered by anything around them; his usual slouched back was straight as a rail, and his eyes restlessly sought answers. Bannon swallowed his concern and tried to emulate the intenseness of the others. He saw Checker's pebble tied at his wrist and wanted to ask about it, but he didn't think he should. He wondered if Jackson and Sonny had noticed—and why they hadn't said anything about it.

The four riders rode silently on, entering a long hollow that opened like a brown jaw with crusted rock for teeth. The trail was easy to read even in the darkness. Bannon no longer thought Sonny had exaggerated about getting close to the gang. He felt it, and touched the stock of his holstered Winchester for comfort. Long shadows within the ravine were twisted and angry, silently warning the riders not to advance further.

From behind them came a scurrying noise, and each man yanked at the holstered pistols on their belts. Checker's eyes rushed through the forest fabric and saw a small, black shape hurrying into deeper woods.

"Must be a possum," he said matter-of-factly, and reholstered his gun. "A bobcat would've stayed to fight."

"Yeah, scared the hell out of me, though," Jackson acknowledged.

"Not me," Sonny said, and chuckled.

"You go on now, possum. We got work to do," Bannon said with more concern than command in his voice. He started to ride away, but then reined in his horse and looked back. He couldn't see any movement in the dark mass of tree and bush. Frowning, he moved on to catch up with the other three.

"This ain't Texas," Bannon observed to himself. "Wonder what folks'd be doin' with a medicine wagon back hyar?" He studied the deep lines in the soft earth like they would reveal their identity.

He caught up with them at a dry creek bed that served as an open spoon inside the stretch of woodlands. The ground underneath them had turned squishy from creek runoff. Their horses' hooves spat tiny spurts of wet mud as they rode. Bannon's eyes took in a bug wandering across a faint hoofprint not quite removed by the rain or the bank's flooding. An owl winged past them overhead; a questioning cry for a mate followed the flapping of its wings into the forest. Bannon looked around but didn't see any sign of the bird, and that bothered him. Jackson had told him that some Indians believed an owl was a reincarnated spirit and that many shadows were too. He shivered at the recollection and wanted to tell his friend that he wished he hadn't shared that piece of information.

"We're only a quarter mile away," Sonny said, and pointed. Breath-smoke followed his arm.

231

Checker nodded and said, "You three stay here. I'll go ahead an' make sure there's no guard waiting for us."

"There wasn't any when I was here before—but Star's the kind that would do it after he got good and settled," Sonny said. "I'm going with you." His tone of voice left no room for argument.

Bannon eagerly asked, "I thought ya done said they's all sleepin'?"

Jackson answered patiently, "Star's a careful man, Tyrel, even if his men aren't. Remember the guard before we got to the Hedricksons?"

"The one that John done kilt?"

"Yes. Likely there'll be a gun waiting along here somewhere too," Jackson said. "John, why don't you let me go—and you two stay? That'll give you room to maneuver if something goes wrong."

"Thank you, Jackson. You too, Sonny. Let me take this one," Checker said as he removed his spurs and laid them over the saddle horn. Then he pulled the Comanche scalp knife from its beaded sheath at his bullet belt, checked the blade's sharpness, and returned it to the leather encasement.

"I'm going," Sonny said, and checked his own gun before returning the weapon to its holster. "I've been down that trail. You haven't."

Checker listened without speaking. Sonny didn't look at him, busy with removing his own spurs. Finally, he glanced at the tall Ranger and Checker smiled. The tall gunfighter tugged on the brim of his rain-lowered hat and said, "Jackson, we should be back in a half hour. If you hear gunfire, we've got trouble. Come careful."

"John, why don't you and Sonny wrap your gun

barrels—like they did at the jail," Jackson advised. "Turnabout's fair play."

"Good idea," Checker answered. "What have we got that'll work?"

From his saddlebags, Jackson produced an old shirt that he insisted they use. They tore it in half, and both Checker and Sonny wrapped their pistol barrels, securing the wadding with rawhide lacings, also from Jackson's supplies. Then Checker and Sonny wordlessly slipped over a low bench of land laced with jackpine. Black trees swallowed them completely, leaving only a faint rustle as they moved into the forest. Like an oversized night cat, Sonny hugged the bench that followed the thin trail. Checker motioned and eased to the other side of the path and became a shadow. If he was right, one of Star's men would be sitting off the trail. If he was wrong, they would have lost only some time.

After tying the reins of all four horses to tree branches, Jackson drew his Winchester from its saddle boot and methodically put in fresh loads, examining each exiting bullet to assess its dampness. He repeated the process with the handgun in his coat pocket. The steady man mumbled something Bannon thought might be a prayer. Jackson shoved a handful of ammunition into his pocket, looked up at the farm boy, and smiled. It was a warm smile, like a father might give his son, and Bannon returned it with a lopsided grin of his own. Neither spoke, and the uneasiness of waiting was broken only by an occasional leaf sliding down the night sky onto their hats and shoulders.

For lack of anything else to do, Bannon decided to remove his spurs so he could feel more like he was part of Sonny's urgent plan. Two quick jerks of the spur yielded nothing; it remained in place on his boot heel. Angry and embarrassed, Bannon stood on his left leg, bent the other in front of his waist, and yanked hard on the unbuckled spur. Suddenly, it popped free and he lost his balance.

His arms frantically grabbed for air that offered no support. The spur flew from his hand as Bannon fell in a sprawl to the ground, the splat of a mud puddle surrounding his landing. A frightened grouse rose from its hiding place and flew deeper into the forest, scaring him with the hurried thumping of its wings. Jackson turned toward him, saw the situation, and quickly turned back to hide his smile.

The young farm boy sat up and reassured himself. "Come on, Tyrel, that were jes' a grouse or somethin'." His attention returned to his task, stating loudly for Jackson's understanding, "That damn spur always bites into my heel." His neck was crimson, and he was glad Checker and Sonny weren't around to see the exhibition. It would have set Sonny off laughing to no end, and who knows what Checker would have thought.

Bannon felt odd about using "damn." What would his mother think? What would Jackson think? The curse word stayed on his tongue like bad milk, and he spat to make it go away. He managed to pull off the other spur easily from his squatting position. That done, he stared at the shivering moon and wondered where his two friends might be, then about the medicine wagon at the hideout, then about the dancing girl.

Suddenly, he blurted, "I jes' can't believe Salome would do nuthin' bad, Jackson, do yah?"

Jackson smiled wistfully. "Tyrel, there are a lot of things in this world that just aren't what you think they should be. If she's traveling with Dr. Gambree, or whatever his name is, I suspect she's part of it. But I figure she has a right to her innocence until it's proven that isn't so. That's the law."

Bannon's face reddened, and he snorted, "Yeah, Sonny was just jealous that she liked me, that's all."

Disgusted, Jackson said, "Come on, Tyrel, you don't believe that."

"I—I . . . no, I'm sorry," Bannon stammered. "I jes' . . . wal, she's mighty purty, an' I'—"

"Why don't you make sure you're carrying dry ammunition," Jackson interrupted, changing the subject. "We're riding to a fight. But we've got to get those kids out before they can use them against us."

"What do ya mean?" Bannon's brittle question loosened his reluctance to talk about the kidnapping. His hand slid along his belt to the newly acquired handgun. He accepted Jackson's suggestion and reloaded as he talked. "Star jes' be playin' a trick on John, right? He wouldn't be a-hurtin' 'em when it come right down to it, would he?"

Jackson stared at the young farm boy for a moment before answering. Even in the dark, Bannon could see the frown on the black cowboy's face. Jackson didn't want to think about the answer, and he took a long swig from his canteen first. His words came slowly, like he wanted to touch and feel each one before it was allowed to go free.

"Tyrel . . . I think he wants Checker to . . . never find them again. Ever. I think we wants to trade 'em to Comancheros—and . . . ride away, laughing. Or leave 'em to starve somewhere. Or maybe bash their heads in with a rock. That's what I think. How long do you reckon a little girl like Rebecca can take this, anyway? How old is she? Three?"

"She's four—and a half. That's a mighty tall hate for any man," Bannon said. He turned aside so Jackson couldn't see the water that filled the corners of his eyes unexpectedly. "Johnny—an' . . . Rebecca. How could anyone . . ."

"Don't stay on that thought, Tyrel, it'll eat up your insides," Jackson soothed. "I know. They've been chewing on me ever since we found out. Had nightmares about every night. What do you think it's doing to John? He's been like a man with the devil at his side."

"But, Jackson, they're just little kids!"

"Star figures they're the way to hurt John the most. If he gets wind of our coming . . . he'll kill 'em first. You saw what he did to . . . Missus Hedrickson."

Bannon couldn't hold back the question that had been preying hard on his mind. "Jackson, what'll John do when he finds Star?"

"I don't know," Jackson said. A stray drip of water escaped from his battered hat and ran down his face. He caught it with a swipe of his shirtsleeve. "Once I thought I knew what he'd do. Now I'm not so sure. Star's pushed him too far. Way past hell. I wonder if Star really knows what he's done. It's like, well, like I've been riding with somebody else. Scary, Tyrel, it really is. John Checker is one strong man, but he's also got a place inside him that no one should go. I guess most of us do. I think Star went there."

Chapter Thirteen

Sonny moved slowly, cursing the fact that Checker could see well at night and he couldn't. Dark trees seemed taller, closer, and more menacing. Propped up by the tallest treetops, the fragile moon was getting weighted down by fragile haze. Cold weather was coming, he told himself. It was a dumb idea to do this, he added. *I could walk right into the guard without seeing him.* His course was through the trees, parallel to the trail and twenty feet from it. A gauntlet of wiry bushes, loose rock, mud puddles, and dwarf trees awaited his advance, in addition to the tree line itself.

Night sounds stopped the moment he entered their world. He watched the ground more than the forest ahead to avoid stepping on dry branches or kicking loose rocks. Beneath his boots, the earth felt like large chunks of soggy sand waiting to slide away from his weight. Yellow and brown leaves from the gathered cottonwoods littered his path and produced crunching noises when he stepped. Scattered spoons of rainwater gurgled when he passed through them. But it was virtually impossible for him to avoid either and keep moving.

A narrow stream—related to the earlier one, only much smaller—meandered across his path, headed downhill. He stepped over its regurgitating bank and a downed branch crackled under his weight. In an urgent heartbeat, he kneeled and waved the wrapped pistol in a semicircle in front of him. *How could I have missed seeing that?* he asked himself. Seeing nothing headed his way, he looked down at the pistol in his fist and realized it hadn't been cocked. Was it smart instinct to avoid the noise of the hammer locking in place unnecessarily—or was he foolishly being rattled? He didn't know the answer.

Maybe I should walk on the trail itself; it's quieter than this, he evaluated as his breathing returned to normal. *What would John Checker do? Hell, Checker would slide through this forest like that damn wolf*, he declared silently. Maybe the shaman was right. Sonny shivered; he had never seen his battle-hardened friend so completely unraveled than at the burned homestead. How would he feel if his sister had been beaten like that? Of course, he didn't have a sister; he didn't have any family. Not anymore.

His vaquero father broke his neck trying to tame a wild horse when Sonny was a baby. A year later, his English mother moved her three sons across the Rio Grande to Amarillo. At twelve, he ran away from home, aftering hearing that his two older brothers died at Shiloh, to volunteer for the Confederate army. His skill with a gun—and his aggressive spirit—compensated for his youthfulness. He saw his mother only once after the War and wasn't welcomed; she was remarried and starting a new family. He shook away that memory. It was of no use now. But yesterday was connected to the photograph of the young woman in his watch lid, and he had to endure that recollection before being able to concentrate and continue.

Questioning whether this made sense, he eased his way through a shallow draw and up its soft banks, and wondered if he should just return to Bannon. The trail itself was empty—even he could see that with the aid of the begrudging moonlight—then he thought he saw movement in the trees ahead. He dropped to his knees and crawled beside a downed tree, magnificent in its death. Moving as fast as he could in this position, he advanced toward where he had last seen a silhouette against a tree. The silhouette of a big man. He had no idea where Checker might be.

Sonny's knee popped against an unseen rock embedded in the ground, and the pain went through him like a silent bullet. In midstride, he stopped and his forehead squeezed into a tight frown to force away the wild ache that raced through his body. His teeth clinched and raked against each other to hold in the cry that wanted out. He breathed hard, as if new air would erase the throbbing. Minutes passed as he let his body return to normal, or, at least, for his mind to accept the new pain. He cleared the last limp branch of the tree and let his eyes dig into the shadows ahead.

The silhouette paused at the top of the ridge and disappeared. A solitary line of sweat crossed

Sonny's broad face. There's one! Was there more? Where? Something touched his boot! He cocked the pistol already in his hand as he looked down. A curious ground squirrel stared back at him. Sonny moved his foot enough to convince the small animal that there were other adventures more worthwhile and returned to studying the area ahead. After a few minutes, he was certain there was only one outlaw, and he eased the hammer down on his gun. That would make him an instant slower in responding, but it would also keep him from accidentally firing his gun if he stumbled.

The huge guard leaned against a tree twenty feet off the trail. His chin lay against his chest, his hat down over his face. A Winchester was cradled in his arms, and it was cocked. Cocked? Sonny looked again to make certain. The outlaw's buttoned vest glistened with remains of a greasy dinner. He was definitely sleepy, Sonny thought, but a man that size would be a lot to handle. Much taller and heavier than Sonny, the guard carried two pistols, both shoved into his waistband. The outlaw's dark beard made him look more intense than his relaxed stance indicated, but the cocked rifle was the most threatening part of the image. The guard's job was to shoot at anything coming down the trail to warn the rest of the gang.

Kneeling beside a log, Sonny watched the guard from twenty feet away, but was careful not to look him in the eyes. He had known of instances where men actually felt such surveillance and reacted out of some long-forgotten instinct. He waited, in spite of his desire to move swiftly. He couldn't risk rushing the guard; there was too great a chance the rifle would go off. One shot would change everything—and none of it for the good.

There was no way he could move through the forest quietly enough to get any closer. Should he wait for Checker to make the first move? Checker was likely behind the guard, or at least closing in on him from the opposite side of the trail. Sonny decided to loop around the guard and come up the trail itself, as if he were coming from the soddy itself. From there, he would act like he was one of the outlaw gang coming to keep the guard company. *It might work*, he observed. The man wouldn't be expecting anyone from that direction except friends. It would also pull his attention away from Checker. For a moment, he wished he and Checker had decided on some kind of a signal to let the other know where he was.

A broken sandstone ledge presented itself between Sonny and the trail opposite the guard, running twenty yards alongside the trail at varying heights before returning to its earthen womb. He walked next to the natural wall, then charged uphill to a more level area and stopped. He was now on the other side of the guard and ten feet from the trail. His breathing was heavy, and he tried to keep his mouth shut to hold back the sound. In the night, any noise would carry.

Suddenly the guard's hat fell off, tumbling to the ground. Sonny stopped in midstep twenty feet away. He waited, applying and releasing the pressure on the walnut grips of his barrel-wrapped Colt. His thumb rested on the hammer. A trickle of sweat announced his nervousness and ran down his face. But the bearded man cursed, picked up the hat, and shoved it back on his head. Sonny resumed easing toward the trail, carefully lifting each foot high and watching where it was headed.

He pulled his derby brim lower on his forehead and wished he were wearing a wide-brimmed hat like Checker's, one that wouldn't stand out as being different. The shadows would have to help him—and the fact that the guard would see what he expected to see: a friend coming. As Sonny concentrated on his hat, he stepped on a brittle dead branch and its crackling filled the night.

"W-who's there? I've got a rifle aimed at your head!" A high-pitched voice followed. *Damn, is there more than one guard?* Sonny wondered in response to a voice that didn't match the huge frame ahead of him. But the only thing he saw was the guard's Winchester swinging menacingly back and forth in his hands, covering the area where Sonny stood.

"Put your damn gun down before it goes off, you fool. It's me, Star. Thought you might like some company," Sonny said, hoping he sounded somewhat like Star McCallister. He held his pistol behind him as he casually strolled toward the guard. The big man flinched, but the message reassured him.

Sonny had figured on pretending he was one of the gang and come smoking a cigarette and whistling. Presenting himself as Star just wasn't what he had planned to do—it just came out. Would the guard hear only what he thought he was hearing? Or would he pull the trigger? Where was Checker? Sonny rushed to close the distance between them, keeping his head down.

Smiling into the night, the guard said, "Glad to have you, boss. Hey, you're not . . ."

In the darkness, and to the big outlaw's right, Checker's hand slid between the rifle hammer and the bullet in the chamber and grasped the gun. The move was a blur. The hammer slammed harmlessly against the back of his hand. Sonny couldn't tell if the guard tried to squeeze the trigger to warn the others, or did so as a reflex from fear. In the same instant, Sonny's wrapped pistol was inches from the man's face. The outlaw's chin lifted to attention and he froze, afraid even to swallow.

"Hiccup and you die. Let go of the rifle real easy-like, then put your hands close to the moon. You let that hammer come down on my hand, mister," Checker growled, "and it hurt. I don't like being hurt."

With a nod to Sonny, Checker pulled the weapon from the outlaw's shaking fingers, then smoothly uncocked the rifle, carefully holding the hammer in place while he removed his trapped right hand. With the rifle in his left hand at his side, Checker took his own Colt from his waistband, withdrawing it carefully so the wrapping would stay in place. Sonny took the man's pistols, one at a time, shoving them into his own belt.

"You don't scare me. If ya shoot, my friends'll know somethin's wrong an' come runnin'," the big guard declared. His high, thin voice made Checker and Sonny smile.

"Who said anything about noise, friend," Sonny snapped. "Our guns are wrapped—just like you had them at the jail. Funny how that'll take the bark out of a gunshot, isn't it?"

"Come to think of it, we don't really know if that wrap will do the trick, do we, Sonny?" Checker snarled. "You could be right. I've never tried it before, have you, Sonny? Maybe there's something about it we haven't learned. Let's find out for sure? Try it, Sonny. Of course, you won't be around to know—but that's . . ."

"H-hey now! D-don't . . . p-please. I—I'll tell you whatever you wanna know. P-please!"

"Start with how those kids are," Checker said. "We'll go from there. Are they all right?"

"Oh yeah, I guess so. Little girl's kinda whiny, misses her ma."

"Of course you tried to comfort her."

"Huh?"

"I'll ask once more," Checker said, his face red with anger. "Are the kids all right?"

Excited, the outlaw spewed detail: The gang was held up in an old soddy several hundred yards down the trail, along with the children. It was their best hideout; no one had ever come close to finding them there. He said the gang had several such places throughout the Nations, but most were near the cattle trails. The Hedrickson horses were corraled there, too. Nobody expected anyone to be so close behind them. Star McCallister said John Checker wouldn't be able to start after them for at least a week, that he would have to care for his sister first. The outlaw proclaimed that no one thought they could be tracked at all after the heavy storm. He said it with a fearful puzzlement that Checker and Sonny had found them. His implied question went unanswered.

In two days they would head south for a Comanchero camp Star knew. He wanted to trade the horses in return for the renegades killing Checker when he finally arrived. Star hadn't made up his mind whether they would take along the children as part of the trade, or leave them behind, or kill them for Checker to find. They would return to Texas where other members of the gang would be waiting.

Sonny's stomach turned with the last bit of information and the question hurled from his mouth: "What's with the wagon tracks?"

The big sentry stiffened and studied Sonny's hooded eyes for a moment, then felt the nose of Sonny's pistol cold against his neck. He blinked, not liking what he saw in either place.

"Well, hell, mister, I'd a-figgered you knew by now."

"I don't spend much time studying wagons."

"That's the damn medicine wagon from Dodge. They was here afore us. It's a straight shot out of Dodge, if'n you don't go the way we did."

"What's it doing here?" Sonny's voice was laced with impatience.

"Hell, man, the doc is Star's brother. Really, I ain't lying to ya." The guard was breathing fast, and his eyes brightened with fear. His voice was like the screech of an old water pump. "Blue's his real name. Blue McCallister, but he goes by that moniker, Dr. Gambree. Saw papers in the jail on him. Lots o' names he done goes by. He an' Star worked out the whole thing. Slick, weren't it?"

Staring at Sonny as if to assure him that his words were true, the bearded outlaw jabbered on, "Blue's got that fancy lady with him. Kinda chocolaty-lookin', ya know. Says she's from Egypt or some-whar like that. Man, she's as tasty as all git out. She don't talk much, 'ceptin' to Blue." He swallowed, glanced at Checker, and continued, "She belongs to

245

him, sure nuff, an' that's one mean son of a bitch. I saw him kill both deputies. He done knifed them Triple C boys, too. Cold as sleet, man. Made Joe Coffey crawfish. Really he did, I saw 'im."

Checker shook his head, trying to force away the guilt for not recognizing his younger half brother when he met him in Dodge. He saw again Dr. Gambree grinning at him, and it became his father's face.

"What about the lynch mob?" Sonny asked.

"Thar weren't none. Leastwise, not really. That fool trail boss, Kayler, yeah, that's his name, he thought Doc and Rand were gonna help him lynch us. The fool didn't see what was comin' until the Doc shot him ri't in front o' us. Never seed a man wrap up a gun like that a'fer. Really keeps 'er quiet, don't it." He realized what he had said and shivered.

"Yeah, I'm afraid so." Sonny wasn't sure if he should believe the man.

"H-hey, man, I'm tellin' you the truth. Kayler carried in one o' them Triple C cowboys, like he was tolt, and then the doc shot Kayler. Star told us everybody would blame us gittin out on a lynch mob. The marshal were in on it, too. He done cock-cocked his own deputy. Yeah, his own man. Blue shot the deputy in the head when we was leavin'—to make sure."

"Why mess with all that?" Sonny asked.

The big guard nodded his head like he understood what Sonny was chewing on. Still nodding authoritatively, he said, "Wal, Star figgered it would give us more time to git away. The marshal was to git a posse together an' go after them Kayler riders. I heard tell they was waitin' outta town somewhar. He was to tell folks that they done kilt 'n' buried us.

He were to arrest them boys fer murder. 'Sides that, it were a quick way to git a bunch o' hosses. Kayler brought 'em from his trail remuda, like he were tolt. Mighty slick, I'd say. Bin real fun to see all that a-happenin'. Were you in town that next mornin'?"

"No. We were on your trail."

The guard couldn't help but return to the question riding his mind. "Star said there was no way anybody could follow us after that goddamn storm we rid through last night. So did Big Tom. How did . . ."

"We're good at it—and you're not," Checker said. "Tell us something worth keeping you alive. We've got better things to do than listen to you windy us."

"P-please," the guard muttered, and studied Sonny's face, not daring to look at Checker. "P-please, mister, I ain't lyin'. Wes is m-my name. Wes M-Morton. I stole some beef, sure, but I ain't never kilt nobody—an' I ain't never hurt no kids neither."

"You're a fine, upstanding citizen. Any other guards?"

"N-no sir. Jes' me, honest. I—I told ya we didn't think nobody was a-comin'. Star said we had to put out guards anyhow. I were the only one who weren't drunk. Everybody was wet as hell when we got in. Shoulda drunk more."

Sonny chuckled in spite of himself. "How many riding with you?"

"Ah, t-twenty."

"Try again." It was Checker.

"Oh, yah, yah, thar be eight o' us, countin' Star. Then thar's Blue an' the lady. Ya done got Ferguson, I reckon. Leastwise, he never came back."

Biting his lower lip, the outlaw turned toward Checker and asked, "You're Checker, ain't ya? I heard Star say you 'n' him, 'n' the doc, were all brothers. He just funnin'?"

"Yeah, funnin'."

"Figgered as much. Ya don't look nuthin' alike. That were your sister's place we, ah . . ."

"Where are they keeping the kids in the house?" Checker asked tautly. "Were they wet? Did they get dried off—an' get some warm food? Blankets?" Checker's following questions were jabs to the man's courage.

"W-well, they're over in a corner, again' the wall. S-sleeping. L-leastwise, they was when I left. R-reckon they was, ah, yeah, w-wet. I—"

A blow from Checker's Colt to the back of the big man's head brought a whimper that became a half-blurted moan. The guard slid down the tree into a heap of collapsed legs and arms. Checker tossed the rifle as far as he could into the dark brush behind him. The clank and clatter made him crouch low in reaction to the noise and quickly look around to see if the sound had been noticed.

"Damn! Why did I do that?" he asked Sonny, and tugged on the brim of his hat as an exclamation.

"Beats me, but I didn't know where the hell you were until you grabbed his gun."

"So I noticed," Checker replied with a glint of amusement in his eyes. "You don't make a very good Star McCallister."

"Yeah, didn't exactly have time to practice."

"It was a smart move," Checker said. "I couldn't figure out how to get close enough until you did that. I, ah, I didn't know where you were either."

"Don't that beat all? Figured you could see everything at night," Sonny said.

"Don't believe everything you hear, my friend."

"John, did you know Star has a brother?" Sonny said, slowly raising his eyes as he spoke, until they reached the Ranger's intense gaze.

Looking off to the south, then back to Sonny, Checker said, "His name *was* Blue. I barely remember him. He must've been only five or six when . . . I left Dodge." He turned back to Sonny. "Dr. Gambree." Checker spat the name like he'd just swallowed alkali water.

While Sonny went for their friends, Checker tied the unconscious guard, using the man's gunbelt to hold his legs together and a folded, wet bandanna to grasp his hands behind his back. He stuffed part of the man's vest into his limp mouth and held it there with another bandanna around the outlaw's face. When the three Triple C riders returned, Jackson advised against riding any closer to the hideout out of concern their horses would smell the Hedrickson herd and start whinnying. Checker agreed, and their mounts were tied to branches and bushes along the trail.

Jackson bound the unconscious guard to a tree with his lariat, examining Checker's handiwork as he did. Bannon didn't see the necessity for doing that: The blood splotch on the back of the man's head meant he wasn't going to be doing much of anything for a while. He shrugged impatiently, knowing it was Jackson's way, but noticed that Checker and Sonny were waiting in appreciation of their friend's thoroughness. Sonny handed Bannon one of the outlaw's pistols, and the farm boy placed it carefully in his waistband. It bothered him for a few moments. What if it slid down to his manhood? He saw that both Checker and Sonny were also carrying additional handguns the same way, so he decided it wasn't something to worry about.

With a sense of pending battle in their throats, the four men headed down the trail. Only Sonny was without a rifle. Only Jackson carried a canteen slung over his shoulder on a long rawhide string. A scrawny string of smoke was caught in the night sky as if weaving the handful of stars together. Sonny explained what they should expect. Gradually, the outline of a grayish-brown sod structure took shape in a tight, shallow valley surrounded by rocky hillsides in three directions and a heavy tree line on the fourth. Row after row of aging bricks of matted sod composed the small house. A lone window faced them on the back side of the house, with its doorway on the opposite side.

Tree limbs were weaved among the rafters, supported with slick grass and laden with large sod blocks. The eastern side of the valley was flat, but bloated with trees and underbrush; the rest was a three-sided bowl of rocky hillside. The wandering creek they had crossed three times had found its way along the same side as the trees. Only now, its true vein was difficult to tell as it squatted across the land as far as the rain's enhancement let it go. The unmistakable shape of the medicine wagon was on the far side of the soddy. Silhouettes of horses could be seen in the attached stable. Tied to the outside of the corral were three steers. Around the house, trees and brush had been cleared away, leaving fifty yards of open space. Anyone approaching would be quite visible.

Sonny rolled his tongue across his lips and said, "That's Hedrickson's herd." Breath-frost blossomed at his mouth. "How are we going to play this?"

"Like you're good at taking orders," Checker said.

"Well, I did ask, give me that."

Behind them, Bannon stumbled and fell, clanging his rifle on the rocks. Sonny turned and put his finger to his mouth to signal silence. Bannon scooted to a walk and went into an exaggerated tiptoe to approach them.

Chuckling at the performance unseen by Checker, Sonny listened to Checker outline a plan. Jackson and Bannon would go to the side of the soddy, around through the tree line. He and Sonny would take the right. He would go to the planked window in the back first to see if anything could be learned. He would go in after the kids, and the others would fan out to protect his exit with them.

With silent agreement, the four men eased down the ridge, through the uneven ground, watching their movement to keep from loosening rocks or stepping on brittle branches that might signal their advance, or slipping on wet grass that would send them sliding. Unsettled terrain of flat chunks of shale had not yet decided if it wanted to be the wall or the floor of this tight land bowl. Erosion from the weather had cut away entire bands of earth from the gray mounds. For sturdier footing, Jackson kept his steps near clumps of long, spindly grass sprouting wherever rock had been apathetic about their existence. They would provide the safest footing, he thought, and pointed to them for Bannon to imitate him. Sonny and Checker vanished off the hillside to the right.

Beside a crowded oak tree, Checker studied the house and the surrounding ground for minutes, reminding himself that to hurry could only get him in trouble or dead. Beside him, Sonny also examined every shadow, every tree, every large clump of grass, and every large rock to assure himself that no additional guards were out. He told himself to tell Jackson of his thoroughness; the black man would be pleased. He couldn't make out much detail in the hillsides that enclosed the cabin, only dark, twisted shapes that could be anything. He couldn't even see Bannon or Jackson, and he knew where they were. A glance at Checker assured him that the former Ranger was satisfied with what was there. If a guard was hunkered down among the higher ground, there was nothing either could do about it. Now was the time to go.

"Wait here. I'll go take a look," Checker whispered. His eyes asked Sonny to agree this time.

With his Winchester in one hand at his side, Checker ran to the sod cabin and stopped beside the lone window in the back and peeked through a slit between the sod and the boarded cover. Only one room, it reeked of fried food, urine, and sweat. A singed, crumbling stone fireplace held a dying fire. Sitting on the fire's edge was a coffeepot, left from supper, mixing the odor of burned coffee with the other smells. A tired candle lamp was doing little to push the shadows into the corners. In the far northwest corner was a stack of rifles and one shotgun.

Lying about the room were sleeping outlaws, their snoring creating a harsh cacophony of snorts, grunts, and whines. He couldn't see the whole room but recognized several members of the McCallister gang. The small Joe Coffey was sleeping in a chair. The negro O. F. Venner was by himself in a corner. What had to be Iron-Head Ed Wells was stretched out in the middle of the room. He didn't see Star. *Where are the kids?* Then he saw a corner of two small shapes huddled under a gray blanket next to this wall, not far from Venner. The slit in the board ended before he could make them out completely, but it had to be Johnny and Rebecca.

No matter how hard he squinted or moved, it was impossible to be sure how many outlaws were in there. He counted three times and came up with a different number each time. He dared not risk attempting to remove the window board for fear it would fall inside and wake everyone. He licked his lower lip as he acknowledged what he had known all along. He had to go in there and get the Hedrickson kids. It was risky—but to wait meant the outlaws could use the children as a shield to get away. Or kill them out of spite when they discovered their hideout was surrounded.

A glance to his right caught movement along the eastern tree wall. Someone in the trees! Another guard! Had a second outlaw seen him? No, it was just Sonny, antsy to join him. With a deep breath for luck, he ran toward the first tree in the string and heard a familiar voice.

"What's next?"

"I'm going in to get them."

"Don't ask me to stay behind."

Minutes later, Checker and Sonny met Jackson and Bannon coming from the other side. Bannon was directed to a spot halfway up the rugged southern slope that faced the front door. He crouched behind a rock alcove that provided cover and a good field of fire toward the front of the soddy with its single window and skinny doorway.

Jackson took a position at the edge of the corral where he could watch the horses and the front door at the same time. He took Checker's Winchester along with his own. The former Ranger didn't want to carry the weapon inside. If trouble happened, a handgun would be faster. He didn't say what they all knew, that any kind of gunplay would likely mean they wouldn't get the children out—or themselves.

With his derby pulled low over his eyes, Sonny hummed "Dixie" to himself and opened the door for a silent Checker. They stepped inside. No one moved. Only the sounds of sleep reached them. Each took a long breath. Sonny smiled and slid to the wall beside the doorway. In his hands were two pistols: only one was wrapped for silencing. He was surprised at how hot it seemed in spite of the breath-smoke that fondled his face.

In the farthest corner, Star McCallister lay sleeping, his blond hair luminous in the night. Just seeing him bothered Sonny, like the man was waiting on him to get farther into the room before waking the gang. Lying next to Star, he saw a man and a woman under the same blankets. Across her waist was the unshirted arm of a man he didn't know but assumed was Star's brother, Dr. Gambree. The woman's naked breasts were exposed above the edge of the blankets. Sonny did a double take and swallowed hard. *Bad time to be thinking about women,* he told himself, and tried to concentrate on the room ahead of him.

His eyes bounced back to her bosom twice as he watched Checker headed into the labyrinth of sleeping men stretched out on the packed-dirt floor. The tall gunfighter walked carefully, trying to step around legs and arms half-hidden under blankets, holding his breath as long as he could before exhaling and going on. Against the far wall was an unused bed, the only one in the cabin. Next to it was a tall bureau with a missing drawer. Although the bed blocked his vision, he could see someone was sleeping beside it. He was certain the kids were there. Yes, the blanketed shape looked smaller than the others. There was an outlaw sleeping close to them.

An arm flopped in front of him just as his left boot was coming down in the same space, and he tried to keep from stepping on it. But the sudden change in movement robbed him of his balance and he careened into the sleeping man next to the arm-flopping one.

"What the hell?" the aroused man growled as Checker's weight slammed against him. Recognizing Tiller, the man he'd shot in the shoulder, Checker kept his head away from the aroused outlaw and mumbled, "Sorry, I was taking a leak. Lost my balance."

"Well, goddammit, be careful," the groggy Tiller snapped, and pushed on Checker's back as he tried to stand. "Do it in your pants next time."

"Yeah, sorry."

Checker stood again, not looking at the man, and stepped over the flopped arm that had caused his fall. At the front wall Sonny's fists tightened around his guns in anticipation of the whole room coming awake. Checker glanced at his own weapons in response; one was holstered, the other still wrapped and in his waistband. His thoughts sought his knife, but the awakened Tiller was not moving, apparently sliding back into sleep. Tiller's filthy shirt was marked with new bloodstains around his shoulder, indicating the wound had reopened. The doorway looked a thousand miles away, and Sonny seemed to be only a nondistinct shape. Sonny waved his gun to indicate Checker should go on. The former Ranger nodded and eased himself around the bed, noting that it had a huge hole in the middle of an old rotting mattress and deciding that was the reason no one was using it.

Next to the wall, snoring loudly, was Tom Redmond. Checker recognized him as a tough former Rebel whom Sonny had ridden with once in a border gang. That was back in his wild days when Sonny Jones was Cole Dillon and wanted by the Texas Rangers. The outlaw had been surprised to see Sonny with the Triple C crew when Star's gang was arrested. His plea to Sonny for help because of old times had been bluntly rejected.

On the far side of the bed, Johnny and Rebecca were together under a gray blanket. The bureau had blocked this view of the room from the outside window. He tiptoed around the bed and pushed his hat back to allow his face to be seen more easily. He kneeled beside Johnny. The boy was sleeping with his arm around his younger sister. Both of their faces were dirty and red; their clothes were layered with dried mud and sweat; their hair was sticky and matted. His throat caught the emotion that jumped into it. *What kind of a man would do this to a family?* As far as he could tell, neither was bound in any way. A few feet away, by himself in the corner, the black gunman Venner was stretched out, snoring. A pistol had slipped from his hand to the floor. Checker studied him to make certain he was sleeping soundly. The trick was to awaken the children—without arousing anyone.

Chapter Fourteen

Placing his hand fimly over Johnny's mouth and holding his body in place with the other hand, Checker whispered into the boy's ear.

"Johnny, it's your uncle John. It's all right. Are you awake now? Just nod. Don't say anything when I take my hand away. We've come to get you and your sister out of here. But you've got to be quiet—real quiet. All right? Good."

The eight-year-old's eyes were instantly wide; his body tensed. Checker's hands moved away from him, and Johnny swallowed. Checker whispered for him to tell his sister the same way he had told him. Johnny quickly obeyed, placing his hand over his sister's mouth. Checker bit his lower lip as the boy began by singing a sweet song he'd heard their mother sing to them at bedtime. She awakened, and her eyes were bright with confusion. She stared at Checker, showing no sign of recognizing him.

Checker glanced away at the room of sleeping men for assurance that nothing had changed. Even the outlaw he'd fallen on was apparently asleep again. *So far so good*, he muttered. He turned back and tried to lift Rebecca to him but she twisted away and whimpered. Before Checker could coax her, Johnny said, "Sis, you quit that, right now. This is Uncle John. Let him carry you out of here. Do it right now, Becky—I mean it."

With that rebuke, she blinked back the advancing tears and held out her arms. Checker lifted her to his chest and stood. He drew the wrapped pistol with his right hand, holding her in place with his left. Muffling the sound wouldn't make any difference now, he told himself, but there was a certain security in its presence.

"It's all right, honey," he whispered. "We're going to get you home."

The last word didn't want to come out, but he forced it and bit the inside of his cheek to keep his feelings in place. Swallowing, he told her, "Hang on tight, honey." She reached around his neck and squeezed. Motioning for Johnny to walk close behind him, they moved around the bed and over to the east wall of the soddy, keeping as much distance as possible from the outlaw he had fallen into. There was no sense in pushing his luck by walking past him again, even though it looked a bit faster. Sonny had moved to the closer side of the wall; he studied the room for movement.

As the Ranger and the two children paused at the fireplace, the brawler Wells sat up from his bedroll. Johnny gasped, and Checker pushed the boy behind him with his right hand, which held his pistol, then swung the weapon toward the big man. Wells mumbled something unintelligible and fell back into his blankets. *Talking in his sleep!* Checker muttered. *Damn!* Checker's gaze returned to the wounded outlaw Tiller he had stumbled over, reassuring himself there was no threat there either.

He kneeled beside Johnny, and Rebecca squeezed his neck to indicate she didn't want down. The boy's dirt-streaked face was grim and determined. *Just like his mother*, the Ranger thought to himself.

"Do you two see my friend Sonny by the door?" Checker whispered. "Remember him when the Triple C boys came to your place? All right, let's go—right to him, Johnny. Watch out so you don't step on that guy's arm."

Johnny nodded and started toward Sonny. The happy-go-lucky drover grinned, and motioned for the boy to advance. Three small steps from the doorway, a fat-bellied outlaw to Johnny's left stirred, and Sonny was the first to glimpse the gleam of a revolver within shifting blankets.

"Run, Johnny! Come on, John!" Sonny yelled, and his pistols were an instant behind the commands, smashing into the shadow. One gun was much louder than the other, with its lead tearing through layers of shirt. The boy hesitated, then ran through the open doorway.

The outlaw's head snapped backward, raising his propped-up, heavyset body momentarily off the floor. His revolver clattered on the hard ground and exploded into the sod wall. Rebecca screamed as Checker raced past Sonny into the night. The gunshots brought the room into a sleep-drugged frenzy.

"Hey! What the hell's going on?" "That's Checker!

Shoot him! Shoot him!" "What's he doin' here?" "Kill him!"

Gunshots blistered the wall and framed doorway where Sonny had been a moment before. Ahead of him, Checker, with Rebecca and Johnny, slid safely into a large gulley, aided by an outcropping of crumbled rock and dried brown grass. Heavy frost-breath encircled Sonny's head as he lumbered toward the same refuge, splashing mud and rainwater to his waist. His derby flew and rolled independently toward the soddy. Bullets whined death songs at his feet and shoulders as he crossed the open yard between the house and hillside. To his left, Jackson's rifle spat rapidly at the doorway from a prone position between the corral and the hill. Bannon's gun answered the attack from above.

Sonny half-dove, half-slid on his knees into the rain-soaked gulley right behind Checker and the kids. Bullets bit at the top of the incline, a foot from his head. Checker was crouched low, trying to comfort Rebecca, who was crying uncontrollably. Sonny looked around and saw Johnny squatted behind a rock shelf twenty feet to his right. Johnny waved, and Sonny returned the greeting, in spite of himself.

"It's all right, honey; you let go now—and Uncle John will shoot back at these bad fellows," Checker said, gently pulling on Rebecca's arm, but she wouldn't release him.

He tried again, and she clung tighter. Hunching his shoulders to recognize the futility of getting her to let go, he peered between rocks anchored to the top of the waist-high ditch. Rebecca's arms remained wrapped tightly around his neck. A silhouette appeared at the partially open door, followed by a gun barrel aimed at the retreating Jackson. Sonny's pistols roared and the silhouette jerked out of sight. For the joy of shooting back, Sonny emptied both guns at the slamming door. Smoke wisps sought escape from both gun barrels.

As suddenly as it was aroused, the house went quiet. Even the candle was blown out, eliminating what little light there was. The lock of the bolt clattered into silence. Checker slowly peeked again, trying to see into the blackness of the lone window. No longer crying, Rebecca studied the Ranger's face; he looked down at her, smiled, and kissed her cheek. His position wasn't the best, and it was time to move before the gang recovered and rushed them. He didn't like the thought of that possibility, especially with Rebecca at his chest.

"Come on, Sonny. Let's go see Tyrel," he said, and signaled for Johnny to do the same.

In the darkness, the risk posed by their movement was slight—and definitely less than that from staying where they could be easily rushed. Gunfire from the soddy searched the gulley for flesh while they worked their way up the ridge-layered hillside. Arriving first, Johnny hugged Tyrel, and he returned it, embarrassed at the show of emotion until he saw the hatless Sonny kiss Rebbeca's forehead as she continued to hold tight around Checker's neck.

"That guard wasn't lying. Star and the medicine doc are in there," Sonny gasped, his body fighting to find enough air to allow for the luxury of speaking. "There's nine of 'em. One less than that now, I reckon." He paused and added, "An' your gal—Salome—she's there, too." He thought for a moment about whether he should tell of her nakedness, then

262

decided against it. Bannon's face was a mixture of emotions Sonny couldn't read, and he decided he shouldn't have teased him.

"That's still a big handful, Sonny. We's only four—an' we got the kids," Bannon noted, avoiding asking about Salome although he wanted to, then bursting out with, "Were she a-sleepin'?" He felt silly.

Sonny grinned and said, "Yeah, she was sleeping. Didn't have much on either. Almost too much for this old cowhand." He paused and said with a change in his voice, "I'm stayin'. Dr. Gambree killed Harry—an' Tex. An' they hurt Amel—Mrs. Hedrickson—real bad. They killed some of my friends on the trail. They're going to have to kill me—or die."

If Checker was listening, he didn't show it. He was watching the soddy grow silent, then studying the small building itself. At the corral, his eyes recounted the number of horses. It looked to him that both Hedrickson and outlaw horses were there. His tired eyes flicked with a reassurance; this was truly a secure camp in Star's mind, and he could understand why. It was only by Sonny's persistence that they had found it.

Jackson arrived, gulping for the thin predawn air that didn't seem to hold enough life for him. His long coat was covered with oozing mud from knee height downward. Both hands gripped a Winchester, his and Checker's. Both were smoking. The canteen, hanging from his shoulder, was half covered in mud.

"Hey, old man, you're outta shape—and you look like you've been playing in the mud!" Sonny teased. "Thanks for the cover."

Jackson's shoulders rose and fell in rhythm with

his gasps, then sputtered, "You should talk, I thought you were waltzing across that yard. I've seen old women faster than you. Did you try to hit every mud puddle out there?"

Sonny laughed out loud and slapped him on the shoulder. Smiling, Jackson handed the Ranger his rifle, and Checker's eyes thanked him. Immediately, Checker's hands went to his double-looped bullet belt to gather fresh loads for the gun. Jackson gave the canteen to Johnny, and he accepted it eagerly.

"I'm sure thankful to you boys for the cover, too," Checker said as he shoved new cartridges into the chamber. "Sonny got downright unsociable and went an' shot one of 'em. So we were asked to leave."

Sonny shook his head and chuckled again. "Hey, that sounds like a song. Shot one and we had to leave. Shot one and we had to leave." He smiled at Rebecca, and she shyly turned her head toward Checker's shoulder, then quickly looked back at Sonny and smiled flirtatiously. Her eyes sparkled with enjoyment at his attention.

"Oh my," Sonny exclaimed. "Are you gonna break some hearts one day." Checker chuckled and kissed her cheek. "She looks just like Amelia."

"Lucky for her she didn't come out lookin' like her uncle," Sonny added, and held out his hands for her to come to him, and she did, giggling. "Come here an' let's give your ol' uncle a rest. All right?"

Checker watched her go to Sonny, and his intense gaze followed her like a protective dog, then moved to Sonny. "I'm not leaving. Star is going to pay for this—and Blue." He levered the Winchester into readiness as punctuation to his statement; built within it was a question he couldn't bring himself to ask.

Sonny answered it for him. "Well, you must be getting deaf in your old age, Ranger. I already told you I have no intention of leaving without them. I'm sure Jackson and Tyrel didn't come all this way to run away, either."

Without further comment, Checker returned his gaze to the silent house, halfway expecting gunfire to open up on them at any moment. As if they were somewhere on a picnic, Sonny sang a made-up tune to the little girl about her hair and flowers. But his gaze reviewed their position and saw his derby lying forlorn against the side of the cabin. It could have been back in Dodge, as far as immediate availability went. He felt naked without it, then chuckled at his own feelings for a hat.

Sonny noticed that Jackson was evaluating the same thing and was comforted by the black cowboy's apparent approval. They were safe from any direct shots, and the hillside behind them would absorb lead, not let it ricochet. Would the gang dare a frontal attack without knowing what they were up against? Star's thinking was often contrarian, but he wasn't likely to try a stunt like that. Too risky. Better to wait and assess. His men weren't likely to like the idea of charging a hillside of rifles either.

"Tyrel, I want you to take Johnny and Rebecca back to our camp." Checker's dark eyes didn't leave the soddy as he spoke.

"I want to stay hyar—with yo'all."

"I appreciate that, Tyrel, but we've got to get them out of here."

He explained his plan. Their best chance to get the

gang to surrender quickly was to make them think a large posse had them under fire. He and Sonny would fan out to to the corners of the ridge: Sonny would go over to the rock shelf on the far side of the pitched-in bowl holding the soddy; Checker would move down the hillside, slanting toward the tree line and firing as he went. He would slip into the trees for final cover. Jackson would maintain this position. As soon as they started shooting, Bannon and the children would move over the ridge and along the back side, then go down into the tree line and backtrack the trail to their horses. He would take them back to their camp and wait.

"We've got to look like a whole posse—and we've got to do it before daylight takes the only edge. Guns in both hands, spread them apart. Make yourself look like two men every time you fire. Shoot and move. Shoot and move. Don't worry about hitting anything. Just shoot. All right?" Checker ended his strategy with a question.

"Are they going to take us back?" Rebecca's voice was thin.

"No, sweetheart, they aren't," Sonny said quietly. "You go with Tyrel now—an' we'll be along shortly."

"I wanna be with you," she pouted.

Without answering, Sonny searched his fat vest pockets for something to give her. His thick fingers found cartridges, coins, leather strips, tobacco makin's, his watch—and, at last, two pieces of hard candy. He took them out and examined their red, rectangular shapes. His fingers brushed away a few specks of dirt, and he sang, "Oh, looky here. Oh, looky here. I found some candy. I found some candy." He stopped, grinned, and said, "Hmmmm, would you like a piece of candy, little lady?"

"Oh, yummy!" Rebecca exclaimed, then grabbed and shoved it into her mouth in one motion. "Is this a special day? Momma and Poppa give us candy on special days, like our birthday."

"Well, I guess it is a special day—for me. Here's one for you, Johnny," Sonny said, and looked to Checker for reassurance that his gifts were approved. "I get to be with you and your brother—an' your uncle John. An' my two friends. That's pretty special to me." His blue eyes joined the wide smile under his heavy mustache.

"I like special days," she said. "On my birthday, Momma and Poppa sing to me and bring me breakfast—right to my bed."

"Well now, that sure sounds real fine. Nobody ever did that on my birthday, that's for sure," Sonny responded, trying not to show his anxiousness.

Rebecca studied him and said, "When we get home, will you come and stay with us? I will bring you breakfast on your birthday. An' sing to you, too."

Sonny took a long, deep breath before answering. "Ah, I would like that, honey, I sure would. But I've got to go home too. To Texas."

"Oh."

Her round, dirt-streaked face puckered, and he thought she was going to cry. Quickly he added, "But not right away, of course. We'll have lots of time to play together. An' lots of singing, I promise."

Rebecca's face brightened. A playful breeze took advantage and dragged her damp hair across his broad cheek.

"First, you go with Tyrel and Johnny, all right? He's gonna play a game of marching behind that hill—an' then hiding in the trees. It'll be fun."

With a kiss on her cheek, Sonny held her out to Bannon. This time, she went without a sound and the farm boy settled her little body into his crooked left arm and held his Winchester in his right fist.

"You be thinking about a song we can sing when I get back, sweetheart," Sonny added, and then began removing his coat. "Here, Johnny, you put this on. It's cold out here. Tyrel, wrap your coat around her, keep her warm."

Shyly, the boy returned the canteen to Jackson and accepted the coat, then shivered as the idea triggered recognition of his discomfort. The coat was huge on him, with sleeves flopping well beyond his hands and the waistcoat reaching his knees. Sonny laughed, and Bannon joined in. Rebecca pointed at the jacket and said, "Oh, that's funny."

"By golly, you look like you could hibernate in there!" Sonny exclaimed, sun lines deepening at the corners of his eyes as he squinted with enjoyment.

"Feels like it," Johnny admitted. "Should I take it off?"

Bannon smiled and said, "If you think that's bad, you shoulda seen what I wore on the trail drive. Got teased every day, seems like. If it feels good 'n' warm, I wouldn't worry about it." He wrapped his own coat around Rebecca, and she snuggled into his chest.

Checker watched from his kneeling position. His tired eyes were renewed by the happy interplay, in spite of his anxiousness to get the children to safety.

Looking up from his new coat, Johnny turned to

Checker and asked, "Are Momma and Poppa dead?"

Checker wasn't ready for the question. He stared at the boy. Knee-high breeches and a full-buttoned vest over a white shirt were layered with trail mud, dried rain, sweat, and black soot from the house fire, and now Sonny's coat. The boy's sand-colored hair was matted with sweat and dirt. Freckles covered the bridge of his mother's nose, and his father's light blue eyes searched for truth in Checker's face. Johnny waited for an answer, standing like a school-boy waiting for directions from a teacher, arms at his side.

"They are, aren't they." The boy's summation fol-lowed.

Standing next to the boy, Sonny spoke first. "Your pa was a mighty brave man. He died, ah, trying to protect all of you. I'm mighty sorry. Your mother, she's bad hurt—but she has a fine doctor looking after her in Dodge. Doc Tremons. He looked after our trail boss after he was shot up. Your uncle John took her into town himself."

Bannon's mouth was dry Texas sand. His emo-tions were a swirl of sadness for the boy and anger that Sonny had told him about his parents. Johnny's face balled into despair. The farm boy watched Johnny's entire body shake, and the tears blister his freckled face. Bannon reached for him with his free arm, squeezing Rebecca's so tightly with the other as he moved that she told him it hurt.

"I'm mighty sorry. Wish it'd all go away for ya, but it can't," Bannon said in a soft voice. "My pappy done left us too. I know'd how it hurts." He patted Rebecca on the back and held her more comfortably.

The boy swung his arms violently to push away

Bannon's intended embrace. Johnny's face was a blur of water as he declared, "Uncle John was supposed to keep us safe. Momma said he were the bravest of all Texas Rangers. Why did he let them kill my pa? Why did he let them do that to Momma? Why did he let them burn our house?"

Bannon's face received the verbal assault intended for Checker and turned to gray stone. Sonny glanced at the stunned Checker and knew this wasn't the time for delay, but keeping the truth from the boy would only make it worse later. Slight movement across one window heightened his worry.

"Why is Johnny crying?" Rebecca's eyes widened as she sought the answer to her question. Putting her hands on Bannon's face, she looked into his eyes, wanting to be told something. She repeated her question: "Why is Johnny crying?"

Biting the inside of his cheek, Bannon knew how the boy felt. When his own father died last year, it was like God had hit him in the chest. He shrugged away those old feelings and tried to think of something to say, "Well, Becky, Johnny's been mighty brave, you know."

"I'm not crying," she responded coyly. "Haven't I been brave?"

"Ya sure have bin, li'l Becky, ya sure have," Bannon said. She waited for more explanation, but got only a mumbled, "Maybe Jackson kin tell ya the what-fers."

Recognizing the fragility of their situation, Jackson grabbed Sonny's arm and said, "We haven't got much time. Help me with Johnny."

"Damn, Jackson, I thought I was doing the right

thing," Sonny said. A frown lined his tanned forehead.

"You did. Come on," Jackson urged.

Sonny glanced at the unmoving Checker and followed Jackson at an urgent trot parallel to their hidden position. Sobbing, Johnny had run to a large, reddish stone just below the crest of the hillside. Nothing hid him from the soddy except the darkness. The odd-shaped rock was as tall as the boy's heaving shoulders as he lay against it. Clumps of skinny buffalo grass slid against the stone and around the boy's legs, seeking companionship, and covered him from the soddy. Jackson looked around, uneasy that their silhouettes would be outlined against the false dawn's glow searching the land for believers.

Without waiting for Sonny, he spoke softly, but firmly, into Johnny's ear. "You're the man in your family now. You have it to do. You'll do it real fine, too. You're like your uncle. He's hurting, too, you know. He loves you and your little sister—and your ma and pappy—so doggone much, he can't stand the pain of seeing you hurting like this."

Johnny lifted his head. No more tears were left, only emptiness, an ache to see his mother and father, to feel their love around him. His body heaved with barely controlled breathing, interrupted by jerky sobs.

"M-my uncle l-loves me?" he asked, turning halfway toward Jackson.

"More than about anything, I reckon," Jackson said. "Now, let's get your little sister out of here. You and Tyrel can slide right over the hill, then through those woods. He'll show you where our camp is. I'm counting on you, all right?"

"Yessir, I'm ready—can I go hug my uncle first?"

Memories of a happy time darted into Checker's strained state of mind and stilled the rage that welled within him as he crouched, trying to concentrate on what the outlaws might do next. He must ignore Johnny's outburst—he must, he told himself. But his thoughts were frozen on an everlasting moment when he first saw a smiling Johnny standing between his mother and father. He recalled the boy walking with him into their barn, eager to tell him about their horses, announcing proudly that they had a horse like his big black, " 'cept'n' it's brown. An' a mare. Probably shorter, too." He saw again the look on their faces when they received his presents brought all the way from Texas. He felt again the love that filled every room of their house and knew he wished it could have been his home. Johnny's anger crackled like hungry flame against those memories.

With a gulped "Uncle John!" Johnny ran toward Checker, swimming in Sonny's coat. Checker spun around, not certain what to expect. His face tightened in anticipation of more anger from the boy. Johnny half-jumped into the waiting Checker, pushing his face into Checker's broad shoulders. Checker held Johnny tightly, searching for comforting words that wouldn't come, feeling the boy's anguish in the quiet crying he tried to hold back. It found Checker's own torment deep within him, where another small boy still lived. Checker shut his eyes and rocked Johnny gently in his arms.

His dirty cheeks streaked with tears, Johnny stepped back and stared into Checker's face and said, "M-momma told me about the button. How she done took it off your shirt when you left. She said it meant you'd come back. I—I took off one of mine. I didn't have one of yours." He reached into his pants pocket and retrieved a small brown button. Checker saw the open slit on the boy's shirt and swallowed the emotion slamming against his throat.

"John, we're losing night fast." It was an urgent Sonny.

Checker looked up, blinked and nodded. He stood, holding the boy close to him. "You take your li'l sis—and go to our horses. Tyrel knows the way. We'll be along in a while. Get yourself something to eat. Got new clothes for both of you in our packs, too."

"These are just fine," Johnny blurted. "They're from our house."

Checker examined again the boy's filthy clothes, measured the determination set on his dirty, tear-streaked face, and said, "Yes, they're just fine."

"I—I lost the knife you gave me. I-it was in the f-fire," Johnny said, the words bubbling out close to Checker's ear.

"That's all right. When we get back to camp, I'll give you mine."

Watching the exchange, Bannon's mind wandered on to Salome, the medicine show dancer. It aroused him to think she was inside the cabin. He imagined telling her of his feelings for her. She told him that he was very brave and kissed him warmly.

"Here, Tyrel, something to read while you're waiting—and, ah, to remember—Never mind." Jackson interrupted the imagined embrace, handing the poetry book from his coat pocket to Bannon.

His face searing and prickly about his daydream, Bannon wasn't sure what to do or say next, but out of his mouth tumbled "Ya be careful now, Jackson. Ya don't move as swift a foot as ya used to, I reckon."

Jackson told Bannon what to do at the camp, where the food and children's clothes were stored, to keep horses readied and race for Dodge if he saw riders other than them coming. He explained that the gang wouldn't know of the camp, so he would have a slight edge if he didn't delay. Unspoken was the fact that the three Triple C riders would be dead if that happened. Bannon listened without comment, understanding the fullness of the instructions and not wanting to deal with their actual meaning.

As Jackson spoke, he held out his canteen for Rebecca to drink from it. She sipped its cool liquid, studying the black man as she did.

"What do you have on your face?" she asked.

"That's the color of my skin, Miss Rebecca. I am a Negro."

"Oh, does it hurt?"

Jackson chuckled and said, "Little lady, how I wish I could answer that." Then he recorked his canteen and added, "God, be with them."

"Were you praying? Momma makes us say a prayer before we go to sleep. Do you want to hear it?" Rebecca asked, leaning away from Bannon's chest and peering at his dark face.

"I've got to go, Miss Rebecca, but why don't you say it for Tyrel. He'd like that," Jackson replied, and spun away. Checker and Sonny were already shadows blurring into the hillside.

"Now I lay me down to sleep . . ."

Chapter Fifteen

The thunder of guns drowned out her little prayer. A string of orange flame blossomed along the hillside as the three Triple C men executed their posse mascarade, running and firing to new positions. With the first crackle of gunfire, Johnny sprang from a crouch and disappeared over the ridge. A few steps behind him was Bannon, hesitating only to glance at the black cowboy firing his rifle in one hand and his handgun in the other, spreading them apart as far as he could. Bannon could make out Checker and Sonny from the flame of their guns and hoped it wasn't that visible from the soddy.

"Come on, Tyrel!" Johnny urged. Bannon swallowed and went over the ridge.

Sonny's movement across the face of the pockmarked hillside was agile, defying his chunky frame. His shirttail wagged beneath his vest. All shirts came with wills of their own and, therefore, would never stay where they were supposed to, he had observed on more than one occasion. His blue eyes darted back and forth from the footing below him to the house as he moved, firing both pistols casually in its direction as he ran. Narrow-legged shotgun chaps and leather cuffs brushed against rock and brush, making noises that seemed louder than they were. At least he had removed his spurs, he told himself. Puddles sprayed their annoyance at his passage as he stomped through them. He absorbed the gunfire from Checker and Jackson behind him without being conscious of it.

From the trees, Checker shouted, "Shanghai, have your boys spread out. Get those torches ready. We'll tear this mud hut apart with lead." His Winchester snapped a succession of quick shots from three different locations.

Jackson answered in a contrived harsh voice, "We're ready, by God. Let's take the goddamn bastards apart." He added his rifle to Checker's barrage, levering his Winchester as quickly as he could.

Sonny smiled. He'd never heard his friend swear before. Almost sounded like the big cattleman. He decided to compliment Jackson when they were together again. Certainly better than his attempt to imitate Star McCallister. Checker's loud growl and Jackson's guttural answer repeated themselves over and over again as the words raced in echo around the small land bowl.

Sonny slipped into a long crease in the middle lip of the hillside. A flint-rock formation curled up in front of him like the wall of a fort. A glance at the house produced no sign of movement. It bothered him. *Did it work? What's Star planning? Has he figured*

*how many we are? How long will it take for Tyrel to get
to the horses with the kids?* Questions rattled through
him, prodding his nerves.

Over his shoulders, the first true blush of a new
day was pushing its way into their world. A stringy
fog slipped into the clearing, wrapping thin ribbons
around trees and bushes. Sonny wished the light
would stay away. He never did like the dark—as
Checker did, he told himself—but now it was their
ally. At least the fog would complicate the gang's
viewing. Checker never had problems seeing at
night. He silently cursed himself for choosing not to
bring his Winchester. A rifle would be more effective
at this range.

Shrugging off the concern, he loaded his holstered
pistol and returned the still-smoking weapon to its
leather sheath, then loaded the emptied gun from his
belt. The butt of the guard's other pistol presented
itself from his waistband. With a wry grin, he
switched the weapon he'd just reloaded to his left
hand and drew the waistband gun. *Count us three
times, you bastards,* he growled. Breath-smoke agreed.
Like a man casually rolling a cigarette, he strafed the
soddy with gunfire from both Colts, keeping his
arms outstretched to give the impression of two men
shooting. It felt awkward and probably looked stupid, he thought, but it might work.

This time return gunfire eagerly sought his position, but he was safely behind the rock wall. He
crawled twenty feet to his right, avoiding a long
crease of rock filled with water, and fired his remaining pistol three times at the same window and
ducked down again. Reappearing five feet to his left,
he emptied it. Checker's following gunfire slashed

Cotton Smith

into the house from the tree line itself. Supporting bursts from a different location on the front crest told him Jackson had also moved. Bannon and the children were within the forest on the far side—or at least that's where Sonny hoped they were. He also hoped the farm boy wouldn't respond by shooting at the house, and he didn't.

He pushed up the leather bands on his upper arms to give himself the feeling of being ready. For the first time, he noticed how scratched the cuffs at his wrists had become. With a chuckle, he ejected spent shells, grabbed fresh cartridges from his pocket, and reloaded the three guns. After he finished, only eight bullets remained in his belt loops, another ten in his pockets. Moving to the right, he crouched and studied the soddy through a jagged hole in the rock frame. Checker and Jackson had stopped shooting—to reload, he presumed.

From the house came a voice uncomfortably familiar to Sonny. "Hey, Cole, that you? It's me, Tom. Told the boys ya'd be the one that'd find us. They didn't believe me." The last words echoed through the small clearing and nestled within the arriving fog.

Sonny couldn't see the broad-shouldered rustler but knew it was Tom Redmond. The guttural rhythm of the outlaw's voice struck into corners of Sonny's brain he didn't want reopened. A time when he cared about no one, only feeding an emptiness that was never satisfied.

When there was no answer, the outlaw called out again, "Come on, Cole, you an' the Ranger ain't got none o' Shanghai's boys backin' your play this time. Saw him 'n' his bunch leave while I was in that damn jail. Who's out there with you—that kid—an' that nigger? Who else? I don't know how ya found us, but ya didn't drag no posse with ya."

Silence followed as the land faintly replayed "no posse with ya" in an echo that tempted Sonny to fire at the closest window, just to be shooting at the words. On the roof, branches shifted and tiny beads of rainwater sparkled in the air for an instant before returning to the naturally built framework. A dark man's hatless head crested above the opening, disappeared momentarily, and then crawled onto it. He lay flat against the roof, not daring to move further. Morning light squeezed around a rifle barrel inching into position. None of the Triple C riders saw him settle behind the row of heavy branches at the soddy's edges.

Adjacent to the back side of the corral, four crouched figures emerged into the morning haze from a small trapdoor on the ground. Covered by a piece of sod lashed to the frame, the hidden entryway was a short tunnel under the soddy wall and into the main room. Star had insisted the gang build such an emergency getaway into every hideout, even where it was illogical anyone would ever find the place. Satisfied they were unseen, one ran for the trees and disappeared into their embracement, another slid unnoticed between the house wall and the medicine wagon, and two eased into the tree line and crept toward Checker.

A black long duster covered the tall man's shirtless chest, dark pants, and boots as he melted into the shadows of the forested belt next to the corral. A crimson sash was knotted at his waist and held a yellowish-handled, short-barreled Colt. Last night's bourbon lay thick on his tongue, heavy in his eyes, and his long hair was snarled from the sleeping that followed. In Dr. Gambree's right fist was a double-barreled shotgun.

He pushed his spectacles in place and observed the moody trees ahead, searching for Checker's position. Several strides behind him came another outlaw, also carrying a shotgun. Inside the soddy, he had proclaimed his desire to kill Checker by himself, but Star had assigned the wounded but eager Andrew Tiller to go with him and sent the mulatto killer, Joe Coffey, after Sonny, along with the black gunman Venner to the roof. Dr. Gambree hadn't protested much about the change. The only two remaining outlaws—Wells and Redmond—were to distract the Triple C riders, then kill Jackson. Neither of them could get through the small tunnel anyway. Star himself would ride away and wait for them at the Comanchero camp, where he had friends who would help them.

Redmond yelled again. This time his tone was friendly. "Cole, tell you what. Ya got them kids. That's what ya came for. Ya can have them hosses, too. Ride away, and we'll head south. How's that for a trade? Otherwise, we're gonna kill all of ya."

For a tantalizing moment, Sonny wished Bannon would fire a few shots as he passed through the tree line on the far side of the clearing. Gunfire from there might make the outlaws rethink their decision about how many men they were facing. But the moment passed quickly. Any action by Bannon would draw gunfire, and that would put the children in danger. Was Redmond bluffing? Or stalling for time? A wolf's deliberate call broke through the early-morning haze and interrupted his worry.

Suddenly, Checker's command tore into the morning shroud. "Either come out now—with your hands up—or die in that mud hole. Your choice. Make it quick." Echoes of his message raced around the land bowl.

Crouching low, Sonny moved to the left side of the crease and squinted through a narrow slit. A steady dripping from a rock lip on the other side distorted his view. The far tree line offered no hint of where Checker might be. Any shadow could be his. He smiled grimly. It was impossible to tell if Checker was in better control of himself than at the homestead, but from his actions it certainly looked like he was the same old Checker again. Sonny would know when he saw him up close.

In many ways, Sonny knew the two of them were alike. Probably that's why they had become good friends. Hard, lonely men who seemed to live from fight to fight, yet without seeking battle. Men who rarely let anyone actually see their feelings. Sonny hid his with an apparent carefree nature; Checker did it with controlled silence. Both approaches were honed reactions to what life had dealt them.

Without warning, he caught himself looking for Clanahan and Tex and gasped at the realization. He missed them greatly. They were friends, and he hadn't had too many of those in his life. Certainly not the bunch he ran with along the border. He breathed deeply, pushing the melancholy through his body and away, and realized he missed having little Rebecca nuzzled against his chest.

Amelia Hedrickson popped into Sonny's mind. He saw her again at the Triple C celebration at their homestead. He had been captivated by her gracious manner, simple beauty, and engaging mind. They had talked for some time that day, mostly about Checker. She had been warm and friendly, as she was to all the riders, he reminded himself. Several times their eyes had connected for an instant more than necessary.

Those tiny emotional exchanges had burned into his mind, like stored treasures to be taken out whenever he wanted and enjoyed all over again. To see her so badly mauled was almost more than his mind could take. He frowned to keep that image from entering and could only imagine Checker's anger. His mind bounced back to Amelia and saw her smile at him. She was the first woman he had found truly fascinating since his Mary died. Faceless whores and dance hall girls had come and gone, bringing only momentary physical satisfaction, but Amelia was so different. The realization hit him that he hadn't thought about Amelia's husband dying, and he felt ashamed about his imagined flirtation with her.

Giving up on glimpsing his friend, he studied a boulder lodged against the lower hill twenty feet away, looking for a new position to shoot from. Scrawny jackpine huddled around it, seeking permission to exist. Otherwise, there wasn't much cover. It wouldn't hide him well, he reluctantly decided, after the initial surprise. Worse, getting back to the relative security of the crease would be difficult at best. He took a deep breath and prepared to shoot again.

As the echo of Checker's words bounced past Sonny, Redmond answered, "Don't shoot. We're comin' out."

The front door opened and Tom Redmond stepped into its frame. He stopped, rubbed an old scab on the back of his right hand, and scanned the hillside. Seeing no one, he loudly addressed the gray rocks at the base of the hill, announcing that the gang had been badly shot up and would be slow coming out. As a punctuation to his statements, he stepped onto the porch, raising his hands above his head after he cleared the doorway.

Behind him came Iron-Head Ed Wells. The huge outlaw paused in the opened door, much as Redmond had before him, and made a comment about having patience and no one shooting. Using the two outlaws' talkative surrender as his cue, Dr. Gambree spat his defiance into the wet ground and crawled where other shadows encouraged his passage within the tree line. A toothy smile defined him—and indicated his pleasure at seeing Checker. The former Ranger was thirty feet away, focused on the soddy's door and the two outlaws stalling for their comrades to get into place. Without looking back, Dr. Gambree motioned for the outlaw to join him. Tiller's pinched face was pale. Wearing a bandolier of rifle bullets and a high-crowned hat, he gripped a Winchester as if he were wringing a chicken's neck. At his shoulder a bright red rosette had formed.

Dr. Gambree looked down at the twin hammers of his own weapon. Slowly, he pulled back each hammer, being careful not to let any cocking noise alert Checker. Earlier, he had advised Tiller not to move through the brush with a cocked gun because it might be easily tripped by the heavy underbrush. Now they were close and would soon finish the legendary lawman. *Farewell, O half brother mine*, Dr.

Gambree said in a singsong voice through clinched teeth. *How sweet it will be to tell Star how I took the life of the great John Checker. Star should be here to see this,* he thought to himself. *He'll never believe I killed John Checker by myself. He's scared silly of him. Thinks he looks like the old man—and we don't. Ha-ha-ha, I've killed a lot tougher men than John Checker. Just like this. They never saw it coming, and he won't either.* Dr. Gambree smiled and could already taste the whiskey that would flow to hear him repeat the grand story.

He was eager for the kill, and his dark eyes returned to the gray place where his intended victim stood. *Now, dear half brother, you die th—* His silent proclamation was cut short by the uneasiness in discovering that the famed Ranger wasn't there. Dr. Gambree listened for sounds of movement ahead of him, any movement. He heard nothing, not even the normal forest talk that a new morning should create. He saw nothing, only yellow leaves shivering from cold, autumn breezes looking for playmates. Groaning at the temporary setback, he decided Tiller should be encouraged to scout to their right. The medicine wagon doctor fought off an evil grin, knowing the command would sacrifice the gang member in order to determine where Checker had moved.

With his teeth clinched, Dr. Gambree glanced at where Tiller should be crouched ten feet or so behind him. The outlaw was standing twice that far away, his arms at his sides. From that distance, Dr. Gambree thought Tiller looked like he'd seen a ghost. Probably just the shadows playing tricks on his expression, the professional killer thought, and waved at Tiller to come forward. The scared outlaw nodded his head and began walking stiffly toward Dr. Gambree. Angry at the man's foolish approach, he mouthed "Get down," then realized Tiller wasn't carrying his rifle. *What the hell is the matter with that fool?* he muttered between clinched teeth, and breath-smoke ran with the curse.

As Dr. Gambree turned back to analyze where Checker might have gone, his mind caught something his eyes hadn't. A second shadow behind Tiller! Checker was behind the man. *My God! How did he get there?* Dr. Gambree returned his attention toward the advancing figure, now barely nine feet away.

"Drop the gun, Blue," Checker ordered, stepping from behind Tiller. His Winchester was aimed at Dr. Gambree's stomach.

Tiller murmured, "I'm sorry, Doc."

"It's good to see you, too, brother John," Dr. Gambree responded as calmly as if they were meeting on a street corner in Dodge. "I would've known you anywhere. You look like our dear old father."

"I said drop the shotgun, Blue. Now."

"Hell, you even sound like the old son of a bitch," Dr. Gambree said, and kneeled to lay the gun before him on the wet ground. "Not even a 'how have you been all these years' to your half brother. My, that's not very cordial. You certainly didn't learn that at home. Oh, I forgot—you didn't have a home. Just a whore's tent."

"Where's Star?"

"Him? Oh, that cowardly brother of ours ran away," Dr. Gambree answered. He lowered the gun to the ground as if presenting a grand gift, but his fingers were a fraction away from the twin triggers.

"He used to do that a lot when we were kids, remember?"

As the last word rolled off his tongue, Dr. Gambree smoothly spun the shotgun toward Checker and fired both barrels. An eye blink ahead, Checker dove behind the frozen Tiller. All of the blast caught Tiller, tearing into his right side and stomach and turning part of his face and neck instantly red. Tiller unleashed a dreadful scream that was more animal than man, and fell headfirst over a bush in front of him. A crimson circle spread on the mud around him.

Flying through the air, Checker returned the fire as he passed Tiller's twisting body. He levered the Winchester twice before he hit the ground. The first shot missed; the second drove deep into Dr. Gambree's stomach. Checker's younger half brother dropped the emptied shotgun; his knees buckled and forced him to a kneeling position. He stared down at the blood streaming from his naked stomach under his coat.

Checker rolled to his feet, levered a new bullet into his rifle, and announced, "Blue, you're going back to Dodge to stand trial for murder." "Gonna turn me into Rand?"

"Rand won't be there."

"Oh really. Who'd I murder?" Dr. Gambree said, his breath coming in stilted gasps and surrounding his face with layers of breath-smoke. He held his left hand against his stomach to hold it in.

"Tex Whitney and Harry Clanahan."

"Oh, those the two fools in the alley?"

Checker inhaled the callous response and stepped around the unmoving Tiller. The former Ranger didn't speak. Dr. Gambree studied his half brother, grimacing from wave after wave of nauseating pain pulsating through him. He was hit bad and knew it. The bullet had ripped through his insides. Feeling weakness spread through him, Dr. Gambree spat blood and his white teeth became reddish.

"Y-you don't really remember me, do you, C-Checker?" It was Dr. Gambree who spoke first. "I—I remember you in that silly-ass tent with your little sister and your whore of a m-mother."

Both hands now pressed against his stomach to contain the agony. His right hand brushed against the yellow-handled Colt lurking in his sash. He grimaced, took a deep, uneven breath cut short by a fearsome jolt of pain, and added, "A—A long way from c-coming out between a whore's legs to a Texas Ranger badge, isn't it, b-brother?"

"Oh, I remember. I remember a snotty little kid who tried to sneak up and poke my eyes out," Checker coolly answered the first question, ignoring the second. "Looks like you haven't changed much."

Behind him came a groan, and Checker swung to meet the new threat. Tiller's face was a red mask, and in his quivering hands was his retrieved Winchester. Checker's rifle spat orange flame three times. Tiller stood erect for a moment as if an unseen giant hand had straightened his body, then doubled over, took a half-step to the right, and fell headfirst into the mud. His Winchester exploded in midair, tearing into the tree leaves directly above.

"N-now, you drop the gun, Ranger." Dr. Gambree's voice was thin but victorious. "Then turn around real slow. I—I want to watch your eyes when I kill you. The last thing you're going to know is me pissing on your face, Checker. N-now drop it and turn around!"

Without a word, Checker threw the Winchester hard toward underbrush five feet away, using only his left hand. At the same time, he drew the holstered, short-barreled Colt with his right and fired at Dr. Gambree without turning, looking at him only as the pistol unleashed its fury. Caught off guard, Dr. Gambree's attention had enjoyably been on the flight of the rifle. Dr. Gambree's too-hurried bullet whistled past the former Ranger's ear as Checker's lead lifted and shoved Star McCallister's younger brother backward. He sprawled against matted brush and weeds, releasing rain diamonds into the air. Checker watched him struggle to get up.

"Blue, it doesn't have to be this way," Checker pleaded. "Drop the gun. Please, drop the gun."

Trembling, Dr. Gambree held the pistol in his right fist and pulled back the hammer with his left. His eyes were blurring and not helping him concentrate. His hands and arms were weak and uncooperative. He couldn't understand why they wouldn't do what his mind ordered. Under his coat, his bare chest now carried two blood flowers flowing crimson down to join the earlier stomach wound. He swung the pistol toward Checker and screamed, "S-Star w-will be impressed t-that I k-killed—"

Checker fired again, and the shot snapped Dr. Gambree backward into the mud with his legs coiled beneath him. Dr. Gambree's gun dropped, nose first, into the mud. The jolt dislodged the hammer and sent a bullet into the soil, forcing the gun back into the air and finally plopping on the ground like a fish from a stream.

With swift strides, Checker rushed to the dying Dr. Gambree and stood over him. Checker's face was twisted with an agony few would understand.

"Y-you going after S-Star?" Dr. Gambree asked. His eyes wouldn't focus on Checker; his breath would come only rarely, leaving only wisps of breath-smoke when it did.

"I have to. He's got to pay for what he's done."

"Y-yeah, h-heard they t-tore up your sis real . . . b-bad. S-sorry, s-she was r-real nice. . . ." Dr. Gambree's eyes closed, and Checker thought he was dead, but they fluttered open and he said, "I—I d-didn't think you were t-this good. S-Star was r-right. Y-you are l-like the o-old man, aren't you?" He swallowed, but blood rushed from his mouth and he whispered, "H-how did you get behind me?"

Checker didn't answer for a moment, then he said, "I am brother to the wolf. He would not let you hear me." Checker held up the pebble tied around his left wrist.

Squinting to try to bring him into focus, Dr. Gambree stared at Checker, then at the small stone, without comprehending. His hand reached out for the pistol lying beside him, touched it, and gave a last gravelly ultimatum. "P-Pa . . . I—I t-told you . . . not t-to hit M-Mother." He gasped no more.

"An old friend told me if I didn't quit fighting my father, I would become him," Checker said, and turned toward the clearing. "Too bad you didn't. It's not a long way from a having terrible father to dying in the mud, is it, little brother?"

Chapter Sixteen

Reacting to the gunfire in the trees, O. F. Venner rose to his knees on the roof, in rhythm to its roar. With his rifle pointed toward Sonny's rock ledge, he noticed too late a shadow at the corner of the hillside.

A syrupy command followed like an invitation: "You'd best stop and throw down your rifle." The black outlaw almost fell off the roof in his hasty efforts to comply, threw his rifle toward the ground, and raised his hands.

"Good choice," Jackson said. "Now jump down."

Venner stared at the ground and finally said, "I be colored, too, can't ya see? Got meself all busted up by a he-bull. A while back, it were." He paused to let his implied plea settle in. "I-it's a long way down there."

Jackson fired his rifle, splitting a soggy branch next to Venner, and said calmly, "Longer with my bullet."

The black outlaw immediately swung over the side and sprawled himself awkwardly in the mud; a stiff leg pushed him off balance and onto his side. Jackson levered a fresh load into his Winchester and ordered the two surrendered outlaws to get rid of their hidden weapons. Surprised at his attentiveness, Tom Redmond immediately removed the pistol from his back waistband and flung it in Jackson's direction. Venner stood, drenched with mud, professed not to have any other guns, and turned slowly around in place to prove his point, limping as he did.

Triumphantly, the massive Ed Wells declared, "There's only two of you now, nigger. That blastin' was the end of the damn Ranger."

"If so, where's that put you? I'm his friend," Jackson replied, and fired at the man's feet, spitting mud on his pants.

Wells jumped back and reached halfway toward his hidden pistol.

"You're trying my patience," Jackson said, levering the Winchester again. "Bring that gun out with only your fingers touching the butt. Any other way and I'll drop you."

At the corner of the soddy, Joe Coffey also heard the gunfire and smiled. John Checker was dead. Now it was his turn to kill. He cut a slice of a fresh tobbaco plug and jabbed it into his mouth. With a push of his tongue, the brown quid nestled inside his cheek. Confident Sonny wasn't looking at him, he returned the plug to his shirt pocket and curled around the back side of the wagon. In seconds, he blended into the hillside itself, stopping behind a struggling oak tree. He had agreed with Star and

Redmond that they faced only three men.

Coffey studied the rock ledge twenty yards away before moving again. A dark hat with a hawk feather in its band lay on his back, held at his neck by the stampede string. In the mulatto's hands was a long-barreled Smith & Wesson revolver. Dangling from his left wrist was the quirt. As much as Star's brother, Coffey liked to kill, and it showed in his sneering smile as he spat a long stream of light brown juice. Dissatisfied with its color, he chewed the tobacco vigorously and spat again. This time it looked right and he resumed his quest.

After two more careful relocations, each placing him ever higher, he was finally above Sonny's rock wall. Sonny's back was to him and only ten yards away. Coffey smiled and knelt. He sighted his pistol, cradling it with his left hand as his right held it. He cocked the gun and was surprised at the loudness. Disturbed by the sound of the shotgun in the tree line, Sonny spun at the noise behind him and fired with both guns at the same time as Coffey's first bullet ripped across his hip.

Sonny's shots drove the mulatto gunman awkwardly against a boulder. Coffey smiled at Sonny, spat a fat stream of tobacco juice, and fired his own pistol again. Sonny jerked from the impact in his right arm, and the gun sprang from his right hand and skittered across the rock shelf. In response, he emptied the gun in his left hand into the staggering outlaw.

Frantically trying to regain his balance by leaning his left arm against the rock, Coffey tried to cock his pistol, but his fingers trembled and his thumb wouldn't do what his mind asked. His chest was a crimson mass. Stretched out on the rock platform, Sonny crawled toward the pistol that had been ripped from his right hand. Blood running from the corner of his mouth, Joe Coffey stumbled forward and rolled down the hill. His head lay awkwardly propped against the rear wheel; his limp legs, twisted under him. His right leg spasmed in the mud and was still.

Pain sprung through Sonny like a swollen spring creek. He breathed deeply again, then again. *I've been hit before*, he reminded himself. *They're a long way from my heart*, he thought and tried to chuckle, steeling himself for the coming impact of shock and loss of blood. The wounds were bleeding steadily and he was becoming woozy in relation to the loss. Shock tugged at his courage and made him want to rest a little. He tried to move, and his wounds screamed at his brain to stay still. He fought back the agony.

Think. Think. Checker is down. They tried to set us up. How many are left? Dizziness came and went as he moved too fast. He sat quiet again, pushing his numbed right hand against his side to stop the bleeding. Awkwardly, he loaded the spent pistols with his left hand, pushing them, one at a time, against his knee for leverage. New cartridges and empty shells became lively things in his shaking hand. A shiny cartridge jumped from his fingers and rolled across the rocky crease, plopping in a tiny circle of rain water. Another bullet followed seconds later, bouncing toward the same puddle but ending its journey inches away.

Finally, he managed to fill both revolvers. He tried to hold one in his right hand, but it wouldn't respond and slid from his frozen fingers to the rock floor. Wincing, he returned the gun to his holster with his left hand, placing it backward in the leather sheath so he could retrieve the weapon with his left hand. The remaining gun settled comfortably in his left fist, and he slowly cocked the hammer. He forced himself to crawl to the small opening in the wall and saw Jackson directing the surrendered outlaw to lie down. *Where was Checker?* Sonny sat quietly, not daring to look at his wounds. He could feel the wetness but not the pain. Not yet.

Lines of blood seeped through his cuff and along the back of his right hand, which lay numb on his thigh, forcing the blood to find its own way off his fingers. Water in a shallow rock spoon beside him took on a pinkish tinge. His side was bleeding heavily, too. He stared at the pistol on the ground without understanding, then slowly squeezed his right hand until it made a weak fist. A hole in his vest pocket caught his muddled attention.

Through the fragmented tear poked the end of a piggin string and a piece of rock candy. He pushed them back inside and became aware his stomach was sore underneath the pocket. He reached in with his good hand and withdrew his heavy watch. Its dull silver lid was smashed in with a deep crease that nearly broke through the metal. He studied the timepiece in his hand, not understanding the dent's significance.

A push on the stem should have released the lid but didn't. He squeezed it hard between the thumb and palm of his hand and the lid reluctantly sprang open. Inside the lid's face, a faded likeness of a young woman stared back at him from eternity. Her cheek was torn away by the severity of the indentation. A spidery crack flooded the glass protecting the watch face. Both hands were locked at 5:21, but he saw only the photograph. It slowly came to him that the watch had deflected a bullet headed for his stomach and death.

Mary, they should have been our kids, he muttered, closed the lid, and returned the watch to his pocket. He smiled, then wondered where Bannon and the kids were. Were they safe? His wounds jerked at his memory, bringing gaps in his judgment. Were they his children? He tried to recall what had happened to them, but the fog in the valley had entered his head.

"Sonny, are you all right?" Checker yelled as he stepped into the clearing in front of the soddy. His voice carried a concern missing from his earlier command.

It was the first indication that Checker was alive since the forest gunfire. A wide-brimmed hat pulled low on Checker's forehead allowed tired eyes to penetrate the morning haze as he assessed the front of the soddy. Long black hair touched the shoulders of his Comanche tunic. His face couldn't hide the bubbling tension within him. The three outlaws in front of the soddy trembled at his voice, like it was a ghost speaking. Jackson smiled, nodded, and motioned with his gun for the roof-shooting Venner to move next to the other two. He complied with an urgent skipping with one leg, dragging the stiffened other limb, and spraying mud on Wells as he stopped next to him. Venner either ignored or didn't see the big rustler's snarling response to being splattered.

"Just a couple of nicks. How are you? Is Jackson

safe?" Sonny replied, forcing himself to yell and
hedging on the severity of his wounds. "There's a
fella with buckskin leggings dead by the medicine
wagon. I think it's that little bastard Joe Coffey." His
head spun and he vomited, then gulped the morning
air as fast as he could, refinding strength with the
new breath.

The surrendered outlaws were stunned again.
Redmond said more loudly than intended, "Sonny
took Joe Coffey? Damn, I knew he was good." Wells
glanced at him and shook his head in disgust.

"Mornin', Jackson. You all right?" Checker said
offhandedly as he walked toward the three outlaws.
His hands were empty, the Winchester forgotten for
the moment. Jackson returned the greeting, assuring
him that he wasn't wounded.

"Tell the others to get out here. Fast," Checker
snapped.

"Hell, man, this here's all thar be on this side of
the Pearly Gates! You be a-killin' the rest," Redmond
blurted, then glanced at Wells for approval.

"Ain't nobody else breathin' in thar, Ranger. Star's
long gone," Wells added, and smiled wickedly. "He
done went through that hole next to the corral. Got
us a trapdoor thar. Real slick-like. Had him a hoss
strung up on the other side o' them trees. Does it
ever' time we bin hyar. Hell, by now, he's halfway
to Texas."

"Yeah, an' the poor doc—an' Joe—an' Tiller, they
used the same hole," Redmond added. "Only, they
didn't go so far, I reckon."

Ignoring the comments, Checker roared into the
dark soddy. "Star, this is Checker. If I come in, you
won't come out. Your call."

Wailing loudly, Salome burst from the front door and past Checker with only a blanket wrapped around her. Within four steps, her bare feet were caked with mud as she ran into the trees to find Dr. Gambree. Checker told Jackson to watch the outlaws while he went inside. As soon as he disappeared into the dark house, the huge Ed Wells dared Jackson to search him. He held up two massive fists in front of him. Hamlike fists were layered with white scars from previous battles. His arms were as thick as his shoulders were wide. Jackson's only response was to point his rifle at Wells's chest.

Redmond called to Sonny over his shoulder. "Sonny, how bad are you hurt? Sonny?"

"Hey, Cole, did the half-breed put lead in ya?" Wells bellowed toward the ridge where Sonny sat. His snarl produced a mouth of missing or yellowed teeth. "How 'bout it, Cole? Did he? Hurts somethin' fierce, don't it?"

Jackson's eyes became flint, and his words were as hard. "I wouldn't be smiling. Looks to me like Star left you boys behind—to hang."

Redmond glared back, taking a half-step toward Jackson. The black cowboy said in his easy way, "Come ahead."

"Hell, thar's only one o' you, nigger."

"Make that two niggers, Tom. Him 'n' me. But Jackson can handle you in your sleep."

The voice was Sonny's. Holding his right arm close to his chest to ease the throbbing, he was working his way down the hill. His boot heels dug into the soggy earth to alter his direction in a zigzag descent, picking his way over rocks, around chunks of flat slate, and between shaggy bushes. Dizziness caught him halfway down, and he went to his knees. He squatted on the hillside for a minute to regain his balance. Standing slowly, he gave up trying to keep an eye on the surrendered gang and concentrated on his descent. Breath was as jagged as his direction, but the downhill momentum carried him beyond the pain and the light-headedness.

Sonny started toward the big outlaw when Checker reappeared from around the corral. He reported to his friends that a small tunnel went under the soddy wall and opened along the back of the corral. He grimaced when he said the door was hidden, covered with grass and dirt. Both Jackson and Sonny instinctively looked in that direction as if they could see around the soddy to the tunnel opening.

"Hey, Ranger, how come you're lettin' a wanted killer like Cole Dillon ride with you?" Wells snarled, glancing at Sonny, then at Redmond, who nodded agreement.

After propping his rifle against the soddy wall, Checker headed straight toward the belligerent outlaw. "I don't know any Cole Dillon."

"Come on, Checker, he's right thar."

"Don't be a fool. I've known Sonny Jones all my life," Checker said in a low, hard voice. "Where was Star headed?"

"Headin' for a big Comanchero camp south o' hyar. We was to meet him thar soon as we took care of you three. Nobody believed Shanghai were with ya," Wells answered. His sneer worked its way to the left side of his face.

Eagerly, Redmond reinforced the news. "On the other side of them trees, he had a long-legged bay mare. Always kept a saddled hoss there when he was here. Did it at every hideout. Iron-Head's speakin' the truth, Ranger."

"Ha-ha-ha! He outsmarted you again, Checker. He said you were his bastard. . . ."

Iron-Head Ed Wells's words were cut off by Checker's driving blow into the bigger man's stomach. Wells wasn't expecting it; he thought Checker was going to talk, intimidated by his sheer size, like most men. The huge man had won many fistfights simply because his smaller opponents were scared that they couldn't defend themselves well. He bent over to hold in the screeching pain. The careful Jackson ordered the other two outlaws to lie down on the ground with their hands and legs spread. His Winchester swept from one to the other as they complied. Sonny guarded them from the other side, brandishing a pistol in his left hand.

Jackson saw Sonny keep his right arm to his side and saw the dark stains on his shirt and pants. He frowned, knowing now was not the time to help him. He wasn't worried about Checker. Actually, he felt sorry for the outlaw. There was no way the big man could have known the fury he was facing. Jackson admitted to himself that he expected Checker to kill the outlaw, if no one stopped him.

Following his initial punch, Checker slammed a knee into Wells's lowered face, pushing down with both hands on the back of his head at the same time. Bones crackled. Wells's arms flailed away from his body; his head swung backward, showing a face covered in blood. He wobbled and threw an off-balance, roundhouse punch at Checker's head. Checker deflected the blow with his left arm; his countering right jab to the bigger man's face popped open a long gash on his cheek. Blood spewed on both men. Checker followed with a left uppercut, snapping the outlaw's chin like it was on a hinge. The two remaining gang members were mesmerized by the violence.

Checker's face was hot fury as he grabbed the outlaw by the shirt so he couldn't fall and hit him again in the stomach. Checker was four inches shorter and thirty pounds lighter but fought with a savage violence the outlaw had never seen before. All his pent-up anger and frustration exploded through the former Ranger's fists. Hatred for his half brothers and his evil father leaped from his soul, eager to destroy. Checker's right fist drove into the man's crimson face, and the crunch of a broken bone could be heard by everyone standing there. A tooth flew into the air and bounced on the ground, followed by Checker's medicine pebble flying from his wrist. Jackson took two steps to the right and retrieved it, taking his eyes off the two outlaws only for an instant.

Completely helpless, the outlaw staggered backward, out on his feet. Checker swarmed after him, slamming punch after punch into his battered frame, holding up the outlaw with his other hand. Finally Checker let the unconscious man fall. He stood over the unmoving body, unaware of his own bloody fists. A lack of air tore at his chest. He gasped again and again to bring what he needed into his body. He looked down at the fallen outlaw and started to grab him again.

"John, he's done. Amelia wouldn't want it this way, John." Sonny heard himself saying the words and didn't believe they had come from his own mouth.

Checker spun toward him, seeking trouble. A deep frown took over his face as he recognized his friend. "Cole, don't tell me wha—"

Checker rubbed his hands together and looked at Sonny, his rage barely under control. Without waiting for a response, Checker charged toward the other prone outlaws and roared, "Which one of you dragged my sister? Tell me now—or I'll kill every one of you sons of bitches with my bare hands."

His eyes were slits of fire. Even Sonny stepped backward from the intensity of Checker's hate. Sonny's voice was thin but urgent. "John, you're a lawman."

Checker turned toward Sonny and said angrily, "I'm not a Ranger anymore, Cole. They took Amelia's children and burned her home. They killed our friends. They killed Orville. They may have killed . . . my, ah . . ." He couldn't finish the sentence, but added, "I—I want every one of these miserable excuses for men to know what hell is. Me."

Sonny ignored Checker's use of his real name and hitched his shoulders to drive away the shiver that followed. Checker strode wildly to Redmond lying on the ground and grabbed him by the hair. The ex-Confederate shook his head feebly and reached for Checker's tightened grip. Checker slammed his left fist into Redmond's arm, driving it away.

The tall former Ranger spat his intention: "I'm going to drag you until there's nothing left but a whimper, you son of a bitch, then I'm gonna hang you." Checker looked up, saw Jackson, and growled, "Get me a horse, Jackson—and a rope."

"No."

"What do you mean 'no'?" Checker's glare tore through his friend.

It was a wobbly Sonny who finally broke into Checker's temporary madness. He stepped toward him, speaking slowly, hesitantly.

"John . . . we've got to . . . take them back . . . ah, to Dodge. If we don't . . . John . . . we're no better than Kayler and his bunch . . . that wanted to lynch 'em. Remember when . . . you said it was . . . the law's job, not ours?"

Checker was surprised at the suggestion. He stared at Jackson, then at Sonny, as if trying to comprehend the idea. Slowly, his fist opened and released Redmond's hair; the man's head thumped on the ground. Not waiting for any argument from Checker, Sonny looked at Jackson and yelled, "Jackson, we're riding out of here now. We're taking these men back to let the law deal with them."

Jackson nodded affirmation, glanced at Checker, and asked, "Are we burying the dead first?"

"They can," Sonny said, pointing at Venner and Redmond.

He shook his head positively, and the motion made him dizzy. He knelt to regain his balance. One glance told him he was bleeding heavily where the bullet had sliced a trench across his hip. He tried to push his fingers on the wound to stem the blood but couldn't move his right arm. Hoping it didn't appear awkward, he pressed his left fist holding the pistol on the bleeding area. He breathed slowly to steady himself. It wouldn't help anything if the outlaws realized he was weakened.

He blinked to make the dizziness go away, stared

at Checker talking, but heard nothing. From somewhere, the soft image of a woman he had loved and left appeared. She held out her arms to him. He started to speak to her, but his mouth opened and closed without a sound. She wrapped her arms around his neck and kissed him. He swayed and toppled over on his knees, then collapsed completely. His pale face slapped against the hard earth.

Checker was the first at Sonny's side. He held Sonny's head and tried to get him to come around. "Sonny. Sonny, come on, boy. Come on," Checker said, patting Sonny's pale face.

"Some colored fellows I know would give plenty to be where I am right now. Ready to shoot a bunch of white men who killed their friends," Jackson said matter-of-factly, his Winchester aimed directly at Redmond, who swore. Venner stared at his muddy boots, then looked up and mouthed "I won't do nothin'."

Gradually Sonny regained consciousness, looked into Checker's face, and asked him, "I-is Mary safe? I—I told her I was c-coming back."

Checker recognized the name from long ago and said, "Easy now, Sonny, easy. Mary's safe. You rest."

Comforted, Sonny shut his eyes for a moment, then blinked them open again as he asked, "J-John? W-would it be all right if I—I stayed in Dodge . . . t-to help you . . . r-rebuild their h-home?"

"I was counting on it," Checker said.

"Y-you think y-your . . . A-Amelia . . . would . . . m-mind?"

Checker studied the pale face of his tough friend, smiled, and said, "I'm sure she wouldn't. Besides, Rebecca wouldn't let you go anyway."

"S-she's mighty . . . J-John, I'm going to sleep now. For a few minutes."

"You do that, my good friend."

From his guard position, Jackson asked, "How is he?"

"He's lost a lot of blood. Real hot, burning up. I thought you said he wasn't hurt bad."

"You know I didn't say that. Sonny said that."

"He's going to need your help. I'll guard these bastards. Maybe one of them will give me an excuse."

Suddenly, Salome appeared at the corner of the soddy. With one hand she held a blanket around her; with the other, she held Dr. Gambree's cocked revolver. Neither Checker nor Jackson moved. Redmond yelled, "By God, you bitch, shoot! Shoot them!"

The click of the hammer on an empty cartridge was the next sound. Then another. Jackson walked over to her and took the gun away. She dropped her arm to her side and her chin sank to her chest.

"Better get some clothes on, ma'am, it's cold out here," he said gently. With that, she let go of the blanket and strutted into the soddy. Each man stared at her proud, bouncing bosom as she passed. Checker told Jackson to follow her and make certain she didn't find another weapon inside. The black cowboy held out his hand and showed the medicine pebble to Checker.

"You keep it, Jackson. It'll bring you good luck."

Jackson smiled and put the pebble in his pocket.

An hour later, a band of riders on saddled outlaw horses left the forested trail and reentered the prairie. In front of them were thirty loose horses, pranc-

ing and nipping at each other to determine rightful
leadership. Tiny worlds of mud spun in and around
long legs and swishing tails. Trailing the herd were
four heavily tied outlaws. All were barefooted—
boots and socks left behind to make it more difficult
to escape. A wobbly Wells was lashed to his saddle
to keep him on, as was the coldcocked trail guard.

Then came Checker. Alongside him rode a stoic
Salome, her face streaked with unwashed tear stains.
Behind them came the steady Jackson, driving the
medicine wagon with the two steers resisting lead
ropes at its rear. His old pipe swirled fresh smoke
about his dark face and worn hat. Across his lap was
a Winchester. In the bed of the wagon lay Sonny
Jones, covered by warm blankets. Jackson had
tended to the feverish gunfighter, cleaning his
wounds and dressing them as best he could with
torn strips of Sonny's shirttail. Checker had taken
Jackson's recommendation and placed Sonny inside
the medicine wagon so he could rest while they
moved toward Dodge, instead of waiting for him to
be strong enough to ride. West of the soddy, a mass
grave had been dug by the outlaws to hold their
dead companions, then a separate one for Dr. Gambree at Checker's order.

The day was releasing control to the shadows as
they came to the Triple C rock ledge camp. Bannon
stepped from behind the rocks, gripping his Winchester. He said something and the two children appeared beside him. Checker squinted and tried to
make out their small faces. Something inside swelled
and wanted out. His shoulders rose and fell, and his
breath quickened.

Bannon's face was showered with relief and he

was eager to talk. He started to speak, saw Salome and halted, took off his hat, and said politely, "Good day to you, ma'am."

She stared at him and spat. He jumped back, although she was twenty feet away. Redmond laughed and said, "Be careful, boy. She's a spitfire."

Red-faced, Bannon turned to Checker and said, "Star McCallister rode by hyar. Nigh on to three hours back, it were. We'd just set ourself down to eat. He were ridin' a long-legged red hoss. Good-lookin' hoss, looked like she could run fer a long day. He 'peared a mite flustered, I reckon. Ya know'd, he's got eyes that kinda flip-flop like butterfly wings or somethin'."

Checker tried to hide his annoyance at the unimportant details. It was Jackson who broke into the recitation. "Tyrel, what happened, boy?"

"Ah, oh yeah. He didn't see us at first, flat out layin' the spurs to this hoss, not that she needed it. I reckon she could run—well, maybe not as fast as your black, John, but . . ."

"Tyrel, what happened?" It was Checker this time.

Slightly annoyed at the interruption, Bannon continued nevertheless. "I laid this hyar Winchester at 'im an' tolt him to stop."

"He done so—but I didn't see he'd got himself a fancy pistol 'til he done showed it to me. Well, sir, that be what we call a Mexican standoff down home. So he ups an' tells me that yo-all are dead an' I should ride on to Dodge—an' he'd go on hisself. I tolt him that I didn't reckon my friends were dead, that I figgered they could be handlin' 'bout anythin'."

Bannon licked his lips, glanced at Salome who was

examining something on her dress, and continued, "This hyar Star, his eyes started to flyin' around, like he can't do nothin' with them. Then he nods an' agrees—and says he was ridin' on. I jes' couldn't shoot 'im in the back. Ain't never shot nobody a'fer. Not even no Injun. Didn't think I could face Ma if'n I shot 'im in the back."

"That was fine, Tyrel," Jackson replied.

"Oh yeah, a'fer he galloped off, he tolt me if'n yo-all did come back, to tell ya somethin', John."

"What was that?"

"He done said to tell you that he were sorry 'bout your sis, didn't figger on that—an' he weren't gonna hurt these kids. Just funnin' with ya. Then he tolt me to tell you to let him go. He wouldn't be botherin' ya no more."

Bannon couldn't hold back the question. "We goin' after 'im?"

"Not now, Tyrel. We're going back to Dodge. Sonny's been hit pretty bad—and we've got these boys in need of a jail. We'll do that first," Checker said, paused, and finished, "Then me an' an old wolf friend of mine will go after him."

The farm boy wasn't sure what he meant, but Jackson nodded and told him to gather their gear. Bannon packed everything quickly on a buckskin that Jackson thought would accept the load. Redmond asked Jackson how Sonny was doing, and he told the outlaw that he was sleeping and would be all right, just weak. The black cowboy thought the ex-Confederate wanted to say something more, but he glanced at the unconscious Wells and was silent again.

Minutes later, Checker helped Johnny onto his

own black horse while he cradled Rebecca in his left arm. Checker's smile was warm; crow's-feet widened at the edges of his tired eyes. Bannon and Jackson held the horse herd back to give them time alone. The outlaws sat unmoving.

Checker brushed off Rebecca's wrinkled, pale blue dress, as if a few swipes would remove the destruction of the trail and fire. She looked down and back to his tanned face.

"Momma will be angry at me for getting dirty."

Checker blinked back the emotion that rammed itself against his mind and stuttered, "S-She'll be very happy to see you. I—I think she'll understand." He quickly changed the subject. "Did you get something to eat?"

She smiled and said that Bannon had cooked them breakfast but she was still hungry. From his saddlebags, Checker pulled a sack of biscuits and two apples. He gave a biscuit to each child, kept one for himself, then tossed the sack to Jackson.

"Sometimes, we get honey on them. Do you have any honey, Uncle John?" Rebecca asked.

"No, sweetheart, I don't," Checker said with a lop-sided grin. "Tonight, we'll have a good hot meal, though, and camp by a pretty stream—how's that? You'll like Jackson's cooking. Do you like apples?"

"Oh yes, apples are good too."

"Well, I've got a bright red one for you," he said, and showed her the fruit, which she grabbed with both tiny hands. "I've got something else, too." He retrieved the rolled blue ribbon from his pocket. "We'll tie this in your hair for the trip back."

"Oh, it's beautiful, Uncle John!"

He put her down, then fumbled with the ribbon

for a few minutes before Jackson came over to help. Without being asked, Bannon watched the outlaws and pretended to ignore Salome. The outlaw Redmond leaned against his saddle. "Boy, ya figger you could down all four o' us if'n we was to git away ri't 'bout now."

Bannon carefully considered the question, glanced at the new Winchester in his hands, and answered, "Prob'ly I'd . . . Well, let's see. I'd get you first. Best I put two in you, real quick-like. 'Round your heart, I reckon. Then, well, I'd be a fool not to be a-goin' fer that big fellar thar, even though he's not lookin' real pert. Mighty easy target runnin' any which way, though. 'Course, he's a-carryin' a lot o' paddin' in his belly, so's I'd best aim fer his head. Seems to me that'd be the smartest thing. Yessir, the head. The other two? Well, let's see . . . prob'ly I'd . . ."

"Forget it, boy." Redmond choked on his words.

Bannon started again. His face was serious, like that of a child reporting to a teacher. " 'Course, John and Jackson would up 'n' be a-firin' by then, I reckon. So's you'd have to figger on them downin'—"

"I said that was enough."

"Sure 'nuff. Anytime you got a question, jes' ask."

When Jackson finished tying the ribbon on a lock of her hair, Rebecca beamed and asked the black cowboy if he had a mirror. He didn't have one but said she would be able to see herself in a stream when they camped. That was enough to change her little pout into a bright smile.

Turning to Johnny, Checker gave him an apple and a biscuit. The boy eagerly accepted both, smiling as he took a large bite of the apple, then shoved part of a biscuit into his mouth at the same time.

"Oh, I almost forgot," Checker said, unbuckled his gunbelt and removed the beaded knife and sheath, then rebuckled it. "Here you go."

He handed the weapon to Johnny, who examined it like he'd been given a box of gold. "Is this really for me?" he exclaimed.

"Yes, you are brave—like a young Comanche warrior—and you should wear what he wears." The boy was scrambling to loosen his own belt and put the sheath in its proper place.

"It's your job to keep it sharp," Checker said, and put his hand on the boy's shoulder. "And use it carefully. It's a man's tool, not a boy's toy."

"I'm the man of our house now, Uncle John."

"Y-yes, you are, Johnny—and a fine one."

Minutes later, they were riding northeast toward the prairie and, ultimately, Dodge. Johnny rode beside Checker, who held Rebecca in front of him. The small boy measured his uncle's every movement and held his reins where Checker did. At the boy's waist, on his belt, was Checker's sheathed knife. He patted it constantly to reassure himself it was still there. The former Ranger's manner softened with their closeness.

He held a canteen to help Rebecca drink, then gave her a small piece of jerky to chew on, explaining she should chew it carefully. He gave another to Johnny. Rebecca advised him that her mother always told them to do that. Bannon rode beside the wagon, occasionally staring at Salome, who was with the four outlaws. Once, she looked back and smiled warmly.

An eerie silence rode with the strung-out band, stealing away words and pushing them inside each man, Triple C rider and outlaw alike. But the chatter of the children brought music to the quiet tension. Rebecca kept a stream of questions going, including asking Checker to sing. After his halting rendition of "The Old Chisholm Trail," she didn't ask again. He couldn't remember any verses that weren't risqué, and making up new ones hadn't come easily to him. Johnny, on the other hand, jabbered about the McCallister gang. He described Star McCallister thoroughly and said the man scared him.

The tall Ranger listened and probed gently to assure himself the children hadn't been harmed. Johnny was certain the unconscious Wells had intended to hurt them but Star wouldn't let him. Checker swelled with anger. A long inhalation slowed its momentum, and he released some of the emotion with the exiting breath.

"Will Momma die?" Johnny asked, tears welling in his eyes.

Checker stared at him and answered gently, "Your mother is strong—like Sonny. I think she'll live—and seeing you two will be the perfect medicine."

Rebecca frowned and began to whimper. "W-where is Mommy and Daddy? I—I want to go h-home."

Johnny studied his little sister for a moment, glanced at Checker, and said, "Becky, you quit that. Uncle John will think you're mad at him."

"Well, now, that's all right," Checker said, unsure of what to do. "Say, Johnny, how'd you like that black?" He patted the neck of the long-legged horse, hoping it would divert attention from the sadness.

"He's a good'un. My pa'd like him too," Johnny

said, and tears came. He couldn't help it; they just exploded down his face.

"Damn," Checker exclaimed, and reached over to put his hand on the boy's shoulder.

Rebecca looked up at Checker and said, "You shouldn't say that word. Momma wouldn't like it."

Without looking at her, Checker said, "I'm sure she wouldn't. Don't tell her, will you?"

"Oh, it's a secret, Uncle John. I like secrets."

Sitting on the saddle in front of him, Rebecca examined his battered, swollen hands and asked about them. For an instant, he wasn't certain how they had become so bruised. Then a cruel satisfaction crossed his face. He told her it happened going through some thorny bushes. She launched into a long story about gettin' into a bush outside their house and asked if they were going home to see her mother and father. Checker tried to think of something to say when Johnny interrupted with a question of his own.

"Uncle John?" Johnny asked, tearing off another chunk of his jerky with his teeth. "One time I heard him say you were his brother—and Mom was his sister. Is that true?"

"Him" was Star McCallister. Air hissed through Checker's clinched teeth. Chewing enthusiastically, Johnny searched the Ranger's taut face for an answer.

"No, he's not, Johnny," Checker said, his words carrying a sadness within them. "He must've been kidding."

"I don't think so, Uncle John." Tiny flecks of spitum fled from his small mouth as he spoke. The black horse turned its ears toward him to assess their meaning. Johnny glanced at the ears and patted its neck.

"Well, he's gone now," Checker answered, and changed the subject. "How do you like that knife?"

Johnny grinned widely and patted the sheath. Checker glanced down at Rebecca. She was asleep, leaning against him as they rode; her small hands lay across his left arm holding her in place. From a mournful place as much in his mind as in the rolling hills around them, he heard the faint cry of a wolf. He smiled and whispered, "Thank you, my brother." Then he added, "Amelia, your kids are safe—and we're coming home."

He saw his sister smile and then turn into the little girl he remembered so well from long ago. Gradually, her face became Sarah Ann's. It seemed like a different lifetime when they were together. His mind went there, to her kiss.

Behold a Red Horse

Cotton Smith

After the Civil War, Ethan Kerry carved out the Bar K cattle spread with little more than hard work and fierce courage—and the help of his younger, slow-witted brother, Luther. But now the Bar K is in serious trouble. Ethan's loan was called in and the only way he can save the spread is if he can drive a herd from central Texas to Kansas. Ethan will need more than Luther's help this time—because Ethan has been struck blind by a kick from an untamed horse. His one slim hope has come from a most unlikely source—another brother, long thought dead, who follows the outlaw trail. Only if all three brothers band together can they save the Bar K . . . if they don't kill each other first.

___4894-9 $4.99 US/$5.99 CAN

PRAY FOR TEXAS

COTTON SMITH

Rule Cordell is a pistol fighter, one of a special breed of warriors spawned by the Civil War, men with exceptional skill with the new weapon, the Colt .44 revolver. Like many other former Rebel soldiers, Cordell finds no place in the post-war world of bitter enemies and money-grabbing politicians, so he seeks refuge in bloody Texas and joins the band of guerrillas led by the wild and charismatic Johnny Cat Carlson. Cordell thinks he is fighting to bring freedom back to Texas, but he soon finds that Johnny Cat and his men are just outlaws out for all they can get. Now Cordell is ready to strike out on his own again, but the road to freedom will lead him through some hard choices and tough trouble. Before he can leave his past behind him, he'll have to face up to it, and the father who turned him to the gun in the first place.

___4710-1 $4.50 US/$5.50 CAN

Dorchester Publishing Co., Inc.
P.O. Box 6640
Wayne, PA 19087-8640

Please add $1.75 for shipping and handling for the first book and $.50 for each book thereafter. NY, NYC, and PA residents, please add appropriate sales tax. No cash, stamps, or C.O.D.s. All orders shipped within 6 weeks via postal service book rate. Canadian orders require $2.00 extra postage and must be paid in U.S. dollars through a U.S. banking facility.

Name_____
Address_____
City_____State _____Zip _____
I have enclosed $ _____ in payment for the checked book(s).
Payment <u>must</u> accompany all orders. ❏ Please send a free catalog.

COTTON SMITH
DARK TRAIL
TO DODGE

Tyrel Bannon knows more about a plow than longhorn cattle, but the green farm boy is determined to become a Triple C rider on the long, hard drive from Texas to Dodge, the "Queen City of the Cowtowns." But this is a trail that only the brave, smart and lucky can survive. Waiting ahead are Kiowa warriors, raging rivers, drought, storms . . . and vicious rustlers out to blacken the dust with Triple C blood.

___4510-9 $4.50 US/$5.50 CAN

Dorchester Publishing Co., Inc.
P.O. Box 6640
Wayne, PA 19087-8640

Please add $1.75 for shipping and handling for the first book and $.50 for each book thereafter. NY, NYC, and PA residents, please add appropriate sales tax. No cash, stamps, or C.O.D.s. All orders shipped within 6 weeks via postal service book rate. Canadian orders require $2.00 extra postage and must be paid in U.S. dollars through a U.S. banking facility.

Name_____
Address_____
City_____State_____Zip_____
I have enclosed $_____ in payment for the checked book(s).
Payment <u>must</u> accompany all orders. ❏ Please send a free catalog.
       CHECK OUT OUR WEBSITE! www.dorchesterpub.com

Man From Wolf River

John D. Nesbitt

Owen Felver is just passing through. He is on his way from the Wolf River down to the Laramie Mountains for some summer wages. He makes his camp outside of Cameron, Wyoming, and rides in for a quick beer. But it isn't quick enough. While he is there he sees pretty, young Jenny—and the puffed-up gent trying to get rude with her. What else can he do but step in and defend her? Right after that some pretty tough thugs start to make it clear Felver isn't all too welcome around town. Trouble is, the more they tell him to move on—and the more he sees of Jenny—the more he wants to stay. He knows they have something to hide, but he has no idea just how awful it is—or how far they will go to keep it hidden.

___4871-X $4.50 US/$5.50 CAN

Coyote Trail

John D. Nesbitt

Travis Quinn doesn't have much luck picking his friends. He is fired from the last ranch he works on when a friend of his gets blacklisted for going behind the owner's back. Guilt by association sends Quinn looking for another job, too. He makes his way down the Powder River country until he runs into Miles Newman, who puts in a good word for him and gets him a job at the Lockhart Ranch. But Quinn doesn't know too much about Newman, and the more he learns, the less he likes. Pretty soon it starts to look like Quinn has picked the wrong friend again. And if the rumors about Newman are true, this friend might just get him killed.

___4671-7 $4.50 US/$5.50 CAN

Dorchester Publishing Co., Inc.
P.O. Box 6640
Wayne, PA 19087-8640

Please add $1.75 for shipping and handling for the first book and $.50 for each book thereafter. NY, NYC, and PA residents, please add appropriate sales tax. No cash, stamps, or C.O.D.s. All orders shipped within 6 weeks via postal service book rate. Canadian orders require $2.00 extra postage and must be paid in U.S. dollars through a U.S. banking facility.

Name_____
Address_____
City_____State_____Zip_____
I have enclosed $_____ in payment for the checked book(s).
Payment <u>must</u> accompany all orders. ❑ Please send a free catalog.
          CHECK OUT OUR WEBSITE! www.dorchesterpub.com

WILD ROSE

of

RUBY CANYON

JOHN D. NESBITT

At first homesteader Henry Sommers is pleased when his neighbor Van O'Leary starts dropping by. After all, friends come in handy out on the Wyoming plains. But it soon becomes clear that O'Leary has some sort of money-making scheme in the works and doesn't much care how the money is made. Henry wants no part of his neighbor's dirty business, but freeing himself of O'Leary is almost as difficult as climbing out of quicksand . . . and just as dangerous.

___4520-6 $3.99 US/$4.99 CAN